THINGS IN THE GROUND

By Sarah Sapp

Published by Page & Parcel Books

For Mudge – my "Dottie"

Thank you for being my adventure buddy through New England graveyards, restricted lighthouses, enchanting gardens, and haunted footsteps.

You are magic.

Today, an estimated one billion people practice witchcraft across the globe.

It begs the question:

Do you believe in magick?

PROLOGUE

Twilight reaches the sleeping pond before the body does.

Swish, stop.

Her limbs drag behind a slogging torso—heavy as dead weight, but only just. A desperate groan shatters the early-morning quiet: *she's alive.*

Swish, stop.

Regrettably alert—hyperaware—despite being locked inside a body that moves like a corpse.

Swish, stop.

Unable to blink, she panics, wondering if she's already rotted... dying and decaying all at once.

Swish, stop.

At the edges of her pulsing vision, haunting cattails beckon by the water like ghosts at a grave— bobbing in suspicious invitation.

Swish, stop.

It spooks her. The end is near. Her bones can feel it.

"I'm sorry!" her mind shrieks, but her silent screams only ricochet off their cage of a skull into a maddening echo. *"I'm sorry! I'm sorry! I'm sorry!"*

But she isn't sorry. She's just caught.

Swish, stop.

And now, as the pond's edge creeps closer, the waking sky warns her, troubling in its promise:

"Red clouds at night, sailors delight. Red clouds at morning, sailors take warning."

Swish, splash.

The first watery step sounds with alarm— slapping back with mud that squelches and smacks— and a quiver whips through the weeds as if the wilderness itself can't stand the anticipation.

Swish, slosh.

Angry fists claw at her—this ragdoll of a body—as they prepare to plunge her under. A final jostle sends a booted foot into view. Her foot. Bobbing with each heave and tug, just like the rest of her. It glares back—a classic wellie with a small heart drawn on the toe—reminding of all her transgressions.

PART ONE:

Lottie

CHAPTER 1

Nightmares are like ghosts.

They haunt.

And for Lottie Lowe, they've taken up a permanent residence. Her mind is a mansion of squatting goblins and grief. Wreaking Havoc.

The woman is a walking haunted house.

They came for her last night, like always. And, like always, she thought she'd be ready for them. That she could hide inside a small closet of her brain, where perhaps they wouldn't find her. Or she might open the door to a new dream—something altogether plain and boring. She'd prefer nothing at all, if it were up to her. Total blackness.

But it's not up to her... and the ghosts seem ever eager to remind her of that.

Now, grateful for the morning but annoyed by the same, Lottie leans into the quietest corner of her cottage kitchen, waiting for her coffee to drown out the mares of the night.

With heavy eyes, she stills, struggling to shake away the ghosts—the memories that visited her dreams.

The smell of sea brine. A pink sky.

A cradled mug warms her palm. She concentrates on its heat.

Stoked into comfort by her company despite a chilling ocean breeze.

Light filters in through the forest to dance upon her cupboards.

Her favorite notebook closes shut to the sweet distraction of another.

Absentmindedly, her fingers stir the spoon clockwise, then counter. She takes a sip, scalding her tongue. Only then is she pulled away from her reveries.

Pain is a powerful influence when it comes to the mind.

"Dammit." The brew spills with a jerk. It lands with a profanity.

Finding the stain to be one of many on her otherwise-washed cotton smock, Lottie proceeds to slip into her denim coveralls anyhow.

"Welp, welcome to the mess, then." A deep breath. "Let's add some more."

Tugging on rubber boots, she gathers wild hair in an easy braid and heads for the door. Pausing, a daily ritual ensues—born out of fear, and now enduring by habit.

At this moment, all doors and windows are locked, and this quaint Tudor home is merely a cottage in the trees. But one toe crosses that threshold, and she can be spotted. Discovered. *Caught.*

She exhales. For these last few seconds, she is a secret. No faces peer in the windows. She is hidden.

Hidden. Precisely her intention. Isolated. Deeply kept.

Practically buried.

In her hesitation, the tarnished mirror above the knotted wall hooks meets her gaze, staring back. The reflection is almost unnerving.

In a past life, Lottie's tresses were wild with reds and aggressively vibrant. Not this artificial honey, rendered by a life in hiding.

And her clothes. *Oh,* her clothes. She still mourns them.

With a flick of her wrist at the knob, the green of her forest grave washes in and greets her. A peek out, a peer about—no watching faces seem to loom in the sea of trees. And, so, she goes.

Low clouds promise midday showers. A soft haze hums over the canopy as an early autumn breeze teases the leaves.

To ready for the rain, she checks the water reservoirs, tripping on a loose brick near the rain barrel—again. She keeps meaning to fix that.

Behind the cottage, the generator is full. The oil glistens.

Next, wood. Despite a sun that's still warm, phantom fingers sneak up on her. Cold and biting. Grabbing the axe and ignoring the chill, she slices through a dozen logs with ease, having practiced for hours on end when first arriving two years ago. She could barely even lift the cleaver then.

"Two years…" she whispers in disbelief.

Scanning the trees, she considers her life and has mixed feelings about it. Two years of hiding. But also, two years of her grandmother's haven.

Back inside, she piles logs by the hearth and gives a good shove to the windows, now hot.

"Oy." A breath. "There we go."

Pausing, she takes in the home. Dottie's home.

Where once there were bare walls, the space now blooms of brushstrokes and color. A chaotic spread of pages, akin to a scrapbook's entrails, dances upon the murals—loose-leaf notes that flap from the open windows. A rainbow of drying blossoms stretches across the ceiling in taut lines of twine. Silk scarves dangle from knobs. An ornate key swings on the bedroom headboard, ribboned and dangling.

The fireplace keystone catches her notice, bearing its single engraved "D." Lottie sighs over it with a graze.

"Miss you, Dottie," she whispers, smacking the air with a kiss.

With that, she heads for the kitchen, eyeing the calendar to cross off another day. The pen hovers over the next, pausing at the bold message meant to be a reminder. *As if I'd ever miss the date,* she thinks.

"SALEM MARKET"

The same bold text covers every Saturday and Sunday. And the season's almost over. Soon, Salem, Massachusetts will close to Market vendors until spring, so she won't have a booth for income—and she won't be able to shop the others.

"Say it isn't so," she whines. Looking to jars of food above the counter, a nervous finger goes tapping. "At least I'll be even *harder* to find," she tries to convince herself, having begun to do her own canning to avoid brick-and-mortar stores. "Can't catch me if I never leave the cottage." *Hopefully.*

9

Something snaps outside, jerking Lottie's chin toward the window. The vision of a splintered door flits through her thoughts in warning.

Only a squirrel. Her shoulders relax.

No faces in the window. No peepers in the garden. Just fresh herbs flirting with the windowsill— ready to be tugged and tasted.

Potted Mint creeps onto the wooden countertop. She pinches a leaf and licks it, thinking a garnished cocktail sounds fabulous. Her nerves could use it, anyhow.

Turning heel, she grabs a pen and notepad for inventory. Down the hall, past the bathroom, into the closet of wonders.

Fabrics and craft guns spill from pockets. A SALEM MARKET VENDOR sign peeks from behind curling ribbon. Trinkets wobble in cluttered stacks.

On a shelf, a framed article beams, praising Lottie's booth and awarding her **"Most Beloved."**

It's a really happy thing—an assurance that she's good at surviving. She didn't just escape; she paved a new path. But the article is also a reminder. A punch to her gut.

They'd asked her to smile at her booth— surrounded by these things that were conjured from her thoughts and crafted by her fingers. Skills she hadn't known she possessed before this life.

But she wouldn't pose for the photo. Couldn't give her name. Because that's not how hiding works.

Ms. Dutton

That's who the booth belonged to. That's the surname she used—Dottie's. Not Lottie Lowe.

Glass shatters outside.

Oxygen turns to lead in her chest.

He found me.

The peace-splintering sound summons memories—shaking hands wielding jagged glass and the sense of a ghost slipping into her skin. Oozing through her blood with an alien energy. Willing her to survive.

He almost got her once.

Hurrying to the kitchen for a knife, she creeps to the window, wondering if he's come for her. White-knuckled and trembling, she scans for an enemy outside. A shadow moves in warning—someone is there. Breathless, she meets their eyes, only to find a deer staring back, playing with the glass bottles sitting in the brook.

The knife goes clattering into the sink with a sigh of relief.

And the rest of Lottie goes collapsing onto the cool tile floor. Scared half to death. Literally.

She brings a pot of Basil down with her. Terracotta cracks and dirt scatters. Lottie just lies beside it, struggling to breathe.

"I wish *you* would die," she whispers, thinking of his face. Only porcelain and dirt witness the confession. "I wish you would choke to death on your cheap liquor and just leave me alone."

Idly, a finger draws in the dirt, tracing three distinct letters.

D I E

One tear slides down a hot cheek. She cleans her mess.

"Get it together, Lottie." Sweat dampens her neck. "Too much to do."

It doesn't help that Paranoia and Fear have become playmates in her haunted-house head.

Shaking it off, she drafts a quick shopping list and tallies costs. And then, like a thief in the night, she pilfers—hunting for stashed-away secrets.

"Insist on sneakery," Dottie would often whisper with a wink.

The batty woman had snuck bills and coins into little hiding spots of dips and crevices all over the home. And Lottie was grateful for that battiness; the stashed-away money had helped sustain her when she'd shown up with nothing but fear and a will to survive.

There's no Dottie around anymore to take care of her. But somehow, the woman still does.

So far, Lottie has maintained that same batty system with the income from her market booth. Especially considering the lack of access to her PO box—and the royalty checks that keep accruing inside it.

Thinking about that too long makes her itch.

She'd love to get her hands on that money—to take what's rightfully hers—but it's too close to the threat.

Too close to *him.*

It's not worth her life. And for now, that's exactly what's at risk.

So she tries not to think about it. Instead, she goes on silly money quests in honor of her peculiar grandmother. Lottie's even developed her own acronym for the hunt: B.U.C.K.

"B. Bathroom mirror."

Inside the medicine cabinet, a white pill bottle hides a wad of twenties. She snags three.

"U…"

In the bedroom, the sheets get a good shove.

"Under the mattress. Check."

Two more bills join.

"C, the 'case of the pillow'," she recites.

Back in the living room, a roll-arm sofa invites her to sift through its soft pillows—and she does.

"Now, K."

The kitchen.

At the top of the pantry sits an uninviting cracker tin, ready to be retrieved. The leafy notes inside slide with their paper-thin whisper.

"There."

It's routine now: rip the list from its pad, wrap it around a handful of bills, and tuck it snugly inside her market day satchel.

Wanting to do one last chore before the rain comes—and the shift to vendor tinkering overwhelms the home—she dons her gloves and grabs the burlap garden bag. Excited toes go wriggling in their boots, as Lottie saves her favorite task for last:

The dirt.

A mist hangs beneath darkening clouds, kissing the leafy things of the garden. The wind whispers a breathy *hush*. Flouncy, butter-yellow curtains waive from the kitchen window. A low thunder rumbles.

Lottie soaks in every bit of it as she tends to the rooted wonders of her grandmother's garden.

Like Dottie taught her, the things in this plot are holy—like all things from the ground. These things that are both alive and life-giving.

Flowers. Vegetables. Fungi.

"They deserve respect," Dottie would say. *"They deserve to be recognized. Named."*

And so, Lottie does.

"Mister Radish," she coos with a tug.

"Hello, lovely Carrot." A good shake from the muck.

"Delicious Onion, thank you, sir."

The disturbed dirt perfumes the air with its earthy scent. Lottie inhales, discerning the aromas of the forest—damp earth mingled with the cloying sweetness of wet bark.

"Now, for my market maidens."

A prized constant upon Lottie's booth table is her array of both fresh and dried flowers, artfully packaged in a dozen whimsical ways.

With the shifting season, she prunes what's left of the Peonies and Daylilies.

"Madame Peony, I've got big plans for a simple syrup and room spritzers." A tug and a toss into the hallowed pile.

"And for you, Daylily, I'm thinking a vibrant salad." Lottie plucks the petals accordingly. "Some to be tossed," she says, snapping the shoots and separating the roots from the tubers, "and parts to be boiled."

In her mind's eye, she can already picture the packaging: floral-wrapped bundles tied in twine.

"People pay for packaging," she assures the lovely things.

Nibbling at her lip, Lottie breathes in the soil. Gloves abandoned, eager fingers reach into the soft earth and explore it like worms.

As if bewitched, she melts, easing further in to savor. To release. To let the energy of the ground draw from her, as if it might cleanse her to the core.

A giddiness bubbles inside her chest. A laugh swims past tickled lips. *This is so very Dottie.* Finding moments that feel like magic.

Magic.

The thought pulls her gaze to the forest— seeking its depths. These trees have always held a magic for Lottie. Looking for it now, she imagines even a skeptic could be convinced it exists.

As if it's present but invisible—an energy suspended, like fog hovering. Ready to be harvested like the flowers in her hand. Understanding it can be wielded—it simply first needs to be seen.

That's the part that gives her pause, though:

Wielding. Spell-casting. Witchcraft.

Magic, she believes in. She can feel it. This place is magic. Her Dottie was magic—she had her own authentic brand of it. The trees beckoned her. The ground invited her fingers into its dirt. The shadowed parts of the forest held mystery.

But to *control* it?

Some cynical bone in Lottie's chest can't fathom this wild thing—this pulsing force that prowls through nature—could be so easily controlled and exploited.

A clang from the sky jolts the world. A presence sweeps through and settles, eerily still.

Magic, she believes in, but magick—the kind conjured by spellcraft—she has doubts about.

CHAPTER 2

The vigor of a Saturday morning fills the market
with chatter and scent—fresh bread, potted plants,
beeswax. Patrons lollygag along booths and dare
themselves to spend their dollars. Produce,
knickknacks, sweets, wine.
As Lottie finishes her table with thrifted décor
and florals, she takes in the buzz. Smiling, she pats her
favorite marketing tool: a framed quote by Dottie.
"If it might make your eyes bright, give it a
go."
Her Dottie was an odd one—odd with intention,
and fully her own.
"Does it hurt anyone else?" she'd ask whenever
brows rose at her ways. *"Ought it to?"* she'd then joke
with a wink. *"Well, then... if it might make your eyes*
bright, give it a go!"
She gave herself permission to try anything that
made her feel more alive. More awake to the world.
As it turns out, it's become a saying to live by
for many—at least for those kindred spirits in the
market.
Here, with colors and textures and endless new
faces, it's easy to pretend the world is soft again.
The vendors are plentiful—with makers and
creators, farmers and bakers, florists and herbalists.

Being in Salem, magickal influences and witchcraft-inspired products abound. And both locals and tourists flock in response. A beautiful hodgepodge, the sellers are as much a medley of textures and colors as their products.

Though skeptical of magick, the craft has always fascinated Lottie. Charts on herbs and their magical benefits have intrigued her, once or twice. The crystals. The aesthetic of it all.

Witches.

History warned of witches, but Lottie's always scoffed. *The irony*. Women condemned for being women—by bloodthirsty Puritans. For midwifery. For herbalism. For knowing what men did not.

Despite her skepticism, she can appreciate a need to balance the playing field. Where there's abuse of authority, perhaps magick is a viable remedy—defense against the evil.

For evil, she has come to learn, doesn't play by the rules.

A shiver finds her shoulder. An invisible tap—like eyes saying, *I see you*.

She looks up, half-expecting to catch someone staring. The feeling lingers, but there's no proof. And after yesterday—thinking she'd been discovered—she can't decide what's worse: she's either going crazy… or she's getting too comfortable.

For a good while, she'd felt safe. Felt *hidden*. But for the past few months—maybe the entire summer—a familiar paranoia had returned. She just didn't want to admit it.

Looking down to the dyed-blonde braid that trails to her waist, her shoulders slump in defeat. Because maybe being found is inevitable.

"Okay." Nervous fingers go strumming. "Nothing's wrong. Back to work."

With a week's worth of work sprawled across the booth at her hips, she takes in her creations. With the mingling of seasons—flirting between summer and autumn—Lottie used up the last of her summer wares and added some autumn flare.

Bundled Sage, seashell candles, and flower vials. Herb packets and garden seed sachets. Stamped tea towels and postcards. Also, the Peony simple syrup and Daylily salads.

Now ready to sit and sip her tea, she relaxes into her chair and breathes in the day.

The sun warms while an autumn breeze creeps in, caressing cheeks. The season of change hangs in the air, peering into the market the way one might stand quietly at a window—silent and conspiring.

Customers are plentiful, and Lottie enjoys the act of watching. It's one of her favorite things to do. It always has been.

Dottie often called her a wallflower—and that tickles Lottie now. Because real Wallflowers are poisonous. Metaphorical ones? Dismissed as quiet. Meek. Too timid to act. But maybe the "meek" are simply more calculated. They understand the weight of words, so they don't waste them. Maybe their silence isn't fear—it's restraint. And if pushed, they can bite back. Hard.

Lottie bit back, once.

Another shiver sends her upright. She realizes too late—she's waded into her mind like a river, easing in to swim. But she hadn't meant to. Now, she's thrashing, struggling to stay afloat. Eyes wild. Breath short. Because she's drowning in her thoughts—and the present is slippery.

The mental current drags up old fears. Thick, familiar, and clinging like mud. Because she doesn't just feel seen. She feels watched.

There is a difference between people-watching and watching *someone*.

One is innocent in its curiosity; the other is intentional. Risky. Watching leads to snooping. To digging. To following.

In her experience, those who follow too closely are reckless. They miss things.

The glint of a trinket pulls her attention. It sits on the corner of her table, curious and inviting—a gold locket. Its aged beauty emits unapologetically, with curvatures and details etched into its face.

She flips it open. Inside, a curled scrap of paper waits. A message, inked in Latin:

Ferre in mente.

The phrase coils in her head. She doesn't know what it means, but the words cloud her thoughts like a dream. The way a lullaby brings sleep.

"*Ferre in mente*," she reads, as if spoken words might clear her fog.

An offered glance shows no one coming back for it. A yawn pulls out of her.

"Wow, I need a nap," she tells her tea as she takes a sip—only to be surprised upright once more. "What the hell?"

Her lips go smacking. Calculating. Whatever she just tasted was bitter and earthy. But vaguely familiar.

"Mugwort?"

Had she truly tasted the herb? *Did I add it in by mistake?*

Sniffing the drink, she narrows her eyes at the intruder tainting her typical tea of Earl Grey with Vanilla and Lavender.

"Good morning, sweet!" a familiar voice calls out.

Lottie stands to meet her friend's embrace, glad—always—to be reminded she enjoys a gentle hug.

"Good morning, Verdilla."

The warm woman releases her, ever in a cheerful tizzy.

"I just wanted to check on you—see if all is on track for tomorrow's *spectacular* soiree?"

"Yes, ma'am," Lottie assures. "I'll get there early, and you'll be good to go."

With a clap of her hands, Verdilla sings. "Wonderful! Thank you so much again. You're always such a treat."

Bashful, Lottie accepts the praise. "I'm happy to help. I always love visiting the Garden. I'll see you tomorrow."

With her silly sendoff, Verdilla blows three kisses and then rushes away in a twirl.

"Oh!" she says mid-twist. "Someone asked for your booth by name. You're becoming quite the coveted vendor. I'm so lucky I get you all to myself tomorrow!"

Verdilla says something else, but Lottie doesn't hear it. She can't through the alarms blaring in her head. Because that old, crawling feeling returns.

Watched.

"Breathe, Lottie," she whispers like a mother calming a child. "You're being crazy," she singsongs. "There are a million people here." *And none of them are staring at you.* "You're fine."

Looking back to Verdilla, she's twirled out of sight somewhere.

Lottie likes her. Verdilla. She was the first to welcome Lottie to Salem, having known Dottie already. They were old friends.

Ever the socialite and event planner, Verdilla noticed Lottie's gift for tinkering and creating and funneled it into purpose—parties, fundraisers, charity dinners.

And Lottie loves it.

Just like her grandmother before her—who savored the remoteness of the cottage but never shied from a little glamour—Lottie imagines she's walking in regal footsteps. She's grown to enjoy her quiet life of isolation… but every now and then, a soiree makes her feel like herself. The old Lottie.

It may not be the smartest way to live her life— drifting between recluse and spectacle—but at least she's *living*. Not just hiding.

Once, back in her other life, she'd even reached the status of Guest of Honor. A soiree just for her. And not because she'd followed in footsteps. Because she'd earned it. Wrote it. An *Author Extraordinaire,* forging a cobblestone path of prose and punctuation that carried her upward.

That was before her life in Salem. And that particular elegance didn't last long.

Lost in thought, she reaches for her tea without thinking. Takes a sip.

Bitter.

Spitting the soured tea back into its cup, she recoils. And then she sets it aside. Because she remembers:

Two pills. A quick hand.

She knows how easy it is to slip a secret into a drink.

CHAPTER 3

Despite a successful market day, Lottie was spent.

Bone-tired, she hurried home, feeling wrong and off-kilter. Normally, she'd treat herself to a late meal at a local café, but not today. Today, she slogged right past her favorite haunt on the way to the transit station.

The wait seemed long. The ride seemed longer. And her final walk through the trees stretched like a dream she couldn't wake from.

By the time she reaches her cottage path, dread has taken root.

Please don't be sick.

The thought of missing tomorrow's event lands like an anvil in her already sinking mind. Down, down. Deeper.

Her legs tremble—so tired, she's unraveling. A shuffling foot stumbles across the cobbled path.

"Damn brick," she curses, knowing it's her own fault.

Finally at the door, desperate fingers fumble for keys. Past the threshold. Almost down the hall.

Once inside her room, she surrenders to the quilted bed.

No dinner. No tea. Just sleep—and it takes her completely.

In the night, she stirs.

And meets resistance.

Something flickers beneath the surface of sleep. Her mind—sluggish and heavy—tries to move the body it seems to no longer control. Efforts stifled.

Exhaustion presses her down, thick and clouding. She tries to turn. Or holler. Or *breathe*.

A panic sets in. Reflexes are rejected.

She can't move.

She can't see.

She feels buried—under mud, or the weight of old dreams, or things demanding to be remembered.

She tries to scream. She thinks she screams. But the sound has nowhere to go. She's paralyzed.

And she's not alone.

Nearby, a presence lingers, circling the foot of her bed.

Her chest tightens. She thrashes in her mind, but her limbs won't answer.

She's helpless.

And something menacing stands over her. Some*one*. They watch her. Some stranger. Some proverbial Other.

The more she struggles, the more it wins— overwhelming in an abyss of shadow and fury.

When she finally gives in—when the pressing weight pulls her under—her body goes slack, like drowning in an undertow. Pulled, pushed, and weightless all at once.

Come morning, she wakes up well after sunrise. An odd thing for her.

CHAPTER 4

She wakes up aching, like she'd fought herself in her sleep. Literally. Like she's been punched, or drugged, or both.

Her head pounds. Her eyes sting.

Checking the clock, she balks. It's so late. Early mornings are her favorite, and this one slipped past like a thief. The mere thought of yesterday makes her dizzy.

"What is happening?" she groans.

Forcing herself upright, she operates on autopilot—until fingers brush the locket hanging from her neck.

"How did you get there?" She remembers slipping it into her satchel, but that's all.

It's a pretty thing. Gold and gilded on a long, fine chain. It's something Dottie would have worn. A way to keep secrets close.

Opening it again, the sight of the inscription makes her woozy. Or maybe it's just the fatigue. The window. Her pillow. The doorway. Everything makes her woozy.

Another groan.

"Don't be sick."

She stands.

A ruined routine is as good as the wrong mix of tea.

Going through the motions is effective, but the day's start is all wrong. Most of the morning has disappeared.

After a quick sip of coffee, Lottie hurries to the trees, already hours behind. But there's always time for this—for exploring. It's the best part of this lifestyle: the challenge to get lost amongst her closet comrades.

Seeking the secrets of the forest, she considers which flowers are primed for picking. Mostly, though, it's the creek she's come for. Her toes crave the cold sting of the stream.

Hints of autumn whisper nearby, but the summer sun still lingers. Warm against the dewy forest floor. A conjured fog dances through the trees in a playful foxtrot. Ghostly swirls snake around Lottie's ankles and curl up to her nose.

A deep inhale does wonders.

Lottie lets her thoughts dissolve, as she breathes in the scent of lichen and wood. The musty aroma of fungi flirts with the hidden flora waiting for her.

Now, to work.

Lottie never hurries once her feet are in the forest. She's learned the sweetest retrieves hide like stashed-away secrets—requiring soft glances and slow steps.

Today, tucked-away meadows yield Blue Toadflax and Bearded Beggarticks. Unbothered forest floor bursts with Fringed Bleeding Hearts. Faraway fields are painted in hues of Virginia Bluebells. Climbing moss spores Black Trumpet Mushrooms, with

Chicken of the Woods nestled along fallen, shushed stumps. Wine Caps crouch in dirt and Reishi grows on hardwoods.

Everywhere, something is in process. Rotting wood nourishes in the same way stinging bees turn nectar into honey. The work is slow and far from simple. But Lottie looks for it, seeking the magic—like Dottie did.

"There are so many hidden things in the forest," Dottie said once. *"Some of the darkest parts seem to hold hushed mysteries, don't you think? Shadows that beckon of curious things. Quiet secrets in quiet spaces. The best sorts of hiding places."*

With her flower basket in hand, Lottie reaches the creek. Wetting a towel, she wraps her pickings to keep them fresh. Careful to avoid the Monkshood nearby—esteemed by her grandmother as *The Queen of Poisons*—she settles onto a rock warmed by a slant of sunlight.

Noting the stream's temperature, shoes get tossed with a muttered "good riddance." The frigid water flows over her toes and up calves, yanking a squeal of laughter from her throat.

The squeals get stuck when a stranger's hand rises from the water. Reaching.

She recoils, heart lurching.

Odd in their extension, the reaching fingers dip toward her. Curiously curled. As if in expectation.

Lottie lunges forward in reflex, assuming they need help—that the reaching fingers seek rescue. Questions rush through her mind like the water that pounds on the rocks at her stumbling feet.

Who are you?
Where did you come from?
Why aren't you trying to swim?
Why aren't you trying to SAVE YOURSELF?

She reaches, expecting cold flesh—but only panic touches her first. It zips through her fingers. Bracing for impact with this Other.

In a blink, the hand vanishes.

Gone. But lingering. Like the ghost of a memory. Or the echo of a nightmare.

Staggering back over jagged rocks, Lottie realizes with a churning gut: no one was there needing rescue in the shallows. No one could've been.

**

Lottie fled home and locked herself inside.

Hiding from the fingers still curling in her mind.

"Have I gone nutty?" she whispers, half expecting the room of herbs and flowers to shake in confirmation.

A roiling heat simmers in her belly. With a shaking hand, dried Lavender fills a teacup. Trying for steady, she brings the cup to her nose, hovering to welcome a slow inhale while her rattling wrists take turns beneath the cold faucet.

"It's just from being tired." Another deep breath. "It was a strange night."

Her breathing slows—strong and intentional. She focuses on the signage tacked near the open window. For the millionth time, she reads the loose page as it quivers from the afternoon breeze.

Soil is to sweeten, as boot dirt is to cheapen. Dirt of bones brings cursing, and a bit o' mud's for sleepin'.

Lottie can picture Dottie standing in the kitchen. Wielding a bowl of potting soil with dirt-streaked fingers. Fingers that threatened to tickle a young Lottie's bare toes. Smudge her cheeks. Darken her nose.

"Do you remember what it means?" Dottie had asked, fingers suspended, fluttering and poised for taunting.

Lottie always remembered the answer to this pop quiz. It was as easy as singing a favorite song. But she'd always pretend to forget, because that meant *fun*. Dirtied fingers chasing. Side-aching laughter. Messes encouraged.

"Soil makes things flourish," she recites now, "but everyday dirt isn't as good. Bone-dry dirt is certain death. And mud, being too wet, makes things wilt."

In her desire to study flowers and herbs, Lottie relied on this daily. She'd recite it over and over again, finding comfort in the mantra. Again, it works—comforting her even now.

Sleep pulls at her. It battles her declining adrenaline. It makes her dizzy.

But there's no time to spiral. She has a to-do list to tackle. And a date with a dress.

Most of the day's pickings soon dangle high, strung up to dry. Others get pressed between book pages. The favorites head for a vase—Lilies from the garden, Larkspur, and Orange Coneflower.

With final touches for the charity dinner, ribbons form bows on vialed favors. Lottie soothes herself by counting the goods three times through.

As she counts, the curl of her hand reminds her of the fingers at the creek. Memory tugs at her, like a nightmare to a dreamer. Pulling. Luring.

She's back at the creek, for a moment—as if it's right in front of her: the curling fingers. *Come hither*, they seem to say, wanting her to follow.

A chiming clock snaps at her back.

Feeling silly—disoriented but also delusional— a throaty giggle comes through with a snort.

"Must be this house," she says to a long-gone Dottie. "It's making me even battier than you were."

When it's finally time to get dressed, she greets the woman in the mirror. Leaving the final touches for last, she grabs a needle and thread. Resolute.

Retrieving a tucked-away box—one that's been left alone and saved for when she feels strong—Lottie swallows. The perfect dress lies folded inside, blemished by a tear that sits waiting to be mended. Now, the moment has arrived.

It's also a risk, she realizes—wearing a relic from her past life. But it's been two years. She wants to find a way to move forward... even if only during special occasions.

With the lid removed, timid fingers slide across the bodice, delicate with embroidery. Hues echo of the forest she calls home.

As her fingers find the hole, her memory finds the rip—hands tearing it apart.

She falters.

"It's time," she decides, and she sets to sewing.

CHAPTER 5

Dusk drapes over the Ropes Mansion estate like a luffed linen. Suspended and hovering. It stretches like a sigh—lingering before its final descent.

Lottie studies the looming home and feels it staring back—watching its watcher. Antique in age but pristine in upkeep, it looks just as it always has. To her.

The memory of her last visit slithers down her spine and straightens her shoulders. "It's not you I've come for," she insists to the mansion. "It's your Garden I want."

In her viridian dress and shawl, Lottie greets the floral arbor around the back. Through to the garden, she emerges like a flower joining in bloom.

Complemented by leaves and petals framing the threshold, she stands vibrant. Stubborn hues of red shine through her phony blonde tendrils—encouraged by the garlands of green. She notices this and smirks, as an image of wild strawberries tickles her thoughts.

"Feeling wild tonight, are we?"

The Garden, as always, is spellbinding.

She first visited this property with her grandmother. It had been the perfect day—the perfect weather, a perfect misty sky, perfect company.

"The splendor is tangible," her grandmother had said. *"I feel a bit more enchanted just by standing right where I am."*

Now, Lottie stands in that very same spot, quietly willing the enchantment to return.

Pathways wind through koi ponds and flower beds. Quaint benches beckon. Shrubs guard a back wall. Blooms spill over like secrets too heavy to hold. It's as if the rainbow waltzed through and left its footprints in every patch.

Alone, she wanders, enchanted as the sky paints the world its final shade of pink.

Footsteps crunch gravel behind her.

A buried memory of Wellington boots creeps up like the undead.

"There you are, love," Verdilla chirps, hurried. She finds Lottie near the back. "Oh, Foxgloves, my favorites." She sighs at the purple bells. "Might be their final bloom of the season."

The reverie breaks. Lottie laughs softly— nervous. *Foxgloves?* She can't remember what she was doing.

"Sorry," she starts. "I meant to find you after a quick peek," she lies.

After handing over a hefty bag of whimsical party favors, Lottie sifts through her clutch for the locket—surprised to find it around her neck. She offers it.

"Verdilla, you know a bit about languages, don't you?" With a quick click, the locket opens and she removes the hidden slip. "Can you read this?"

Verdilla leans in with her glasses and an accompaniment of fluttering fingers.

"Oh, um, 'Think of me.' Along those lines. You know, dear,"—she smiles teasingly—"the purpose of a locket."

"'Think of me,'" Lottie repeats, left in the tailwind of Verdilla's typical tizzy.

As twilight arrives, guests gather in the Garden. It glows of oil lamps and strands of lights—an ethereal paradise. Friendly greetings find familiar faces. Waiters wander and glasses clink. And pop-up bars multiply like mushrooms.

"Nothing loosens wallets like liquor," she murmurs.

Lovely Verdilla taps her glass, poised on a platform near the mansion. Overlooking the garden and its well-dressed guests.

"Absolutely beautiful evening, isn't it?" She invites. Guests humor her with warm cheers.

"Tonight, we honor the vulnerable. The children and youths in state custody and foster care. Inspired by our dear Dr. Craven's call to 'Sow Selflessly.'"

Polite applause follows.

"Just like this Garden," she says, "beauty and growth take time. And love. And tending."

Heads nod. Glasses raise.

"And so, in support of such a worthy endeavor, we welcome you to an immersive experience. Our theme tonight, *The Secret* Garden, reminds us: every child holds hidden beauty. And we must help them bloom."

A hearty applause, now.

"So, come check in under the arbor," she adds, excited, "and you'll be gifted a special key. It opens a secret, meant just for you." Eyes twinkle. "Enjoy!"

Drawn like moths, the crowd drifts to the arbor. One by one. Ushered through and up the steps, eager patrons trickle inside.

Lottie lingers by a Rosebush. Not much one for close crowds. When the rush settles, she claims her filigree key and champagne flute, as she's welcomed into the foyer.

Memory hits like a slap.

In this same dress, in this same place, she'd been offered a glass of champagne upon entrance. A hand found her back, pushing her forward.

A phantom pressure strokes down her spine. She swipes both the touch and the memory away. Suddenly, she stands in the coatroom, forgetting why she came in.

But she plays the part—finding a hanger, shedding her shawl. Back to its spot, she wedges the hanger and its items between a plain sweater and a patterned raincoat.

Figuring such a fancy event warrants another swipe of lipstick, a dip into her purse rewards Lottie with a gold tube.

And gardening shears.

They startle with a metallic chill, cold to touch. A few loose petals wink from inside the bag. Lottie smirks. She doesn't remember packing the shears. But it's the sort of thing she does every now and then.

Then she considers the locket around her neck. How she keeps forgetting she's wearing it.

"You two aren't the worst things to be surprised by," she whispers. "Especially you," she assures the shears. "You never know what you might need to cut."

A tremor runs through at the reminder. Recalling how her wet hands once trembled as she clutched the sweet sanctuary of a severed water weed.

Dinner is pleasant.

Seated before a grand fireplace, all heads turn to Dr. Craven for a toast. He speaks of humans and nature—how both can harm or heal. Lottie's stomach twists. She knows that truth too well—and is far more familiar with harm.

Reaching for a notecard at the center of the table, she welcomes the distraction:

The Legend of the Little Lunatic

Ages ago, Neglect bore a child.

With matted hair and grime-covered skin, this child was labeled a feral little girl.

People scoffed. Peers shunned her. Caretakers kept their distance.

Nightmares grew where love had been denied. There was no telling which was worse: the horrors of her mind, or the horrors of her reality.

*The Man in the Moon became her only
friend. She whispered to him, danced in the
dark with her fears, and made monsters her
friends.*

*She became the little lunatic. Wild.
Watchful.*

*Let us be better, for the vulnerable. Let
us be company worth keeping.*

Dr. Craven finishes with this:

"When nightmares become the sweet dreams of
a scared child, society has failed. Often, the younger the
child, the bigger their monsters. Let's be better than
those monsters. Let's work together to do right by
them."

Glasses clink in affirmation. Lottie ponders the
lunatic parable, wondering who wrote it. It's an eerie
little tale.

"Like what you see?" Verdilla whispers into
Lottie's ear. Lottie almost snorts into her glass. "He
just moved here at the beginning of the summer."

"I think you like what *you* see," Lottie retorts
with a smirk.

"A decorated scholar and esteemed
psychiatrist," the woman swoons. "And such devil-
may-care charm. Did you see his hands? Scarred all
over. And he cares about kids. Oof! So handsome."

He takes his seat to a humble *hear-hear*, and the
food arrives on cue. Attention shifts to things like roast
sauce and ice cubes.

Lottie eats quietly, content to observe. She knows most here by type, if not by name. Artists, therapists, benefactors. All orbiting Verdilla.

Diligently listening, she keeps to herself—an expert at blending. At becoming a wallflower.

"No one pays attention to the quiet ones," her grandmother would say. *"Except, perhaps, the quiet ones."*

As bellies fill and conversations wane, Verdilla the final event. Each guest is encouraged to find the secret their key unlocks. Bodies disperse—some up the stairs, others through the home, and most back out into the Garden.

Lottie seeks the path of least resistance. She heads upstairs.

"I hope Nabby leaves us alone," a woman whispers ahead of her. "A friend of mine swears the ghost pinched her when she visited."

The escort on her arm rolls his eyes in jest. "Scared of a little pinching, are you?"

The woman swats his hand away with a giggle. Lottie hangs back, careful to give the lingering couple their space—and also curious of this alleged ghost.

A framed write-up tells the story of one Abigail "Nabby" Ropes and her legendary hauntings since her death in 1839. History claims her petticoats caught fire in the upstairs room.

"Women and dresses," Lottie sighs to herself, eyeing her own and noting the freshly stitched seam.

She's never been one to give ghosts much thought. But after the afternoon's run-in with that eerie

Other and their curling fingers, she knows enough to realize: she doesn't know plenty.

At the first immersive room, she finds a live painter—busy at work with watercolors and gouache. Abstract florals come alive on the canvas. Bids are encouraged as visitors gawk.

Back downstairs, guests craft flower crowns. Several pairs of hands work busily, picking through and selecting those prettiest.

Lottie stifles a giggle, recognizing the selection to be funeral flowers—suggestive of death. A sly smile slips past her lips, amused by the oversight. Death disguised as décor—beautiful but morbid. Appreciating the silliness of it, she pockets a crown.

Still seeking the secret to her key, she wanders to the garden. Near the arbored entrance, a fashioned Mary Lennox reenactor performs a live reading of *The Secret Garden*. Special editions flank her garden stage.

"I am sure there is Magic in everything," the feigned orphan reads, "only we have not sense enough to get hold of it and make it do things for us."

Delighted by the verse and a connoisseur of classics, Lottie buys one. She's read it thrice, but she loves adding to her collection. Her ankle bends, tripping her in reminder: that collection is lost.

The last time she saw her precious bookcase, its contents wound up as collateral damage. Because he was in her home. And he's ruthless.

And she's never been back.

Shaking off the grief, she rallies. "Books can be replaced," she reminds. *Unlike bodies.* People. No one can substitute another.

Strolling on, others find the secrets to their keys, unlocking boxes of Lottie's treasures. Her gifted favors.

There are packaged teas honoring the locale. Bottled Wishes of dried flowers. Floral hair pins and boutonnieres. Florally things for a floral occasion.

Back at the arbor, a Tiny Library smiles from inside the leafy tunnel. Encased by books for kindred spirits, a little box sits on the small shelves. A match.

Inside, a delicate silver spoon beams like the moon. The end holds crystals and gems. Beneath it, a note thanks her.

Dearest Lottie, thank you for sharing your Gifts with others. I saw this spoon and thought of you: beautiful, unique, and quite mysterious. It is an authentic antique, surely made for magick.

Lottie grins. "It seems it's been an evening for enchantment."

Taking a seat on the nearest bench, she studies new spoon and her new book. For a moment, she's content. Hopeful. Maybe even happy.

Then it shifts—the night.

For a fleeting thought, the night air felt like a friend. But now it's different. Warning of foe.

That chill returns, tapping at her shoulder. *I see you.* Coming from the bar.

"I knew it," she chastises, regretting her decisions.

Perhaps her dyed hair and wallflower-only ways are not good enough. Perhaps this dress of her past life is, in fact, a death sentence. Perhaps she was always going to be tracked down. It was only a matter of when.

With a bracing swallow, she meets the eyes that pull at her. There he is, twisting whiskey in his hands. Its contents swirling to her churning gut.

He smiles, and her breath locks.

But then a shaking relief. Because it's not him. Not yet.

But the stranger's steady stare sends Lottie a sobering reminder she is ready to leave.

CHAPTER 6

Grateful for her lonely cottage, Lottie reverts to a recluse. For now, there is nothing and no one to bother her, or notice her, or *watch* her. She can rest.

She wakes more restored, but the fog in her head lingers. Thoughts pump like syrup—slow and thick.

Greedily, she inhales a Lavender steam and cradles a mug of Mint tea, chasing clarity. Outside, the air is crisp as autumn creeps closer. But a reluctant warmth loiters. Garden scents coil with the breeze—Lilies and Honeysuckle.

"Winter is going to steal you away," she says to the flowers. "I'll miss you," she assures, as a plucked Honeysuckle gets tossed into the mug she holds. "Maybe I'll do infused soda for the final Market Day." A sip. "Or tea."

Back inside, Lottie falls into her rhythm. Jarring teas and experimenting with mixes. Snipping Mint from the sill for therapeutic chewing. Hanging bundles of herbs to cure. Painting. Gluing. Ribbons. Twine.

Soft instrumentals sing from the record player across the room. Sometimes the radio. Occasionally the television.

Sound keeps her company as she does her daily doings. But still, her energy dwindles quickly.

Monday passes quietly.

Tuesday still follows with fatigue. Despite best efforts for tonics and tinctures, there's no relief. Whatever it is may be no match for herbs alone—but she dreads the idea of going back out. Not so soon after Sunday.

Hoping Wednesday will be promising, she presses on. Strives for routine. Pushes through exhaustion and lethargy.

But her bones ache. Heavy. And her dreams leave her so tired. Like there's a residue left behind, and she can't scrub it clean. Can't think straight. Or feel herself.

Lottie makes it to lunch.

Figuring a light bite might help, she gives herself permission to prop up her feet. Just twenty minutes. Watch the news. She'll go back to market crafts soon.

Instead, hours later, a nightmare rattles her awake. A certain pair of boots dissipates slowly, lingering. Like the residue. Like grime.

The news is still on, and it hums with a story that catches her breath.

"The son of a Gloucester fishery owner was found dead in his home this morning."

Lottie lurches upright.

"Discovered during a welfare check prompted by an anonymous caller," the anchor says,

45

"the deceased has been identified as Wellington Stacey. Known to some for his heavy drinking, the death has been ruled an accident—alcohol poisoning."

Stunned, she can't move. A picture of Wellington Stacey's face sits plastered on the television.

"Wells…" It comes out as a breath.

"Plans for the memorial are in flux," the anchor continues, **"as some immediate family members are currently at sea."**

Memories flood in an assault of disbelief and confusion. The woman with the microphone keeps talking, but Lottie can't hear. She can only exist. Her tired mind feels too feeble to find reason. Like navigating shore-breaking waves—it's a struggle to fathom what's real.

I didn't mean *it,* she thinks in a panic. *I said… I wished, but…*

Something festers inside her, sour and spreading. Rotten. It makes her woozy.

She *did* mean it.

The screen cuts to a shot inside his home. A bottle of whiskey sits by his bed—an expensive one.

"You don't drink fancy," Lottie reasons to no one but herself. "You're cheap. You drink the bitter stuff."

And then she sees them: postcards.

Lottie gulps.

One card displays Larkspur. One shows Foxglove. And one Lilies.

Bile rises, as her gut roils with a knowing warning.

Stumbling to the closet, she yanks down the clutch she'd taken to the Garden. Remembering the shears.

With a growing suspicion she opens it—fingers trembling.

Loose petals of Larkspur and Lilies rest at the bottom. The same shades as those she'd arranged in the bouquet on her coffee table. The same flowers she'd handled just before the soiree.

And nestled beside them: her gardening shears. Purple remnants cling to the blade. Foxglove. The flowers she'd stood beside when Verdilla found her.

Breath catches. Her hands go cold.

Racing to the bookshelf, she pulls out a weathered field guide on flowers and foraging.

Larkspur:
Poisonous Parts: Entire plant. Concentrated in the seeds.
Symptoms include: Weakness, drooling, abdominal pain, paralysis, and death.

Lilies:
Poisonous Parts: Leaves, seeds, flowers, and roots.
Symptoms include: Vomiting, diarrhea, loss of appetite, lethargy, and dehydration.

Note: Lily poisoning can cause kidney failure, which can be life threatening.

Foxglove:
Poisonous Parts: Leaves, flowers, and seeds.
Symptoms include: Drooling, vomiting, seizures, dilated pupils, and death.
Note: This toxin can cause the heart to slow down or become irregular.

The facts stare back at her like a mirror she can't escape. And a message is written in its fog: *Murderer.*

Her chest tightens. Her knees give.

She can't explain why, but she feels it. Deep in her blood.

Lottie has done a wicked thing.

A HISTORY:
TWO YEARS PRIOR

CHAPTER 7

The blank page suffers victim to flustered taps. Strumming fingers. Their owner lost in a daze.

Lottie has written scenes. Scribbled notes. But there's no story yet—no beginning, middle, or end.

So the first line of the first page stares back at her—waiting.

Eyes follow thoughts, as both roam for inspiration. Wandering past the high restaurant windows, they hover over a distant sailboat. Rocking in the distance. Caught in an evening storm.

A story has been building in her mind for some time. In the same way a florist might arrange a bouquet. Daydreamed visions pop into her head at random— summoned by a photograph or sparked by a song, like scenes of a movie. And she collects them eagerly, storing them in her journal for safekeeping.

The assortment is dazzling.

As she sifts through these scenes—arranging them this way and that, as if each is a stemmed flower—she can tell this story of hers is almost finished. Almost ready to be told, but not yet.

Something is missing.

To liken it once more to a bouquet: it's the ribbon. The perfect ribbon is missing. The thing that ties it all together. That makes it complete.

Windows clatter as a deep thunder rolls across Gloucester. Mounted blue mermaids go jittering. Hall lights flicker in warning.

The restaurant crowns a swanky hotel above the churning sea. The disturbance rattles some of the more fragile guests; audible frets rise from the nearby lounge. A few patrons chuckle nervously.

Lottie smirks; she loves this weather. Unlike the traditional take on storms and bad omens, Lottie's always found an angry sky to be a comforting one. Ever since she was a child, storms have meant good things were coming.

With a glance to the bar, the superstition seems to hold true. Because there it is. There *he* is. The perfect ribbon.

The *thing* her story has been missing.

"What's up, Stace?"

A rain-soaked man shrugs off his wet slicker, revealing an unbuttoned Henley. His smile is so genuine his eyes crinkle.

Accepting a gesture from the bartender, Lottie watches as the two men greet one another with an enthusiastic embrace and settle in for a moment of catching up.

"Ey, you cut your hair." The bartender slides over a glass. "You clean up nice for a fisher."

The newcomer—"Stace"—clicks his tongue, running his fingers over damp curls. They're dark. The color of black coffee.

"Yeah, old man said I was looking *'homeless'*."

Everything about him reminds her of the cozy drink—warm, inviting, and lively. As if caffeinated.

He takes a swig from the glass. "That's the word he uses for my brother, so… definitely meant it was time for a change."

The two laugh like he made a joke. Lottie sinks deeper into her seat, suddenly focused only on his lips and how soft they look. How they might feel to touch. To taste.

They look delicious.

The thought makes her swallow… and then sit up a bit straighter. A whisper in her mind warns she's gaping like an open-mouthed fish. But she can't help it; she can't look away. And she doesn't want to.

Inspiration has struck. He is her Muse.

The bouquet of scenes she's already drafted gets tossed into a mental sea of wildflowers. Imaginings flurry through her mind like petals in the wind. And she's torn between scribbling them onto her pages or tearing her gaze from this man who keeps the scenes coming. Like a faucet of fresh water. Flowing, fresh and invigorating.

A novel writes itself into her mind—a garden compared to the bouquet it once was. The whirlwind of thoughts sends her breathless.

"Your chowder, Miss."

Startled, Lottie chuckles nervously and thanks the waitress. The soup is hot and savory, clearing her mind with its scent. Allowing focus.

She writes.

Wreaking havoc upon the pages of her journal, she scribbles down inspiration. Scenes buzz through her mind like bees loose in a glasshouse—flitting against the panes. Tapping. Rioting.

Pausing to massage her aching wrist, she glances to the Muse. He's slipping on his raincoat.

Perhaps it's the cocktail she's been sipping for writer fuel, but without a second thought, Lottie follows—like a fish on a hook. Caught and trailing at his mercy.

With not a single bite taken, she fiddles with her wallet to cover the bill, knocks back the rest of her drink, and skips after him. Thoughtless. Pushed by instinct.

And instinct tells her to know more.

Taking the stairs to race the elevator down— hoping he's not heading to an unknown room—she enters the foyer and waits.

The evening has shifted to night. Coiled clouds deepen in contrast to the yellow shine of streetlights. The harbor's perimeter glows through thick mist.

Pretending to make a phone call, Lottie puts her cell to her ear as hands clasp her shoulders.

"Ope, sorry, Miss. Excuse me."

It's him.

In the dim light of the foyer, he turns in his apology and offers a smile. The sight of it makes her belly jump.

"No worries," she whispers too late. He's already dashed out the doors.

Hungry for intel, she watches. Satisfied, she conspires. Because she sees it. He's shown her.

He drives off in a truck stamped with a maritime logo. Lottie watches, knowing exactly where he's heading:

The Fishing Village Company

The words root in her mind like a title. Like a beginning.

CHAPTER 8

The in-person research begins the very next day.

For the sake of the story, of course.

After staying up into the small hours of night—with this man's face caffeinating her daydreams—Lottie now tiptoes about a buzzing fishery. Itching to spot her Muse.

Her stomach jostles with every step. Because he isn't just a daydream anymore. He's remembered. Memorized. She has a mind full of memories to pair with him.

Fantasized memories, sure… but memories, nonetheless.

Memories of his hands in her hair—well, her character's hair.

Lips. Skin. Breath.

Scenes that wrote themselves through the night until she woke aching.

Something about him unlocked something within her. She's changed. Things happened to her in the night. The Lottie of today is not the same as yesterday's.

Fantasy may be false to those outside of it, but the dreamer doesn't know the difference. Lottie's pulse is proof. It quickens the second she spots his truck pulling in. And there's no going back. He impacts her *everything*.

Her mind.

Her body.

Her want.

Suddenly feeling exposed, she loses nerve and panics. Checking her pockets and purse in desperation, she searches for a stray nip—hopes high.

"Dammit, Lottie," she groans. "Should have grabbed one." Liquid courage did its job yesterday. "Should've grabbed two."

Ducking behind crates at the loading dock, she watches from the safety of *secret*.

It's him.

There's light in his face—the kind that shines with fulfillment at a job well done. He walks the dock with easy confidence, shoulder-to-shoulder with workers in waders. They move in a rhythm with the waves that rock them. And Lottie just watches.

For days, Lottie admires from a distance. She learns of his life, but keeps to the periphery.

When night falls and she can't stand the distance, she scours the internet—wanting more.

Surely, someone like him would leave a digital trace. Because he's not just Stacey. He is *a* Stacey. The family who owns the juggernaut of a business that *is* the Fishing Village Company. But, no.

And it's maddening.

No social media, no casual snapshots. No family pictures. Just a sparse article naming the company's owners and their two sons. And the occasional breadcrumb of Mrs. Stacey's appearance at charity dinners, or fundraisers for the Maritime Museum. Not even a crew photo. The man is a ghost.

Relief returns with dawn. Every morning, back at the docks, she watches him again.

Others call him "Stace." Or more formally, "Stacey." It's obvious he's well-liked. Respected. Maybe partly due to his family name, but his own merit is there.

It's evident in his early arrival and late departures. His modest lunches and cajoling camaraderie. People like him. He's a friend. He welcomes others into his tiny trawler docked nearby, and shares in laughter over an offered drink. He runs errands without being asked. He takes pride in his work. He smiles.

God, how she dreams of that smile.

She wishes she had the gumption to approach him.

"I'd like to know you," she could say. "Would you like to get a coffee?"

But she doesn't.

She just watches.

She just writes down her wishes, guessing at the exact color of his eyes. Wanting to count his crow's feet while he delivers an eye-squinting grin. She imagines the smell of him—salt and cedar and skin. Then it feels real. He is her lover.

Night after night, she sinks into him on the page. Tantalizing banter. Soft caresses. Yearning lips.

She aches to meet her fantasy in the daylight. Yearns for it. A need.

Until then, she bleeds, pouring herself out onto blank pages. Staining them with lust, passion, and tragedy.

And then she goes back each day for more.

After a month, he sets off into the blue abyss, joining the voyage of a deep-sea fishing vessel. Forcing Lottie to focus.

With trembling fingers and a hollow chest, she finishes it:

The story.

Her story. And his.

CHAPTER 9

After a long night of final tweaks and hours of edits, Lottie laughs with her agent over a late-night toast. The relief is electric—weeks of writing, rewriting, doubting, and rewriting again. And now: a finished draft.

"I'm sitting with a legend in the making," her agent announces to the bar that's near closing. "Remember her name, everyone. Lottie Lockwood. Author Extraordinaire."

Lottie flushes, red-cheeked and startled. But the applause washes over her like a warm surf. This is a big moment—and she's grateful someone is making it feel like one.

But soon, the distraction will end. And waiting beyond the bar's glow is the thing she's been dreading to face:

Dottie's death.

It happened a week ago, right after Lottie had visited for a respite in the forest. Everything had been fine, and then it just... wasn't. It wasn't bad, either. It was just over. She was just gone.

The news was jarring. A new reality. Lottie ran from it—diving deeper into her fantasy instead.

Leaving a very real grief to be dealt with another day.

But now, that monster of pain lurks outside the bar. Ready to curl its cold fingers around her ribs and squeeze.

With a final shot, Lottie steels herself. Readying for the inevitable.

After following her agent to their comped hotel rooms, she grabs her bag and journal and turns back into the night. Wanting to walk.

Despite the heels, she walks for hours.

Aimless wandering, it turns out, keeps the mind quiet. She doesn't note where she's going or care about strange men on corners. She ignores the chill. And just walks.

Content to be mindless.

It's only when the sky begins to lift from twilight to gray that she stops. Because her calves throb. And her feet scream.

Spotting a bench that faces the black sea, an open seat waits—empty in invitation. In the distance, boats in the harbor rock on calm waters, soothed to sleep by their mother ocean. Docks groan in soft snores. The cool darkness is quiet.

She sits, finally still—ready to face the monster that followed.

It meets her in the silence, reminding that she's alone. Then it slides over her skin. Sinks into her lungs. Squeezes—as expected.

Drowning.

That's what it feels like.

Her body fights it—this onslaught of emotion—but it pours over. Up and out. Demanding to be felt.

She feels all of it.

Every bludgeoning memory.

Every tear.

Until she is nothing but wound. Raw. Open.

Beaten numb, she struggles for a ragged breath and faces the sky. Looking for Dottie. For her magic.

"Here I am," Lottie whispers. "Where are you?"

With trembling hands, she wipes wet cheeks. As the sunrise stirs, she breathes. Deep and long. Past the grip of grief and anguish. No longer drowning.

"There you are," she sighs, noting a tangible enchantment. The quiet allure before dawn. *Hi, Dottie.*

With her notebook ready, she writes. A final salute to her grandmother.

"You're a beauty," she hears with a startle.

Jolted from her musings, she glances up to find a slickered fellow approaching.

"I'm sorry?" She squints, seeing only a silhouette against the sea set to fire by a rising sun. But she does a double take—because his slicker seems oversized and he wears no pants.

"I said, 'you're a beauty!'" He welcomes himself to the other end of the bench. "As is the day!" A single finger offers an epiphanic salute to the sky.

Her heart lurches. Mouth dry. It's him.

Stacey.

The man of her literal dreams.

Him.

In shocked reflex, a subtle hand slides over to give herself a quick pinch—because he must be a dream. A sweet, welcomed dream, with a smile so unexpectedly refreshing.

"You're—" she breathes, speechless. *Is this real?*

She wants to tell him how his eyes are different than she remembers—having relived that fleeting moment in the hotel foyer where his hands brushed her shoulders. Up close, they seem lighter. In the carousel of her memories and daydreams, they were darker—merging with his midnight lashes. But they're not so dark; they're a cozy hazel. And there's a sleepiness to them that makes her want to snuggle into his neck and breathe him in and rest.

He smiles at her. She tries to count those happy squinting wrinkles.

"You're?" he asks, waiting for her to finish.

A traitorous heat crawls up her neck as she realizes she's been *gawking*.

Horrified, she panics. "You're not wearing pants," she blurts. Lips bend into her mouth in an attempt to hide. *Wow, real classy, Lottie.* "Sorry." She blinks to shoo away her problematic thoughts. "My head's kind of—it's a strange day already."

Sadness returns with the recall. She swallows it down. Because he's here. This is real.

Turning more fully toward her, the fellow crosses one of his naked legs and bobs his Wellie-booted foot.

"I love strange," he says, easy as anything. His confidence melts her. "I'm Wells."

"You're well? That's good."

Amused, he extends a hand in proper greeting.

"No, I'm Wells. Wellington."

Checking the name sewn into his slicker, she accepts his hand with a twirling stomach but raises an eyebrow.

"Not Stacey?"

"Last name," he shrugs. "Family business."

She knew that.

"Nice to meet you, Wells. I'm Lottie."

Still holding her hand, his smile widens just for her. Thinking about it sends a quake of pleasure down her backside.

"Nice to meet you, Lottie. Are you cold?"

In heroic fashion, he slides the slicker off his own shoulders and onto hers. She breathes in the warmth with a dizzy head.

"Thank you," she manages. "Not heading to fish?"

She notices his curls have grown longer since he's been away. And how they're now adorably riotous atop his head—messy from bed.

Mirroring her gaze to the horizon, Wells sighs. "Not likely a fishing day, actually."

"No?"

"You know…" His hand offers a rolling motion, as if it might summon a universal knowledge. "'Red skies at night, sailors delight; red skies at morning, sailors take warning.'"

"Ah." A confidence seeps into her from the warmth of his slicker. "But you're not a sailor. You're a fisherman."

Feigning an eyeroll, he turns back to her. "And you're a redhead, I probably should take warning." He chuckles. "That was... dumb." He laughs again.

"But, really... What are you? Or, *how* are you? You seemed very..." Pausing, he studies her. "Thoughtful." With an apologetic sweep of his head, his eyes skirt to his lap of boxershorts. "Before I interrupted, that is."

Nodding in silence—along with the bobbing boats and the stirring bay—she readies herself to say it out loud.

"My grandmother died," she whispers, trying for control. "She always said, when she passed, I should go 'seek something grand and find inspiration in the beautiful.'"

Thoughtfully silent, Wells watches her easily. As a fresh tear stings her cheek, Lottie forces an apologetic smile. "Like I said," she sniffs, "been a strange day already."

With a quick grab of her hand, Wells gives her a playful side-eye and asks the most terrifying question:

"Do I have permission to provide a distraction?"

CHAPTER 10

Her incredulous smile is all the confirmation he needs.

Wells scoops up her heels, bends low, and offers his back in playful invitation. Lottie laughs—bewildered and delighted—and climbs aboard. The two giggle from the seaside bench all the way to the café down the road.

Every second feels like a dream.

Lottie clutches him tighter, half-convinced he's the only thing keeping her tethered to this fantasy-turned-true. Fingers twitch at the closeness of his hair, wanting to rake it. Her nose closes near to his neck, wanting to breathe him in. To make sure he's not a hallucination. A delusion.

It makes her wonder if manifesting is real. She's heard people talk about calling their desires into the universe. She's whispered her wishes into the wind for months now. Maybe the wind has been listening.

Arriving at the café, he eases her down and she's breathless—from the smell of him, from the touch of him, from the *reality* of him. All smiles, he props open the door with a foot and grabs for her hand, lacing his fingers through hers—and lacing her insides likewise.

Despite a long night of no sleep, Lottie requires no coffee. She thought it before, and she feels it right now: he caffeinates her. *Forget coffee*—he could keep her going for days.

Taking a seat, she loosens her hand to free his. But he doesn't. Instead, his grip tightens.

"I hope you don't mind," he says, as his teeth shyly play at his bottom lip. "I get to be the guy holding a pretty girl's hand." He shrugs. "I'm enjoying it."

She hides an aching smile into a palm and leans over a propped elbow. "I don't mind."

He leans in, and she thinks he might kiss her right here in the middle of the café—like a scene from an old movie. But then he pulls back, holding the freshly retrieved wallet from the slicker she still wears.

"What'll you have?" His eyes twinkle with a playful rascality.

"Um," she tries, still recovering from what she thought was a near-kiss moment. "Coffee and a scone would be amazing." She may not need the caffeine, but she'll welcome it. "Thank you."

With a wriggle of his brow, he strides to order in his boxers, sleep shirt, and fishing boots… and Lottie thinks up a few scenarios for book number two right there.

With the order bagged to go, Wells returns with an outstretched hand. And Lottie—now back in her heels—accepts it eagerly.

They seem to walk aimlessly. But soon they stroll near her rental home, tucked away on the cozy cape that neighbors the harbor and kisses the Eastern Point Lighthouse.

Still early, the red skies from before have shifted into their promise of gloom. Lottie unwittingly flexes her hand in excitement—squeezing Wells' in the process.

"What was that?" he grins.

Too happy to hide it, she lets a laugh out. "It's just... a good day." Mimicking his side-eye from earlier, she specifies, "Good distraction."

Giddy, she hides in her coffee cup and takes a sip without tasting anything.

Squeezing her hand in mimicry, Wells raises his coffee in toasting fashion.

"Agreed. It's a good day."

Soon, she spots her home, tucked into the trees beside Niles Pond. A fleeting consideration teases her—images of soft kisses in her doorway and hot breaths tangled in bedsheets.

"What are you smiling at?" He peers into the distance, trying to follow her gaze.

But Dottie's words of warning bite through the daydream:

"Only a few things are yours in life, only a few things you have control over. Your name. Your home. And your secrets. Hold close what's yours for safekeeping. Insist on sneakery."

Blinking away the voice in her head, Lottie tries to dismiss the misplaced reverie. "Oh, just something my grandmother said."

"What was her name? What was she like?"

With a readying sigh, she contemplates how to respond.

"Well, I called her Dottie."

She will likewise keep Dottie's true name a secret, just as Dottie did. The silly woman, always insisting on *"sneakery."* The reason Lottie's penname is Lottie Lockwood instead of Charlotte Lowe.

"She was… my best friend. And a living legend." The recall of her passing makes the word "living" bite back. Lottie swallows.

Gently, Wells dares to pull her into him, offering a comforting squeeze. Lottie lets him.

"Lottie and Dottie," he tries, testing the way it sounds—and then teasing his bottom lip with grinning teeth. "I bet you two were quite the pair."

They make it to the lighthouse.

The sky has turned steel gray, the sea below it charcoal and frothing. Waves crash. A sea breeze sprays.

Lottie inhales the salt and mystery. Out of habit, she heads for a favorite sitting rock, and Wells follows with interest.

"Come here often?" he muses.

"Oh." Turning bashful, she offers, "I live nearby, so… yes, actually."

"By all means," he winks with a sweeping arm. "Lead the way, my lady."

He never does unwind his fingers from hers.

Feeling confident in her heels, Lottie overestimates the angle of rock and stumbles. Cursing internally, she tries to laugh it off—but a slight moan escapes tight lips instead.

"Are you all right?"

Kneeling beside her, he offers his aid.

"Just clumsy," she strains. "My ankle."

Gently, Wells holds her ankle and shifts it this way and that, seeming to catch how Lottie's night-out high heels lengthen her extended bare leg.

In welcomed cliché, Lottie notices the way the skirt of her dress teases at her thigh, hiked from the clumsy commotion. She also notices Wells... and how his eyes capture the same. They travel the route from her ankle to her knee, hesitating at the hem that seems tempted by the wind.

That question of manifesting returns. *Maybe...* A quiet, internal will asks the wind to slide the hem even higher. To tempt a soft touch.

His hands stay put, but his eyes linger—and something inside her ignites. The mere thought of *him* wanting *her?* It makes her shiver.

Triggered by the movement, Wells blinks away invisible thoughts.

"That feel okay?" he asks, not yet looking back at her.

Flushed with a newfound boldness, she leans forward, using his shoulders to balance—fully aware that her thigh brushes near his cheek.

"Yeah, I think it's okay. Thank you."

Wells returns to his seat beside her looking dazed. Dizzied. "Happy to help." His eyes squint so sweetly.

"Your turn," she demands, as she crosses the leg nearest him to let hemlines fall where they may. "Tell me something about you. Or something about your family."

With a click of his tongue, he surrenders what feels like a secret.

"Well, not much to tell. I... make do. I've got a brother who makes things a little harder than I'd like them to be, but,"—he kicks a rock—"family, right?"

There it is. That optimism. That endless smile.

Clearing his throat, a shy smile plays at his lips and he taps her bare knee with a soft finger. "Tag. Your turn again."

Her skin burns where his finger touched. Deliciously inflamed.

"Family?" Is that what they had been talking about? "No one else really worth mentioning." The reality of the words helps to sober the rest of her body. "I never knew my dad. And my mom is dead."

"Wow, I'm sorry."

Surprised by a lump forming in her throat, Lottie doesn't say anything. She just watches him, falling into her pattern easily, savoring him bit by bit.

And this time, he watches her. Slow. Intentional. Real.

The moment is wonderfully long, as they linger on one another—assessing lips, searching eyes, curious about the other and of this feeling of being enchanted. Of feeling bewitched.

"Lottie." He swallows.

Her breath catches. "Mmhmm?"

Tickled by his thoughts, Wells chuckles into the surreal morning. "I just... you're really pretty." He rubs his face. Laughs a bit more loudly.

She wonders if he might kiss her now. Wonders how he'll taste. His lips. His tongue. Then she dares

70

herself to beat him to it, eager to throw caution to the
wind—and then the wind makes its move first:
    Spraying them with a sobering sea breeze.

CHAPTER 11

Lottie scurries hand-in-hand with a dripping Wells. Two sets of teeth chatter as they laugh and fumble their way to her nearby home.

Quick with the keys, they greet the warmth of the foyer with audible sighs. A trail of droplets follows them to the laundry room. Ready towels afford further sanctuary.

"This is a really nice place." His eyes scan about as he ruffles his dark curls until they're wild. Damp, but still seeming soft. So soft, her fingers itch to touch them. "What do you *do*, exactly?"

Unable to stifle her pride, she laughs at the reminder that she's officially living her professional dream.

"Well, I work for a book agency," she starts, hesitant to say the rest out loud, "but... I'm also an author."

And you're my Muse. Here. In my house.

A tender heat swims through her belly as she recounts fantasized details that he alone inspired.

"Wow. Really? What do you write about?"

Now that heat creeps up her neck—this time, embarrassment.

A nervous laugh skitters past her lips. "Um, I like to write about all kinds of things. Suspense, mysteries… romance. The best stories have a variety, in my opinion."

Grasping that an untold something lurks in her explanation, Wells raises a knowing brow. "Well, consider me impressed."

He keeps his eyes trained on hers as his fingers move on with other matters—like peeling off a soaking shirt.

Lottie tries not to swallow audibly.

"Um, are you a, um…" Words fail as her thoughts flounder. "A… reader?"

How many times has she wondered about the softness of his skin?

What freckles or sun spots sit in secret, out of sight?

Scanning his person, she drinks in the sight of him, wanting to collect and cork this moment. This reality.

He's leaner than she would have thought—but then she remembers: he just returned from weeks at sea.

"I'd read yours," he grins. Then, holding open the dryer, the grin turns playful. "Want to toss yours in, too?"

"Oh." *Oh. Oh. Oh.* Her eyes dart to her dress— miraculously dry, thanks to his slicker. "Actually, I just need to towel off." *Coward.* She swallows.

Taking her towel, she runs it over cold legs and wet hair—realizing with slight horror that she must be a *sight*. No sleep, tearful morning, humid day… sea breeze.

"Use as many towels as you need, I'll… be right back."

Dashing to her room, she turns to the mirror in a fluster. It's not *terrible*. She could use a splash to her face. Some taming of her curls. Fresh clothes.

Back in the laundry room, he's pulling out his boxers. Part of Lottie wishes she'd had the wherewithal to "do a load." Because then he'd have to stay longer.

Towel-ridden. And then not.

He drops his towel, and Lottie nearly dies on the spot. Ducking out of sight, breathless, she hollers from the hallway.

"Want anything? Water? ...Whiskey?"

Emerging in dry clothes, he crosses his arms. A twinkle catches his eye. "Whiskey, eh? I'll have what you're having."

With a twist toward the kitchen, she leads the way. "Whiskey it is."

She pulls the bottle from the shelf with a pout.

"Ah." Holding it up, she groans. "Finished it yesterday with my agent."

Leaning close across from the counter, he conspires. "No worries. That your car out front?"

Thank the universe she took a taxi to the bar last night.

"That it is."

She beams. Another thing to do together. Another excuse to keep him close.

"Shall we?"

Hours later, they've skirted most of Gloucester Harbor—walking hand-in-hand once more.

Giggling over their not-so-stealthy liquor sipping, they roam along beaches and roadsides. The liquid warms them and turns them silly. A perfect complement to the whirlwind of a day. It dissolves any awkwardness. It fills them with a comforting abandon. They're cheery, and glassy-eyed, and *good*.

As the crisp and cloudy day darkens, the atmosphere turns dreamlike. Everything is heightened: the pressure of the sky, the wetness of the world, the briny scent of the ocean. Mist. Touches. *Him.*

The ground now glistens. The streetlights flare—magnified by the moisture in the air. Then the sky rips open with a clang, and the world gets a washing. They look to each other and laugh, welcoming the storm.

Lottie feels spellbound. As if she's not just in a dream—she's chasing it.

Following that whim, she pursues it. Chasing it harder. The magic of the day. Spotting a bench, she leads him toward it. He doesn't protest. They pause and she steps up, silent in her endeavors. His sleepy eyes watch her—glossy with drink and squinting in the rain—and a lazy smile dips into his lips. Curious, he waits.

"Why so blurry, Mr. Murray?" he drawls with a drowsy smile.

The nonsense makes Lottie's light head swim. "What?"

"Sorry," Wells chuckles. "It's nothing. Something I say to myself when the drink…"

Lottie takes the bottle and welcomes herself another tip. "When the drink hits just right?"

"Precisely," he concurs. Then, he goes bashful—biting his lip. Visibly charmed by her closeness.

"I've been aching to do this all day," she whispers, and she takes hold of his neck. With one hand, itching fingers slide into his curls. Easy, they rake through. He relaxes into her.

His forehead buries into her chest, warm and intimate against her skin. Can he hear her heart racing?

Another rake. His black-coffee curls gather and pull as she tugs—from the top of his forehead to the nape of his neck. A shiver trembles through him.

She smiles.

"You make me dizzy, do you know tha—"

A pair of eager lips interrupts.

Mouths meet, hot and heady. Her lips part his and she melts into them. He tastes like whiskey and warmth. With a groan, he melts, too. Hands grip her hips. Steadying. To keep it going. To make it last.

Breathless, he pulls away, but holds her tight.

"If I want to see you tomorrow," he starts, then pauses to pull her closer, "and I do, desperately, want to see you tomorrow…"

She looks away shyly and laughs. He turns her chin back to him, meeting her eyes.

"Will it help or hurt my chances to invite you over?"

**

She followed him to his trawler houseboat, swept along in a current of wonder and lust. The houseboat she's admired from a distance, watching him be a friend to so many. The houseboat that is modest, and welcoming, and warm. The houseboat she's written about, with paragraphs of passion and sensual imaginings. That houseboat. His houseboat.

Inside, it's just like him: cozy.

The kind of cozy that could easily morph into riotous lust for the night—and then serve a steaming cup of coffee over tousled sheets in the morning.

Her gaze flicks from the bed to him. And her body grows hot.

"Can I interest you in a dry tee?" he offers, extending a large shirt with a smirk. They seem to have bad luck with water.

Accepting it, she mirrors him. "Thank you. I think we're oh for two."

"Worth it," he shrugs charmingly, just as thunder rumbles.

Donning the draping shirt in the water closet, a whale swims in the reflection—decaled on the tee. A line of text pulls Lottie's lips at their corners as she reads the classic quote:

"It is not down on any map; true places never are."

"Moby Dick," she muses, appreciating the seafaring story. "So, he *is* a reader."

After changing—delighted by the excuse to tempt with bare legs once again—Lottie finds Wells at the counter.

He smiles over a plate of crackers and cheese. "Hungry?"

"Very, actually."

"Perfect. We're going to play a game."

With a snort, she challenges. "Oh, are we?"

"Yep. Whoever wants to eat has to earn it. A cracker for a question."

They take a seat at the alcove table and settle in.

"Okay, I'll bite," she welcomes—and steals a cracker.

"Hey, hey, hey." He guards the plate with mock offense. "First question: Tell me a secret."

The wind wails outside the little boat as if in warning.

Incredulous, she chucks a cracker at him. "That's not a question."

"Fine. *What* is one of your secrets?"

Turning thoughtful, she braces herself: *Should I tell him?* Should she give herself away so completely? Should she dare touch the magic flame that seems to smolder just for them? Or would that snuff it out and scare away the desire?

"I've..." she starts, but her heart beats into a frenzy. Like the rain at his window.

His smile drops. "I didn't mean to—"

"I've noticed you before."

There.

She said it.

And now she's thirsty. So thirsty. She reaches for a water on the table, quenching her thirst and drowning her embarrassment.

78

"Oh?" His cheeks pin back to where they were—plump and happy. "Go on, you have my complete and undivided attention."

Unintentionally, her eyes dart to the journal peeking out of her bag. "Nope. I answered. I get a cracker." She takes one.

Following her sight, he spots the culprit. She blanches. "No!" she shrieks, mortified. "No, no, no. That's not allowed!"

She lunges for the journal. He follows. They collide and tumble—tangled in a battle of limbs and laughter.

"Oh, come on," he sings. "I don't get to know?"

Breathless and burning, she wiggles free. Pitifully, she tries to stare him down with her "serious" face.

"It's not *all* for you," she tries. "Or, I mean, about you. It's…"

Mercifully, he relaxes his grip on the pages of guilty pleasures. Extends it as a peace offering.

"Forgive me. You've got me curious, but… you're right, it's not mine to read."

But part of her wonders what might happen if he did—if he were to read about the fantasies she's written. Maybe one of them would come true. Maybe he would read it and want it. Every part of it. But… maybe not.

"It's just…" *Ready or not.* "I've noticed you… a *lot*." Maybe she can just start with something small. "And I've liked noticing you. And you're sort of…"

Does she say it? Does she dare?

"You've inspired some of my writing, actually."

Full-beaming pride smiles back at her. "Really?"

The sky clangs and clatters against her taut nerves.

Cautiously, she flips to a page in her journal. That first page of that first day—spotting him in the hotel restaurant. No fantasies. Just *him*.

After that day, every moment of the memory went into her journal—detailing what she'd seen, what he'd said, how he looked... how watching him made her insides giddy.

"Here," she offers, forcing gumption through her fingertips.

He accepts it gratefully. Sets to reading.

She watches him like a storm chaser eyeing cloud formations. Trying to read his face.

His jaw tightens.

Thumbing through the pages, he stops. Pausing. Rereading. His eyes dart about in chase of something— but what? Emotions flicker all at once, and she can't tell if he's pleased, bored, disgusted...

Her stomach churns. He seems angry.

She can see it. Something simmers in a fiery blaze. Stifled but fuming.

"Lottie."

Her name lands heavy. Hearing him say it like that makes her chest feel open. Vulnerable. Exposing the lifeblood of her pages. The crimson ink that has seeped from her soul.

Unable to speak, she lifts her brows. Waiting.

Closing the book, he pins her in place with a steady stare—holding her with nothing but his eyes.

"Which do you like better?" he asks. "The person you've watched… or the person in front of you?"

The fantasy or the reality?

Lottie's throat goes dry. How could he think any such thing? But then his sterile face eases into that gentle, sleepy grin. Her shoulders relax. With a tug of his shirt, she pulls him in closer. Answering.

He lets her. She encourages how their movements shift the shirt she wears. Hiking hems and baring thighs.

He pulls back. Her grip tightens in protest.

"There's something *I've* been aching to do all day," he says, stealing her words from earlier.

With caressing fingers, he touches the soft skin above her knee. In a trail up her thigh, he tickles. Tantalizing.

With a gasp and a sigh, she fusses at him.

"You're such a tease," she tries, but only a whisper makes it out.

Then he closes in on her, connecting their mouths and following her invitation.

They rock with the boat. And then the boat rocks with them.

CHAPTER 12

The night was bliss. The sleep was deep. The boat was cozy.

Now, early morning, Lottie's body demands water. From the alcohol, the activity—all of it.

Slipping out of bed, she retrieves a cup from the table and slips on the slicker. Spotting a marker inside the ajar junk drawer, she snags it—and his boots. A plucky mood takes over.

Outside, the air is crisp. The day is clear and fresh and open. Fishing trawlers pace the distance, already hours-deep in their day. Two sailboats take to the waters. The day is awake… and she's ready for it.

With the marker cap at her bared teeth—from an inability to stop smiling—she bites it off and sets to drawing. On the toe of his boot, she colors a small heart—a reminder of her that she hopes sends him grinning.

"What are you doing?"

Turning, she finds him watching with a sideways smile, amused. She almost chokes on the cap at his presence—finding him even more attractive than yesterday. Already "fresh." Shaven. Awake.

Classically caffeinated.

His eyes are brighter today. His smile is somehow even more adorable. It's like she's seeing him for the first time all over again.

"Just enjoying the fresh air."

Eyeing her ensemble, he scratches his coffee curls that somehow seem shorter. "Ah, and my slicker, I see."

Confused, she joins in the assessment and cocks her head. "Well, I didn't figure you'd mind, since yesterday—"

His smile drops. His eyes go cold. And he looks toward the windows. And Lottie notices the way he's fully dressed, and holding a packed bag, and looking a lot more like the *him* she'd fantasized over.

In following his eyes to the windows, she sees a sleeping body still inside the boat. Her stomach heaves.

"Wells," he growls.

She could throw up right this very moment. Because that wasn't *him*.

Wells isn't "him."

This person is him.

They're brothers.

…They're twins.

Already inside *his* houseboat, the person she can only assume as the original "Stacey" hollers at the sleeping Wells. Demanding answers.

Meanwhile, Lottie struggles to stay upright. Sneaking into her shoes, she slips her belongings over her shoulder and flees before she faints.

"Dammit, Wells!" Stacey barks. "When are you going to pull yourself together. D'you treat yourself to the cash in my wallet again, too?"

The actual Stacey is holding back. Obvious restraint. Fuming.

"A *girl*, Wells? You brought a girl to *my* home?"

The sleeping brother struggles to wake, and Lottie spots the emptied bottle of liquor. Stacey snatches it in disgust. It had been nearly half full last she'd sipped from it.

Wishing she were the size of a mouse, Lottie finally rushes out—but not before hearing the devastating truth that pulls it all together.

"This is why no one wants you around," Stacey seethes. "This is why dad is tired of you. You act like this is about who's the favorite? Wells, *look* at you. You just keep doing this *shit*. Drinking. Stealing. Mooching." And then, with the finality of a slamming cabinet door, "When are you going to stop acting homeless and grow up?"

With adrenaline surging through her, memories connect. Logic settles. Realizations become painfully clear.

Lottie runs to the bench—the same one from the morning before—and collapses onto it. Her mind thrashes like sails in a gale: directionless and snapping. She should have known. The oversized slicker. The longer hair. The different eyes.

She had justified every variance, but she'd been an idiot. She wanted *him* to be real, but he hadn't been. Not the way she'd thought.

Her stomach coils once more at the realization that he knew. He *knew*. He read the journal, detailing every ounce of the original Stacey and even commenting on his "homeless" brother. There's no doubt he knew; he undeniably realized she had seen his brother that day. Had detailed the *other* Stacey. Had been inspired by the *other* Stacey. Fantasized. Wished for.

Not Wells.

And then he let her believe…

A violent reflex launches her forward, only to find familiar boots nearby, taunting her with a freshly drawn heart.

"Sorry about him." It's Wells. "He likes to get high and mighty."

"Stay away from me," she spits, struggling to sit up through her shaking.

With eyes still glossy from drink, Wells surrenders to his knees in pleading fashion. "What? Why? Don't—" His breathing turns to pants, and his eyes turn murderous. "Don't let Brooks ruin things."

Brooks. Brooks Stacey. She had never even learned his real name in all her sleuthing.

She could slap Wells. "*Him?*" Words almost can't be found. "You let me believe you *were* him! You're… that's…"

"*You* said I was better," he barks back. "I asked you—and your body answered."

Nauseated and enraged, she watches him and wonders: *What kind of sociopath justifies something like that?* And then, for a moment, she tries to still believe in it; she tries to hold onto a morsel of the hope from yesterday—of the magic and whirlwind enchantment. She tries to look at him with new eyes and see someone she could forgive…

But all she sees is *wrong*.

The months of fantasizing and pent-up angst somehow convinced her that yesterday was inevitable. She believed she had manifested something that was meant to be. She was naïve, and wishing for romance.

The fantasy of yesterday was assumed against the backdrop of the man she'd made *"him"* to be in her mind. And a stranger was never meant to fill the role. The fact that yesterday was just random has tainted everything.

Now, his pantless legs are pathetic. His bedhead, borrowed. The slicker? Not even his. He's a drunk who probably stumbled out of his brother's houseboat the day before after a drunken night before that—just as he's doing right now.

Yesterday, she walked in the footsteps of a fantasy.

Today, that fantasy is collapsing.

And Wells...

He started as collateral damage.

But he finished the night with welcomed deceit.

He's literally not who she thought he was—and he knew it. She saw him realize—the anger that flashed through his features, the epiphany unfurl as he read, as he understood it was the *other* Stacey all along...

Maybe there still could have been a reality for them that night—not of the assumed Stacey but with the real Wells... but he didn't give her the chance to choose. Not honestly. He didn't offer her the actual choice of himself over the fantasy of his brother.

He lied to her. And then he took advantage of her.

She vomits.
At the thought of him.
Of herself.
Of the lie she let in.

CHAPTER 13

Wells didn't like her answer.

More than that, he refused it.

Curled up in her office, Lottie wonders about the concept of manifesting now more than ever. The story she wrote is filled with passion and romance. And those are the two things she focused on during her days of daydreaming. But the story is also sweetened with suspense and tainted with tragedy—and she fears she may have manifested more than she meant to.

Because on her desk, once again, is a letter. Paired with pages from her soon-to-be-published book. A copied manuscript that went suspiciously missing in the days following the drama with Wells. The rejection.

The mere notion that he may be creeping nearby sends spiders down her spine. Pulling up her knees, she readies to read what he wrote.

At first, they were almost romantic. *Almost.*

Now, they're borderline threatening.

Lottie,

You're only fooling yourself at this point. Look at the proof in the pages. YOUR pages. We could literally be a dream come true, but you're getting in the way.

Stop it.

Yours TRULY

Attached to the letter are pages from her book—highlighted, underlined, defaced. Scenes he believes mirror their time together, though entirely misplaced.

Replaying that day, hour by hour, Lottie itches to tear her hair out.

She should have known better, even if only in the cliché of it all. Her documented dreams and written-down fantasies were so much more enthralling than this unoriginal romance. She and Wells were *boring*. There was no real spark—just a sprained ankle, a borrowed t-shirt, a blur of grief and longing mistaken for love.

It's all just so maddening—and he keeps it going, wishing for more.

The fantasies fill the pages, and he's trying to force the fantasy to fill their lives. But that's the thing:

He's trying to force it. And she's not interested.

**

It lasts for months. Letters. Anonymous calls. Lottie's unraveling.

Paranoid notions of a hidden lurker follow in the shadows.

She considered going to the police, but what would she say? A man she slept with once is sending letters made of her own words?

To keep her job safe, Lottie does her best to keep up appearances. To seem normal. She ignores the letters delivered just for her. She sticks to a plan: *Just until the book is published.* Because it's so close... in the final stages with the publisher. Almost there.

She installs an alarm system.

She keeps her eyes peeled.

She ignores unknown callers.

She never goes out at night alone.

And more than anything, she misses Dottie— her emotional haven.

By the time Lottie learns of her novel's launch date, her wits are already unraveling. Because they've been stolen from her: autonomy; normalcy; her happy life.

In wine-heavy reflection, she grows angry. Furious. She *knows* better. Manipulation, and coercion, and deception—these are tactics she has studied and applied to her stories. These are things she's *sworn* to never fall victim to.

This is not a relationship she has agreed to, yet he has assumed some power over her. As if she were so meek.

Resolute and infuriated, she decides she is done with it. She is not his, and she never will be. And she tells him so, leaving a message for him in the only sure way she knows how while keeping a distance. A text.

With a quick unblocking of a number that had incessantly bombarded her for days, she announces her annoyance, declares him to be a stalker, and orders him to leave her alone.

The reply chills her: "You stalked first."

She blocks him again. For good.

Let him seethe in silence.

**

In the following days, things were different.

A fragile silence crept back in. Normalcy—or something like it—returned on tiptoes. Careful and cautious. She congratulated herself for being so bold.

And then *the* night arrives—her night. And much arrives along with it.

CHAPTER 14

"It's happening," she sings to herself, tickled and giddy. "Tonight is for you, Lottie Lockwood," she whispers at the front door, making her way inside.

"You mean Charlotte Lowe," she hears from the porch swing behind her.

Wells.

Frozen at the threshold, Lottie's heart riots behind its cage of bone as she realizes he's been sitting right outside her front door, silent and waiting.

"Hi," she says, somehow managing nonchalance despite a heavy tongue that sinks into her throat. "What are you doing here?"

Rising with a knowing smile, he extends a package as if nothing is amiss between them. In quick assessment, her heart goes from rioting to downright spiraling, twisting into her stomach as she sees what he's trying to do. His outfit—a formal suit and tie. That can only mean:

"Well, I'm escorting you to the big event, of course."

Lottie swallows, noticing that his eyes seem wrong. Glazed, even—not just sleepy. Glossy and red.

And then there are his shoes, out of place and inappropriate... but entirely intentional. Because they're *the* boots. His Wellington boots with the heart drawn on the toe. The heart she herself drew to remind him of her... back when he was a different *him.*

Feeling stuck, Lottie waits, afraid to let him in but also fearing what might happen if she refuses. Something in his expression seems wild, tonight. Reckless. With silenced panic, she proceeds forward, wondering if it might simply be best to let him escort her. Perhaps a public break up would be best. This is her night, she reminds herself. *Don't let him ruin it.*

"I'm not ready," she insists, as she tries to steady her shaking hand and unlock her door. With a mental force that nearly makes her sick, Lottie curses her own thoughtlessness. *"Just like a secret, hold what's yours for safekeeping. Insist on sneakery."*

She literally led her demon to her doorway.

"Oh, Charlotte—I mean *Lottie,*" he says, baiting her. "You're my person. I wanted to surprise you with a gift to make the night special. Tonight is *your* night. I wanted to help make it all about you. So... here."

With the box outstretched, Lottie lets him follow her into the foyer and she opens it. A beautiful green cocktail dress sits inside, embroidered with elegance.

"It's gorgeous," she assures, hating to admit it but finding it true. "I love it."

"Just as you are gorgeous. Just as I love you."

Bile churns. Uncomfortable, Lottie looks to the time and tries to gather her thoughts.

"Oh, gosh, I need to get ready."

Leaving him no time to respond, she darts away, closing her bedroom door and turning the lock. Relieved by the fact that a room full of people is expecting her arrival, she summons a faraway serenity and tries to simply focus on getting there. *Just make it to the event.*

**

They make it to the event.

Entering a room that dazzles of sophistication and celebration, Wells ushers her through, his hand on her back as they cross the threshold of the Ropes Mansion, and Lottie accepts the champagne offered upon entrance.

"She's here!" a voice booms through the speakers.

All turn to the night's royalty and applaud her. Lottie Lockwood.

"Please welcome the reason for tonight, and the author of the coveted debut novel, *Wild Where We Grow!*" The applause resumes, and Lottie laughs at the praise, finding it all to be surreal.

And then the hand on her back tightens at her waist, pulling her in and plummeting back to reality.

"Congratulations, *Charlotte*," he breathes at her ear. "You did it."

Finding strength in the crowd, Lottie frees herself from his grip and greets her coworkers at the agency, joining in excited chatter with the novel's publisher and literary gurus.

"Who'd have thought our own little Lottie would be hiring big agents instead of just working for one?"

Warmed by the welcoming smiles and familiar faces, Lottie finds a breath and relaxes her shoulders, not realizing they were tensed.

"I thought it," she responds in jest. "I definitely *never* considered that you're connected to the biggest publishers in the country."

Her boss rolls his eyes in delighted mockery. "Oh, right. Not because you love reading stories or helping other struggling writers to make their dreams come true."

She laughs. "Exactly."

Feeling happy now, she wades into the moment, like toes into a river, careful not to be overwhelmed by the life force of the night or the current of the commotion.

In apprehension of its end, she glances to her back, paranoid by that too-familiar feeling of nearby eyes watching her.

Wells sits at the bar, studying her, twisting a glass of whiskey in his hands. He's telling her he knows. He knows she's trying to be rid of him. Somehow—and she is certain—he is telling her she can't leave.

After an hour of cocktails, and praises, and polite greetings, Lottie is pulled away from the elbow-rubbing praise by a yank of the arm.

"I think it's time to go, Charlotte," he says, spitting out her name every chance he gets, insisting on assholery.

Embarrassed and now annoyed, she jerks her arm back. "You're drunk. *You* can leave whenever you'd like."

As soon as she'd said it, she knew it was a mistake. Not untrue… but a mistake. His eyes grip hers with warning, and then he composes himself, without another word, and walks away.

He doesn't come back the rest of the evening, but she's doubtful of its permanence.

As the dream-come-true night comes to a close, and friends and fans congratulate her with farewells, she savors the moments by being one of the last to leave. It isn't until she finally exits, noting the empty street and locking doors, that she realizes:

He left with her car.

**

By the time she makes it home—and seeing no sign of her vehicle—she angrily stalks toward her house, enraged by his insistence on ruining this night. Apparently, her anger blinds her; as soon as she unlocks the door, Wells appears at her back, pushing her in and shutting the world out.

She forgot to set the alarm. Earlier. He hovered, and she couldn't get away quick enough… and she forgot.

"You're drunk," she hollers in disgust, noting the stench on his breath and the haggard insanity in his eyes. "We can talk about this tomorrow."

"You know you're the bad guy, right?" His words slur, and his eyes seem to drip with the same liquored weight, pulled down into their own frown. "That this is all *your* fault."

Outright infuriated, Lottie's challenge slips past her lips before she can think better of it.

"*My* fault? It's *my* fault you're stalking me and showing up drunk to *my* special night? Get over yourse—"

"Yes!" His roar bellows with such force that she stumbles into an alcove. Cornered. "Your pages. Your body. That day together. It's like you've *bewitched* me. And now you're TORTURING ME."

"You lied to me!" A heat pounds through limbs. Her voice cracks with fury. And fear. "*You* ruined everything when you chose to PRETEND TO BE YOUR BROTHER!"

His breath hitches. A maniacal twinkle catches in his eye. Then he laughs—too loud, too staged. Contrived.

"You don't even *know* my brother, so why the hell should it *MATTER*?!"

He towers over her now, blocking her in as if he might make her feel small.

Adrenaline courses, as Lottie questions the best option of getting away from this. From him. He's deluded, and now he's drunk. There will be no truth-telling if she wants to avoid the temper that seems ready to explode through his flexing fingers.

"You're right," she acknowledges, trying for steady. "That is true, I don't know him." A pain prods at her gut—one of embarrassment.

I don't *know him.* She, herself, had been delusional.

"Let's just…" Risking contact but hating the confines of his cornering, her nervous palms press

97

tenderly into his chest. A vibration beats into her fingers, and realization forms a knot in her throat, lodged and choking… as she recognizes a heat of rage radiating where her fingers touch. "Let's sit down." She can barely whisper now. "I'll pour you a drink."

She listens, waiting for his response, too fearful to look at him. But the stillness lasts for too long. Her eyes dare a glance, fearing a glower from above, but instead, it's worse:

He seems to savor.

As if to avoid being distracted, his eyes sit tightly shut while his chest jitters beneath her touch. A small whine whispers past his lips, as if tortured. His flexing fists inch toward her waist, seeming to likewise dare a touch in response. He takes a breath, and a vein in his neck pulsates like a ticking clock. Or a ticking bomb.

"I've missed you," he breathes. "I miss you."

Now desperate, her feet move to freedom, and he lets her, though hardly.

"Take a seat." A deep breath. "I'll bring you some whiskey."

His throat clears. "Bring two." An attempt at ease is evident, tainting his words with a hollow falsity. "You'll be joining me."

She brings two.

She walks to the living room.

She sees he's made himself comfortable, having shed his boots by her bedroom door.

She takes a seat.

"Cheers," he tries, holding out his glass in invitation. "To… second chances," he ticks, "and making *new* memories." He grins.

Finding it difficult to act like his words don't make her cringe, Lottie swallows a gag and offers what pitiful fake smile she's able to. "Mmhmm."

The fumes of the drink make her head spin; she's already so dizzy from a night of champagne. And, now, she's tired too. It's late. Her fight-or-flight senses have been triggered enough to keep her on edge. And there's no telling when this human-sized bomb will go off.

Chancing a glance to his eyes, she tries to read them in the same way she'd tried to read them that night on the boat. She had seen a spark of madness then, only she hadn't understood it. She hadn't recognized it. But now she does.

"If you were to give me a second chance," he starts, watching the whiskey swirl in his glass with a twisting wrist, "I really do believe we'd be perfect. I mean, I *know* what I did was wrong—the lie was wrong—but…" His brow furrows and his other fist clenches. "Everything else was *true*, right? It's not my fault that you thought I was someone else. I just thought you were… incredible, and—"

Now distant in reverie, she watches as his eyes swim over that day, and she almost feels sorry for him. Almost.

"And I just don't understand why you won't give *us* a chance. A real one."

Because I don't want to give you a chance, she wants to scream. *I'm not interested in there being an "us." I just want you to leave me* ALONE. *You make me want to pull my hair out. You make me feel sick. You make me fucking terrified.*

It's her turn to speak, but she doesn't know what to say. She doesn't know how to get out of this. There may be no getting rid of him tonight, so her options are dwindling. He is not going to be reasonable. He is not going to leave willingly.

Does she try to pretend?

Does she hope to discreetly call the police?

Does she wait for him to fall asleep into a drunken stupor?

Looking to the whiskey bottle, it's nearly full. Remembering their night together and the amount he drank then, she bets that outcome would be a very slow-coming one. And it's already nearly three in the morning.

Finding no reason to pretend she's not as exhausted as she is, Lottie leans into the truth of it. With a rub to her brow and a massaging of her calves, the heels she's been wearing for hours slide off and she stands to excuse herself.

"I'll be right back." She yawns. "Let me change. Just a second."

It's impossible not to catch the intensity in which his fingers dig into the arms of his chair, but he says nothing. He gives a nod, and she doesn't care to pretend she's asking for permission. This is her home. This is her life.

Plans of escape race through her thoughts as she forces her legs to move slowly. To avoid seeming too eager.

My keys are on the kitchen counter. My purse is on the kitchen floor. My phone is in my purse. Maybe a neighbor is home. Maybe I can pretend to fall asleep. Maybe I can crawl out my window.

In the mirror, she catches his hand flick over her glass—dropping something inside.

A pill.

Her mind screams. *He's trying to drug me. He's going to—*

Before the thought finishes, his eyes lock hers and a spark of rage flames. Caught.

"Get back!" she screams, bolting for the bedroom door as he jolts from the chair.

All at once, her stomach twists in a way that seems to pull the blood from her legs. She can't feel her feet. Can't feel her knees. Can't tell if she's still standing or being held up by something else altogether. Her body is numb—moving on instinct—but her mind is awake. Terrified.

Snatching his boots with quick thought, she slams the door shut and locks him out.

Feral pounding ensues.

"I'm just trying to get you to RELAX!" He hollers through the thundering slab of wood. "I'm not trying to be a monster. I just need to remind you how we are together. *Really* together!"

Her insides roil at his meaning. *You think if we have sex like we did that night, that all will make sense again—that all will be right in the world?* She nearly laughs at the hysteria of it all. *You think* raping *me will convince me that we should be together?*

With adrenaline overwhelming her body like a visiting ghost, an unfamiliar strength surges and she acts. Heaving her treasured bookcase sideways, she hopes to barricade the door. Books and notebooks spill out, the shelves emptied—no match for him.

Wrought with alarm, she tries to wedge the case between the door. But the lengths are awkward and her strength wanes.

A fist flies through the middle of the door, sending Lottie's knees buckling.

"Just give me a CHANCE, CHARLOTTE!"

Lunging for her window, she throws anything she can grab and heaves, trying to break it. When it finally gives way, the largest shard is salvaged, wrapped with a shirt and wielded at the fiend who's just unlocked her door and shoved himself inside.

"Get back, you fucking deluded piece of shit."

She holds the weapon high, ready to put up a fight. His eyes may look murderous, but hers feel it; a wild ferocity zips through, rattling through her core and making her see red.

Something about the sight of her causes him to hesitate, and she takes advantage, ready to speak the truth or die trying.

"You know, right now, it's just the *lie* of what happened that makes me sick to my stomach."

Every second she can breathe sends an unsteady inhale into her lungs and a godforsaken shaky exhale out.

"But if you were to…" She motions to the living room—to the drugs. To the reality that he was about to try and rape her just to get his way. "If you even *dare*," she seethes, "I swear to you I will *never* have a single thought of sympathy for you. There will be no fond memories. The thought of you will make me cringe. The idea of your touch will make me want to vomit." A sober and steady stare, now. "There will be NO going back."

The hostility in his features doesn't meet his eyes. His shoulders bulk, and his fists clench, and his veins rage, but his eyes plead—and that's the most unsettling of it all. Some part of him demands a stillness, and he seems to contemplate, all while a white-knuckling fire builds inside. But then his gaze settles on her weapon of glass, and a glint twinkles in his eye that kicks at her legs in reflex, and that is her mistake:

She reacts too soon.

Her spurt of movement sends him lunging for her. He pounces, and he curses. She flees, and he chases. In quick chaos, lamps are thrown. In anger, side tables topple.

He yanks at her dress. "I bought this," he snarls past her panic. "I'll take it back."

Irate, she rips it herself, pulling at the seams in a promise to be no one's plaything. No one's dress-up doll.

"You can have it, you drunken rapist bastard!"

That only douses the fire in his eyes, now fully enflamed into madness. With a plunge, his long arms grab at her, and his fingers find the hole in her dress. Catching, he yanks at the fabric, pulling her closer and kicking at her legs with his own, forcing her to collapse.

Her head plummets into the bookcase, and then there's black.

CHAPTER 15

Lottie comes to with a throbbing head and aching limbs. Weak. Battered.

A weightless sensation dizzies her, making her head feel heavy. Impossible to lift. But when she does, a waft of whiskey burns through her nose and nausea crawls up her throat. A pointed disgust lingers.

He's carrying her—Wells is carrying her—and a dozen stifled thoughts clatter inside her beaten mind.

"God," he groans, though he sounds far away. "I can't even look at you."

The words sound gruff... almost pained. But before she can make sense of them, her ears are ringing. Because he dropped her.

Like a ragdoll.

The ground feels rough with rocks and water weeds.

Water.

The realization surges through her like a cold bath, frigid in her veins. *Why are we by the water?*

Something tugs at her—some pesky thing, maybe an animal—but she's so tired. And so pained. So many thoughts battle in her head. Memories. Mistakes. The overwhelm nearly drags her back to the void. But not yet.

The thing—the animal—doesn't leave. Something nips at her shoulders with a soothing rhythm. The nearing sound of water soothes like a white-noise lullaby.

Water.

Realization courses like a canal.

WATER.

She understands, all at once, that nothing is tugging at her; she is *being* tugged. There is no animal. There is only a madman.

Pulling.

Yanking.

With painstaking efforts, her eyelids struggle open to notice red embers from the rising sun searing overhead, lighting to fire the grand abyss that hovers above… a sky that threatens of hellfire. Her mind screams, but no sounds slip out.

It isn't until the shock of water rushes over her—as maniacal hands hold her under—that adrenaline finds her again, slipping into her skin like a ghost once more. Grasping. Grappling.

Kicking free, she lunges to sitting, finding relief in the shallow shelf of the water, grabbing at anything with a newfound might.

Wells curses and seems to slip, pulling them both under.

Water greets Lottie's screams with strangle. Choking. She punches and flails. Needing to survive.

Yanked back upright, her fight resumes—but then his grip loosens. Air floods her lungs.

Pain blinds her, but dread fuels her legs. An impossible energy carries her to the edge of the trees that beckon, beyond the reaches of the pond's greedy fingers. Safe, she collapses—like prey playing dead.

As if lifeless, she lies, grateful to blend in with the trees. To become one with the woods.

What just happened...

Bewildered as to how she'd gotten away, Lottie listens for his nearing steps. Instead, she hears only Wells' wails. Somehow, something pained him, and he cries and curses her name, promising he'll find her.

In caution, she peeks through the foliage that veils her in secret, finding the sun to now have risen over Niles Pond, surprised to find her predator cupping his face, sobbing and sunken to his knees.

Only then does she realize one of her hands feels ablaze, burning as if blistered. Gripped within and vibrating with her trembles, she finds a white-flowered weed. Not yet knowing its name but realizing she must have swiped his eyes in her thrashing, Lottie weeps over its burning embrace in gratitude, pledging then and there to train in the physic of the flowers.

PRESENT DAY

CHAPTER 16

The riddle of the flowers on the postcards dizzies Lottie's mind into a carousel of color. Her fingers itch to read or research, but what is there to seek?

Certainly, she must be out of her mind.

Why should she have any connection to Wells' death? If she had, why would she have chosen the approach of poison? Why can't she recall cutting these flowers that have made their presence known from the bottom of her bag? What did she do with them after their harvest? How would they have arrived to—and then been ingested by—Wells?

She doesn't even know where to find him.

But she's always feared he could manage to find her. Should his father permit him any of his access to resources, Wells would have great threats at his disposal.

It's the reason she never returned to her house. It's why she fled to her grandmother's cottage.

It's a fear that cost her a dream promotion with her agency.

It's a reminder that makes her gut churn when she considers cashing a check on a novel inspired by a delusion.

It's why her honeyed hair has been diluted from its wild red.

It's why she now goes by Lottie Dutton, borrowing Dottie's surname, relieved she'd at least kept Dottie's secret close.

In desperate search of inspiration, she scans the cottage as if answers to her questions might lie hidden within the flowers and herbs strung about the walls—or stuffed inside the modest bookcase of small stories and studied texts. In a corner of the kitchen, she spots her teaspoon gift, promised to be "surely made for magick," and the concept triggers the memory of Mugwort in her market tea.

Mugwort, within the mystic community, is admired for aiding in dreams and divination.

Retracing her days, it was that market day that she hurried home, sinking with fatigue and waking up late into Sunday. It was the next day that she saw strange visions of hands reaching out of creek beds. It was that night, at Sunday's event, that she must have cut and collected Foxglove from the mansion's Garden.

Perhaps she'd been slipped a spelled tea… but, why?

When Lottie began her journey of learning this new way of life—studying herbalism, and mycology, and how to forage within her new forest home—she quickly understood the overlap of mysticism and witchcraft was inevitable. The community of practitioners appreciating both the medicinal and magical properties of herbs and flora were heavily influenced by traditional practices once considered as wickedness… when, often enough, it was mere midwifery.

The skepticism returns as Lottie considers. *Magick.* It seems almost wrong—a perversion of truth. But perhaps she is holding herself back. Maybe there is a deeper option than the shallow commercial magick she *thinks* she knows. Maybe together, they go deeper. Stronger. Magick and magic—tied together like a rope, anchored in mutual appreciation.

"I bet you dabbled in it, didn't you, Dottie?" She whispers to the cottage itself, often imagining her grandmother hovering within its walls, eternally at home. "No doubt," she decides.

And just like that, it seems a path has opened up that Lottie must follow—at least, until it dead-ends. She settles to pursue answers through magick. She's not sure how or what the endeavor may entail, but she feels certain enough by the surprise of Mugwort in her tea that something mystical is at work.

"It is only logical," she assures herself, feeling silly. "To fight magick with magick."

Recalling much but forgetting much more, Lottie scans her grandmother's bookcase, wondering if, in her hundreds of glances through the years, she might have missed a text for the moment's conundrum. With no clear option dancing to be noticed, she instead takes to the pages of a nearby journal and jots down what she remembers.

It's even less than she thought.

Honey—happiness and...

Mint—luck, courage, and...
Lavender—peace, clarity, and...
Roses—love, and...

Not even the basics of the basics. She can recall the practical benefits of Chamomile, Marigold, Rosemary, and Sage... but in the world of magick? Her mind feels muted. Alas, it seems there are some errands to run.

CHAPTER 17

On a quaint, forgotten street corner between an alley and a pub, a modest little bookshop sits and waits for the wandering toes of curious minds. The charm of a characteristic disarray greets newcomers—at first with overwhelm, then with comfort. And an encouragement to become lost.

Some new releases and bestsellers line a shelf in a back corner, out of sight and meant to be ignored. They are lesser here. They collect dust as their allegedly inferior counterparts are touched and tickled, curiously perceived as customers seek something unique and misunderstood.

Used, aged, and weathered, the older books on the dustless shelves hold histories in addition to their stories. They've lived stories of their own. And now, the person whose soul feels seen and known when holding one of these bound kindred spirits walks away with a new friend—and not just another book to flip through from start to finish. No. These books are sought after, not simply accepted. These books are for getting lost in just as much as the shop in which they sit.

Likewise, Lottie finds herself getting lost in memories, strolling down the shelved aisles in reverie as she pictures her Dottie just ahead of her, sifting through "secrets." That's what she called the books that spoke to her.

"Some of these gems are the best-kept secrets," she'd said to a young Lottie at her heels. *"They're not only marvelous reads, they've got magical notations. Like letters passed from one reader to another."* With a chuckle to herself and a whistle at the works in her hands, both eyeballed the lovely antique covers and admired the prints and filigree. Dottie's aged but still-wild curls washed over her shoulders as she read, seeming to hold their own curiosity and ignoring the butterfly clip that attempted to secure them back. Her weathered fingers caressed the cover and pages. A breath of fascination sat suspended on her wrinkled lips. Everything about the woman radiated wonder.

"Like just here, inside this cover, there's a message to 'the reader who's lucky enough to find this next: read it while alone in the woods near Dead Men's Fingers.'"

At the time, Lottie had been both intrigued and perplexed by such a notion, and Dottie had guffawed at the look on her granddaughter's face.

"Oh, Deary, it's a secret—a code. Come. We'll get it, and I'll show you."

"Can I help you find something, Miss?"

An associate pulls Lottie out of her head and back to the present, blinking and embarrassed.

"Oh, yes, actually. Um…" She struggles to find her words and her reason. "I'm looking for… something on magick?"

Referring to the text the way a scientist might consult notes from a study, Lottie finds her nose in a book the rest of the afternoon. *Magick.* The introduction isn't what she expected.

Earth magick is no show of sparks or levitation. It's a contract with nature.

Settling into the sofa, she sips her tea and keeps reading.

It flows from a desire to do good—or bad. To give what you wish to receive.

Okay, nothing scary yet, she decides.

It's about making your wishes and wants known to yourself and whoever you pray to. The Universe. Your God. A Great Unknown.
Spellcasting is putting an action behind your "Please."
It is not a science of ingredients but of resonance. Tools help. Timing matters. Intention is the lifeforce—the emotion pulsing beneath the surface.

Then, in the margins, Lottie finds a scrawl of ink in what must be the previous owner's handwriting:

The magick will find its own way. So long as you mean it.

Appreciating the sentiment, she flips ahead, looking for the fine print.

The warnings.

The trouble.

And there it is:

Magick is a mirror, not a maker. It clings to emotion, wearing it like borrowed skin. It gives you what you already are, just magnified.

So be warned:

Cursing others comes back on you.

Ill will meets ill will.

"Okay," she decides, snapping the text shut. "Don't curse anyone. Got it."

And she begins.

In flipping to the index, she looks up "Mugwort." Finding the expected relation of visions, she's rerouted to "dreams," "psychic," and "sleep." Then she's sent to corresponding herbs, flowers, crystals, and symbols. Finally, she lands on the subject of spells and rituals and intentions, somehow satisfying this endeavor that seemed so silly at the start.

Her research leads her to local shops, from general stores to markets for mystics, and her arms quickly fill with purchases of pretty things and oddities for her approaching activity. By the end of her errands, she feels rather pleased, figuring even Dottie would applaud her efforts.

Aside from the objects for her pending endeavor, Lottie excitedly includes the purchase of henna and beet juice for the first task of her evening. For too long now, she has stifled her hair to be dulled and diluted for the sake of disguise… but it doesn't matter anymore. The threat has been extinguished, though hard as it is to believe; she can finally be *herself.*

So, with a smile, she stares at her reflection, fingers tracing the phony blonde she hid behind. Hid— and never healed.

Tonight, she'll bring back her true colors. Her true self.

No more hiding.

With giddy fingers, she lathers a vibrant goo of red juices and brown paste into her curls. The messiness makes her laugh. It feels like childhood.

When it's done, a long-lost stranger appears in the mirror, happy to be home. The reflection smiles back at her. She feels better already.

"Now," Lottie murmurs, finding *logic* to be a more precarious thing today than yesterday. "I just have to… do it. I've got to *use* the magic… to *make* the magick."

CHAPTER 18

As the filtered light of evening trickles past windowpanes and into rooms with a golden warmth, Lottie sits on her bathroom floor with a readied tub and a tricky task ahead.

An assortment of objects litters the tiles—strategically selected and carefully placed—and she takes a deep breath as she settles. Hoping for a sign. Wondering just exactly how she is to simply "begin."

In the quiet waiting, she considers the extraordinary within her ordinary. A claw foot basin awaits her, as she figured a soothing soak would be needed after this. Though a simple thing, it steams—melodic in its existence, untamable—like dancing souls escaping for a final dalliance with the world.

A slight smile finds the corner of her lips. *"Everyone—and everything—can be a little bit wild,"* Dottie had said, standing right here where Lottie now sits, brushing out the leaves from a young-Lottie's tousled head after a day of playing in the trees. *"And us women?"* she had finished, with a wink. *"Especially so."*

"Be a little wild, Lottie," she now whispers in invitation. "Wild things don't overthink. Just… play."

Given that permission, she begins. With a bundle of sage made for markets, she lights the tip and watches it smolder—snaking out smoke to join in the dancing steam from the tub. Swirling in harmony.

"Sage to cleanse," she breathes.

Striking a match, a silver candle kindles, slowly and with purpose.

"Silver to represent dreams."

Noting the crystals that sit in position, each one is offered a careful caress.

"Citrine, for clarity. Amethyst, for intuition. And Labradorite, for psychic abilities."

Reaching for a favored teacup, she cradles it with eyes closed—focusing on intentions while the warmth of its contents calms her thoughts.

"I think I drank a spelled tea, and so a tea I'll brew. I want to brew a magick tea, to better know what's true."

Stifling a giggle at her attempts to rhyme, she breathes a slow inhale and narrows her focus.

"I *want* to know what's true. I want to know what's happening. I want to make a tea to battle the spelled tea I drank."

Tossing in herbs as if she's done it a thousand times before, their familiar scent brings comfort. These little leaves she's tended.

"Rosemary, for dream recall moving forward."

In goes the Rosemary.

"Peppermint, to clear the mind and aid in prophetic dreams."

Quickly, Peppermint trails.

"And Mugwort, to battle what may have started this by bonding that spell with this one."

In final touch, she finishes, stirring the tea with the gifted crystal spoon. Trusting that magick will follow. Without meaning to, she stirs clockwise, then counter—bringing in the good and banishing the bad, just like Dottie taught her.

The realization tickles a faint curiosity.

Lottie's done this for years—the stirring. She's had the habit since childhood. But she's never assumed it might be anything more than a silly superstition. A fun ritual, just because—like wishing on a star or crossing your fingers for good news. Now, she wonders.

With a sip and a sigh, she takes to the tub and sinks. Allowing her body to steep and go soft, just like the leaves in the teacup.

Outside, a wild wind summons a storm. Lottie smiles at it. She's not so certain storms mean good omens for her, anymore—not after that first night with Wells—but there's still a comfort to be found in a chaotic sky.

With the activity outside her window a lulling comfort—and the mingling of herbal aromas and bath steam fogging the room—Lottie finds a moment of peace. It greets like a sweet, forgotten memory, reminding her of Dottie the way everything in this home does. The reminder leads to reveries, and the reveries allow her thoughts to drift toward sleep until dreams take over.

In the night, she wanders toward a greatly feared thing, though she can't put words to what. Passing grass that shines in the moon, wet from rain, she continues on, next climbing boulders that cause her bare toes to stumble. Coming over a rise, she arrives to some unknown place of rocks and sand, and a brisk wind tangles her vision with violent red curls, caught and ravaged.

Suddenly, at the edge of still waters, she leans over as if peering into its depths, and a face stares back, framed by a floral crown. Realizing it's a reflection, she's startled by a stranger's face. Dark eyes stare up at Lottie, different from the hazel of her own. They hold her there like an anchor, stuck taut and struggling to pull free.

That's when the fear sets in. Stealing away her sleep and swallowing the dream.

Awareness rattles her awake.

Lottie struggles, breath ragged.

She fights a chill that grabs at her legs, frightened by the sudden bite. And the world confuses her. She's no longer in her dream. And she's no longer in her tub.

She's not even in the cottage.

She stands now in the roaring stream of the river—frigid after a fresh storm—cloaked by the darkness of night... alone and afraid.

PART TWO:

Imogen

ONE WEEK EARLIER

CHAPTER 19

A lone woman wanders, accompanied by a wood of trees in the same way a single soul can exist alone within a crowded room. Under a gray sky, the tall and looming beasts of bark and branches watch her, quiet in their rooted stillness, as if curious about her presence—wondering from where she came and to where she'll go.

She is easy to note, with red hair that hollers out against the shifting greenery of the woods around her, readily spotted. The rest of her seems somewhat skittish, with eyes that jump and search. There is a wildness about her, evident too in her wind-rioted curls and bloodied knees.

Noticing her injuries, the woman greets the grassy wooded floor with a sigh, stretching long and sifting through the bag she holds. Prepared for such a moment, she retrieves the necessities for dressing these wounds, cluttering her lap with bandages and ointments, as if she's done this a hundred times before.

Perhaps, she reckons, remembering years of tree-climbing. But not amongst these trees; these aren't the trees of her childhood. She doesn't know the names for any of these, but she knows they're different; there are no Bald Cypresses or Mangroves or Live Oaks like those of her Florida home. Nothing drips of Spanish

Moss or glistens like Sawgrass marshes. These trees aren't evergreens. They don't smell of pungent moss or have that particular variety of musky peat. They don't seem so wild.

They're brittle, with rough bark that breaks from the cold.

But the leaves aren't terrible. They seem to be changing with the season, like a final last breath to surge a climax of life and color before they rest until spring. She can't remember the last time she watched a shifting of the trees—if ever.

Distracted by a falling leaf, her fingers resume their rummaging, and then her breath catches. From the bottom of her bag, a secret envelope glares up at her. With great caution, she retrieves the message she'd not known was slipped inside the burlap pocket.

"It can't be…"

The wooded world stirs only slightly, otherwise suspended in the moment, waiting for eager fingers to break the waxed seal, blood-thick and heavy with importance. Finally, fighting past a sickness that creeps its way through her gut and roils with a painstaking curiosity, she fiddles with the envelope. Intrigue shakes at her fingers.

Miss Imogen Rose,

Your research into our Society has caught our attention. We, the collaborative of the uncommon and extraordinary, invite you to begin the Initiation. Where dreams and desires roam, we follow in fulfillment.

However, heed this and be warned: Fear and fatalities flow in our wake.

To accept our Invitation, you must complete the Tasks we ask of you. Do well.

The Coterie

Imogen reads it a dozen times, forward and backward, her wild eyes pacing, quick and then slow. Finally, she surrenders to the ground, dizzied with a heavy head, filled with the uncertainty of disbelief and the euphoria of hope.

"It's real," she whines and then laughs all at once. "I can't believe it. The Coterie is real."

The canopy above her head shimmers and then swims as her vision blurs with hope-filled tears. Her heart drums to the beat of bewilderment as the promise of the impossible dances through her mind.

'*Where dreams and desires roam, we follow in fulfillment.*'

She's only ever wanted one thing since the innocent age of nine. She's only ever dreamed of one person... desiring that he might find her, beyond the sleeper's state of dream-walking and memories missed. Hoping again and again she might wake up to find him creeping through her window with that ageless smile of his and crawling into her bed once more, safe in the security of one another.

For years, that was all they needed—each other.

Their foster home filled and emptied and filled again, ebbing and flowing with the tide of broken families that ensure welfare workers' salaries in every county in every state. With foster parents who were esteemed in their fields—with doctorates and publications—their home reflected their notoriety. It was big. And they filled the rooms with kids.

For Imogen and Dinny, the system stuck them in Florida. But their placement didn't matter; it only mattered that they were placed together. And for a few sweet years, they were.

She looks for him in the trees.

Today and every day.

No matter the patch or place—for she is certainly no longer near their Florida home—the trusty pillars of bark and leaves are ever-inspiring as their shadows whisper of secrets and Imogen wonders if any of them have been shared by *him.* He was always telling secrets to the trees as he lobbed over their limbs and swung from their branches. They allowed for hiding, and climbing, and spying, and dreaming. They were steady.

Acknowledging the state of her knees, she slumps at the reminder of age and a childhood lost; the trees aren't so gentle with her these days. They don't hold the same welcoming warmth they once did.

But they're still here.

Aside from one another, their closest company was the forest where they played, eating meals in its shade whilst leaning into the trees' ready arms, mothered by their mere reliability. The brown and green beasts witnessed seasons of endless laughter and encouraged moments of childlike bliss.

Her only childhood was with them and him. With the trees and Dinny.

She looks for him now, seeking secrets within the canopy… looking for a wink from the forest that may be friend or foe. She can't put words as to why, but she feels like he might still be found within them—even here, today, in woods that are not hers, near trees that are not theirs… as if he might be hiding, waiting for her to find him.

In a startle, she pops up to resume her pilfering, wondering of the Task mentioned in the letter, concerned she might have missed something.

At the bottom of her bag, another envelope sits—smaller and tucked away, like a secret. Now with directed movements, she rips it open and reads speedily, hungered with an appetite for knowledge and starved until satisfied.

Her disbelief and hope fade away as an eerie dread bleeds in and takes over. She has discovered the first Task… and everything within her fears what is to follow.

CHAPTER 20

Come a new day, Imogen seeks a swamp.

In a waterlogged wetland, foreign and unfamiliar, she trudges through tall grasses and maneuvers around trees as emergent weeds reach for her skin with sticky tendrils. Gatherings of moss form a floating slime, sporadic upon an otherwise stilled water that sits quiet, perhaps to keep from disturbing the death and decay beneath its surface. Haze from a gray morning sky sinks and settles on her shoulders, slipping around her neck, threatening a slow strangle of what fresh breath lingers. She holds it, fearing all is foe, curious as to how easy it might be to fall victim to murder by the mire. A crisp wind blows and the world seems to whisper a warning. *Hushhhhh.*

Imogen halts, pausing at a smaller pool, bordered by a wall of weeds beneath a coven of gathered trees. The trees lean into each other with a sickly stretch, like witches at work with gossip and cackles.

"Here it is," she sighs shakily. "The Cauldron of the Swamp Sisters."

With bated breath, she waits, frozen in fear, as she tries to muster even a coward's courage. Winged things buzz about in a symphony of droning melodies, accompanied by the occasional croak of a toad and tick of a beetle. Cicadas surround the swampland, but their sweet summer song of yesteryear now instead resembles a sounding alarm, shrill and jarring. So many living things exist around her, but the atmosphere of life feels of a funeral's fashion, with melancholic wonders regarding the death of the day. That death, in her opinion, is the loudest thing of all. Everywhere, in this moment, it is the dead and decaying that haunts her thoughts. It is the question of what lies beneath, but the certainty that it is no normal, living thing.

Stepping closer, she stifles a shriek and surrenders her toes to the quagmire, forcing the first step in crossing the threshold from mundane to magick.

"'Enter the world of the witch.'" Her whispers waver. "Check."

The drumming of her ribcage joins in the moment's song, as she questions what the world truly holds—never having reason before to believe she'd ever be in a place like this.

She's wondered of magick for as long as she can remember but has often been wary of it. Fascination only focuses on the initial "wow," but her thoughts have lingered on the "what ifs." *What if it* is *real? What if it's full of danger? What if it's full of hope? What if that hope can be devastating?*

A whisper so slight, it's an accident: "What if this is how I find Dinny?"

As if rallied by her words, the swamp cauldron begins to stir, with water as rhythmic as her hurried heart. It bubbles and burps like a simmering stew and then spits and festers as the muddy waters rise with their splashing.

The strangulation sets in, as the low haze stifles her breath with its grip at her throat. Oxygen seems out of reach, and the thick muck of the mire struggles against her resistance, weighing down her toes and creeping toward her ankles.

And then all else seems to pause when a slow, sly hand emerges from the bubbling pool, with wicked fingers curled in expectation.

"The Swamp Witch," she breathes in disbelief, sending away the last of what was left in her lungs.

As the hand reaches, it steadily moves closer, causing recoil with every inch. Desperate, Imogen manages a swallow of air before nearly going limp into the unhallowed grasp. Recalling that an Offering is first required, she rushes to retrieve scissors from the pack on her back. In anxious hesitation but hurried by dread, Imogen grabs a lock of hair and gives herself the benefit of a quick count. "Three, two, one." *Snip*. Taut tendrils go limp in her fist. Like a wilted red weed.

"What will you do with it?" she begs, as she extends her reach to the hand of the witch, terrified of what possible curse might come from fresh curls.

In silence, the filled fingers close, and the outstretched arm slowly sinks to the depths below, returning to whatever underwater lair awaits. Imogen watches in relief, ready to be rid of the eerie Other. And then, in dismay, she remembers the rest of her Task.

"Wait," she hollers after the hand. "What comes after the Offering?"

Reflexively, the young woman rushes to follow, and then, as the swamp cauldron riots and bubbles with a fresh threat, she retreats, reminded of where she is and what she's just seen. Now seated in the swilling grasses, she watches as the water belches until subdued, and she wishes she could flee… but she wishes to join The Coterie more.

That's how she'll find Dinny. She's certain of it.

Within the ghostly pool, an odd thing emerges, tossed amongst the magickal torrent and tipped in the direction of Imogen's presence. Quickly, ready to be rid of this place, she dips in her hand and grabs it, snatching at the new promise of hope. Then she flees, shaken to her core with a mixture of anxiety at what may follow and adrenaline founded by relief.

The swamp waters slow her down, slapping at her legs with heavy muck. In fear of being followed, she turns back, wondering of the witch. But it's different, now—the Cauldron.

Breathless but curious, Imogen waits. Watches.

The eerie lair that boiled mere seconds ago now sits still as glass, as if no witch or otherwise dwells down below.

"That's quite the trick," she whispers to the Swamp Sisters, all the more motivated to finish this Task and never return.

Distancing herself from the swamp witch and her trickery, Imogen finds a fallen tree and sits to rest. The stump sits decorated with clusters of fungi. In greeting them with a ragged breath, they smile back at Imogen with a congratulatory salute.

"I did it," she breathes, a sheen of sweat at her brow.

The day is lighter, and the solemn sounds of before now take on a different tone, morphing the atmosphere to greet her with a welcome that warms instead of warns. Now that she can focus enough to appreciate what surrounds her, splashes of color can be spotted all about—from the mushrooms at her side with their autumn hues to the bright flowers that beckon in the distance, forming their own sea of yellow.

"Swamp Sunflowers," she breathes, her smile wide. She knows them well. She's loved them ever since her first day with Dinny.

**

A Memory:

She was six years old and wild. Uninhibited. Like the weeds.

Her resolve was strong and often unexpected, but she danced in the hot summer sun when she thought watching eyes had wandered elsewhere, swaying with the breeze and smiling at a dizzied mind. Her ferocity was a quiet one and many overlooked the value she brought. But Dinny saw it.

"These are for you."

Those were the first words he'd said to her, as he offered a fistful of Swamp Sunflowers beside the largest tree in their foster home's backyard forest. The Bald Cypress watched in anticipation, as Imogen questioned the smile of the older boy who studied her, waiting.

She had seen him the night before, joining their motley crew of an ever-morphing family for dinner. At that time, he was just another addition, older than she—

132

nine, or so—and likely one she needn't waste worries or wonderings on. Older kids didn't do much with the younger ones, and she'd rather not be bothered, anyhow. Adults often brought anxiety in their announcements, babies rarely stayed more than a week or two, and few kids remained long enough to be considered friends. Whether families reunited, or kids moved to be with distant relatives who decided to take them in, or there was the occasional disruption or runaway… it didn't matter the circumstance; it just mattered that most everyone was temporary.

So, Imogen kept to herself. She didn't have any family to fight for her, over her, or to be rid of her; so long as she didn't cause trouble, she was one of the few to stay longer than any of the others. With that fact, this six-year-old had unconsciously created a habit of isolating herself, wanting more and more to simply play alone within the trees instead of being overstimulated by the constant banter and chaos of the hectic household.

But until now, no one had cared to question her tactics; no others bothered to step in her way and force the possibility of friendship.

"I'm Dinny," he said, with his bright smile unwavering, "These made me think of you, so… here you go."

Desperately shy, Imogen accepted the flowers but said nothing. It was only her thoughts that were loud and unapologetic as they rioted with queries and challenges.

"I like to tell people the nice things that I think about them," he explained easily. "Because usually it makes people smile, and I like when people smile. Someone told me one time that I have pretty eyes, and that felt good to hear. So, I wanted to tell you about the flowers." He swallowed and kicked his heels, still smiling. "They have bright faces and I like to look at them, and you have a bright face and..." He paused and both went blushing—he from bashfulness, she from staunch surprise. "Well, I saw you dancing and singing earlier, and... I think we should be friends."

Certain her flushed face now matched her hair, Imogen struggled to swallow and turned away, confused by how to behave at a moment like this.

"I didn't mean to be weird," he assured. Even at her back, she could tell his happy smile still filled his cheeks. "Um, what are you playing? Can I come with you?"

Looking to the flowers she now held, Imogen felt a wave of pride wash over her, foreign but fantastic. Someone saw these beautiful things and thought of *her*? What a thing.

Now smiling herself, she turned and offered a timid shrug and then a slow, steady nod.

"We're allowed to go all the way to the water," she said in invitation.

His smile faltered in bewilderment. "To the *ocean*?"

Finding his countenance to be comical, she giggled and felt the urge to grab his hand. For some reason, she let herself, and he followed her lead toward their new destination.

"No." Shy again, she stayed ahead of him, afraid to meet his eyes. They were pretty, indeed—

green, like jade, and bright, like sun spots in the trees—and looking directly into them made her feel nervous, somehow. "The little pools."

She hadn't known the name for them then, but the little pools were pockets of wetlands belonging to the Everglades. The children of this foster home were allowed to wander at leisure, so long as they stayed out of trouble, and this allowance afforded Imogen time and opportunity to venture into Mangrove forests and freshwater marshes, where natural canals of winding waterways dipped and danced within mossy foliage and sopping grasses.

When they arrived at the water's edge, it was Imogen's turn to watch Dinny.

In a sudden frenzy, he rummaged through his pockets upon spotting clusters of Beautyberry, bright and vibrant in their purple and blue brilliance. Pulling out small tins and canisters from his pockets, he retrieved these berries to then crush and inspect.

Imogen wanted to ask what he was doing, but instead she settled to watch, hoping she'd understand soon enough. In quiet intrigue, she stooped behind his shoulders, as he squatted upon a stump and used a pipette to add drops of water to the forming purple paste. Slowly, the realization settled, and then it landed with a guffaw, as a world of possibilities opened up before her.

"It's paint!" she laughed, tickled. "I want to try!"

Delighted by her interest, Dinny offered his assistance, instructing and encouraging with every fresh berry. Easily, she had perfected what would have felt impossible on any other day, and the pride in her eyes made his beam, too.

"Here," he grinned, as he presented a paintbrush, pulled from his trusty pocket. "Now, we can do this."

Without hesitation, he dipped the brush into the fresh berry paint and then set about decorating the nearest canvas: a pad-leaf Spatterdock plucked from the water's surface, pulled from its stem. His strokes were swift and effortless, and suddenly the leaf that was ordinary just moments before had transformed into a masterpiece of purple flowers extraordinaire. It was whimsical and mesmerizing.

Doubtful of her own efforts, but ever witty and ready to play, Imogen put her loaded brush to her lips, then planted a kiss to her palm and chuckled. Satisfied, she displayed her creation with a twinkle in her eye, feeling suddenly confident in this new friendship.

As if reading her thoughts, Dinny mirrored the spark in her eye with his own, as he set about to painting his lips the same. Both understood the assignment:

The Kissing-Palm-To-Cheek War commenced.

In a tizzy of movements and laughter, the two battled with purple lips and smacked their palms again and again as they dipped and dodged to plant their painted kisses upon the other's cheek but tried to evade just the same.

It was a moment Imogen hadn't realized she craved, and even as it was happening, she missed it. She never wanted it to end but knew it must. Even at six years old, her young mind was wise enough to understand that most things can't be bottled and kept, so Imogen resolved to settle for being happy in the now. She would think about this moment for years to come, but as it took place, the details were brought into focus—like how the daylight was soft as a summer evening approached, how the harshness of the afternoon sun had lifted, allowing a more breathable air to replace the sticky humidity of the midday hours; how Dinny seemed to enjoy her as much as she was enjoying him, noting the way his eyes squinted into their own upturned smiles. She promised herself she'd remember the sound of her own laughter as it sang the chimes of childhood from deep in her chest.

It was a stunning moment, and though it ended, it was only the first.

"Oh, someone's coming!" Dinny had dropped to an emphatic whisper as he stretched his neck to assess their options. With a smile and a wink, he now grabbed her hand, and they waded into the water, minding the fish and breaking the rules.

They hid from their intruder, who happened to be just another kid from the home—one of the few who'd been there longer than Imogen—and they waited with breathless giggles as the oblivious girl inspected the aquatic life and puttered with vials and tiny nets.

"It's just Kenzie," Imogen whispered, envious of her foster sister's trinkets. "Oh, man, I always wanted to try one of those nets."

Dinny nudged her with a playful hip as they spied. "Why don't you?"

With high brows, Imogen shook her head. "No way, Jose. They're from Foster Dad's office. We're not allowed." Then, in a deeper whisper, "Kenzie just sneaks them anyway."

While her own brows stayed hiked, Dinny's brows went wiggling. "Rules are for breaking, don't you know?" His smile went all the way into his eyes. "If Kenzie got one, I bet you can, too. I'll find one for you, okay?"

Delighted, she accepted with a vigorous nod, and Dinny watched happily as his new friend's flushed cheeks puckered and plumped.

Dipping her head back and slipping deeper in for a bath, Imogen let out a long breath she hadn't realized she'd held, though it may have been stuck in her chest for years. Her whole life. Back upright, she met Dinny's gaze as he watched her with a side smile.

Kissing his palm once more, he gave a quick but gentle touch to her cheek. "Kiss, tap. Now you're my best friend."

Knowing nothing else to say, Imogen echoed the same, and it was as simple as that.

**

Staring at the field of flowers, Imogen grows sad at the happy memory. After that first day, two things became tradition for a good while.

First, no matter the day, if Swamp Sunflowers were in season, Dinny found a way to bring at least one home for his best friend, comforting her young mind with the assurance that she was not forgotten. Someone thought of her, and it was someone she loved. Someone found her worthy of remembering. Every day.

Even better, though, was their new language for one another. The night after that first day, Imogen had never slept so soundly—because Dinny was there. After lights-out, he snuck into her room with careful tiptoes and crawled into her bed to cuddle his best friend.

"I hate sleeping alone. Can I sleep with you?" he'd asked.

They snuggled in and found comfort in the other's warmth. As Imogen began to doze into his chest, Dinny whispered a final, "Kiss, tap," as he pecked his palm and patted her sleepy head. That small gesture became a part of their every regimen. If ever they were to part, one would hunt down the other, run to their side, and give them a quick, "Kiss, tap" in farewell.

In a house with revolving doors inside a life with great loneliness, their friendship with one another had become a miraculous medicine. They'd found a home within this house. They'd found each other and had claimed one another, and that was even better than most. Many don't get to choose their families, but they got to... and they chose each other every day.

"Kiss, tap, Dinny," she whispers to the flowers. *I still choose you.*

Quickly remembering he's the reason she's here, and that the need to be "here" is now complete, Imogen returns focus to the glass jar in her hands, finding it filled with many things—one of which is a message.

"Message in a bottle," she gasps.

With eager fingers, careful of the bottle and its contents, this new note unfolds with caution, and she scans the parchment for an ink that holds promise. As hoped, it congratulates her, and she welcomes it. Then, as expected, a new Task follows, and she swallows down a rising bile as she takes a slow, brave breath.

"Well," she readies, "I'll need a new dress."

CHAPTER 21

A shopkeeper's bell sings of Imogen's entry. "Hello?"

The charm of the store settles upon her like a deep dream. Dim in its lighting but dazzling in detail, racks of dresses clutter the quaint room of dark beams and wooden flooring, close but chaotic. It's as if the gowns themselves danced in the night, requiring no host to fulfill their purpose.

Tiptoeing through, Imogen spots a small work desk at the back, busied with papers and textbooks and studious things, with dog-eared pages promising the return of its steadfast reader. Strands of lights twinkle all about, seeking sequined bodices and sparkling shawls with their shine and washing the store in a soft glow.

Just like a dreamer, Imogen's mind summons up recall of childhood magic and mysteries left unanswered; the dazzle of the room reminds her of an enchanted place she's certain she explored as a child, though as she tries to grasp at it, the memory turns to mist, vanishing out of reach. But then again, her memories and dreams seem to blur often and blend into each other these days, and now she's not certain what exactly it is she wondered at all.

In trying to find it again—that vanished memory—she digs into her mind and remembers it's nightmares she's been having lately. And always of Dinny.

Becoming her own worst enemy in the night, dreams of the trees she's always loved would morph into a monster, snatching Dinny up and swallowing him whole, hiding him away for no one to find.

In her waking mind, though, she can find him again; he's there in her memories, smiling his bright smile.

As Imogen walks on, a tall mirror catches the light about the shop and tosses it back. Stepping up to it, the reflection is startling. The quick glimpse of her appearance sends a phantom pain biting at her wounded knees, causing a flinch.

"Hi, Miss, sorry," a voice stutters from the back. "Hi, welcome."

Possibly near her age, a young woman scurries through the creaking door beside the desk at the back. Her features seem youthful enough, but something in her stance suggests a weightiness. Perhaps it's the appearance of heavy shoulders that pull forward, suggesting they've possibly carried more burdens than peers the same age.

"Ah," she breathes through a kind smile, "how can I help you?"

Imogen pauses in her answer, stalled in thought at the way this woman wears only lipstick. It reminds her of childhood. It was the way Foster Mom wore her makeup. Simple but bold.

"Everything okay, Miss?"

Embarrassed by her staring, Imogen blushes and comes to. "I'm here to buy a dress," she declares proudly.

With a sweep of her arms, the clerk gestures to the room and smirks. "I think I can help. We're drowning in dresses."

"In particular, something, um…" Imogen hesitates, trying to remember the wording of her next Task. "*Ethereal*."

"Hmm," the shop clerk pauses, turning all about in thought. "Angelic? Or… more mermaid?"

Delighted, Imogen affirms her assessments. "Mermaid, definitely." The notion of such a thing sends a titillating energy dancing into her bones.

"Here," the clerk offers, a glimmer in her eye as she watches the customer.

Handed a gown, Imogen holds it out and searches for a breath that's gone missing. "Wow," she mouths. "It's perfect."

"I have to admit, you've got me curious, Miss. What's the occasion?"

Startled by the inquiry, Imogen tries to play for nonchalance, knowing secrecy is of the utmost importance. "Oh, just a costume thing," she says shyly.

"Your knees, Miss," the clerk strays, now looking down to a trail of fresh blood. "Are you all right?"

Rouge overwhelms Imogen's cheeks.

"Oh, uh, yes," she stutters. "Perks of being a tree climber." She shrugs. "Comes with the territory of adventuring."

Though the trees used to be so much kinder to me.

The woman smiles heartily and gives a concurring nod. "That does sound like a worthy cause. And, you know," she continues, leaning in for emphasis, "pain is proof you're transforming."

Imogen smiles and nods likewise, turning back to the dress and praising it with soft eyes.

"Is that The One?" The clerk seems to notice the way it bewitches.

"It's stunning."

"All the dresses in here have a name. That one is *Imogen*."

Dumbfounded, Imogen looks to the woman for jests, but she shows none. "*Imogen*? That's *my* name."

"Ha!" The other guffaws. "Well, look at that. Imogen, meet Imogen. It's meant to be. And I'm Mac." She extends an energetic hand in friendly offering. "Pleased to meet you."

Imogen accepts it timidly but with grace. "And you."

Then, with a look to her watch and a head-scratch for memory, the clerk glances to the back in angst. "Wait, ah… are you also a Miss Rose?"

Turning to answer, Imogen nods. "I am."

With that, Mac disappears to the back with a finger raised, returning with a package in hand. "This was left for you."

In brown wrapping, subtle and unassuming, a box extends toward Imogen. A familiar crimson seals it closed.

144

She accepts it with a knot in her chest and intrigue in her gut, not having expected to hear from Them until her completion of the next Task.

"I'll wrap up the dress for you, if you're ready."

Now quite distracted, she nods absentmindedly, handing over the gown and accepting the package. Eyes glued.

Once left alone, she eagerly opens, removing the lid to reveal a vibrant, floral head crown. It's breathtaking in its beauty, but it's the note that steals her oxygen:

In honor of the ghosts. Do well.

The Coterie

**

A Memory:

On her eighth Halloween, Imogen was a monster. Dinny was a ghost.

"You're not Franken*stein*," Foster Dad reminded, "you're Frankenstein's *monster*. The *wretch*!"

She sat and giggled as her foster mother dabbed at her face with green paint that chilled and tickled. Halloween was an exception to the monotony of everyday chaos that came with this foster placement.

Every year, the parents helped create costumes and everyone participated. Leading up to the festivities, decorations were crafted and hours were spent with sticky fingers and explosions of glitter trailing all about the home. For mood-setting, lights were habitually low and candles flickered upon dim walls, smelling of pumpkin and cinnamon. Pots often simmered atop the stove, filled with cider fixings like apples, oranges, and cloves. The single television in the gathering room played in loops of seasonal classics and eerie movies. Cheesy wooden posts and well-worn signs and garlands embellished the entryway.

"Hold still, Doll, I'm almost done."

Imogen huffed a flustered sigh but smiled through it. This was the first year she'd get to go *out*. This year, she was considered one of the Big Kids.

In an effort to contain her excitement, she glanced about the home from her seat at the dining table and assessed the many costumes that had turned little kids into goblins and ghouls. With all the costumes being handmade, each one had that unsettling finesse that comes when something isn't "quite" right. Some masks had wonky eyeballs that drooped or sat crooked, some painted faces revealed the intent of the look but fell short, some fabrics didn't fit perfectly, and some makeshift props appeared more grotesque than gory. But Imogen loved it all—every eerie, odd part.

Before her, Foster Mom wore a witch hat and glitter, while Foster Dad wore the counterpart costume of a warlock. Appropriately, he set to stirring a cauldron in the kitchen, as the younger kids who would be staying home took turns to partake in the cookie-making and "potion" treats.

"I know you're sneaking up on me, Dinny," Foster Mom announced, as she finished the last dabs of Imogen's face. She and Imogen both turned in time to see a sheet ghost with arms high, frozen and then relaxing with a whine.

"Aw, come on."

Imogen giggled, able to hear the smile even in her best friend's disappointment.

"Dinny, look at me! I'm a *wretch*!"

Finally free to move, her excited little body danced and wiggled and jazzed all about.

The darling ghost mirrored his best friend, and his stitched-on rosy cheeks bounced upon his own as he laughed. To complete the face, his ghost eyes were big with embroidered black detail and the mouth O echoed the same.

Silly in their costumes, the two quickly entered into their kiss-taps, and Dinny soon wore a black kiss mark on his stitched cheek, thanks to the dead lips of the dancing monster.

Ever distracted by the enchantments inside their own little world, the two giggling fiends took a breath as a whine sounded from the nearby stairwell.

"You look like an old hag," a boy named Jones snickered. He was bothering Kenzie, who Imogen could tell easily enough was an Igor of sorts. A minion. "You just need a cane... and some lipstick!" The boy snorted. "At least then you'd look like an actual *girl*!"

Kenzie glared back but didn't say anything, but everyone could see her cheeks turning red.

"Jones, you're a *dead possum*," Dinny hollered toward the stairs. "Lipstick could do *you* some favors!"

A flicker of a smile flashed across Kenzie's features. That made Imogen smile at Dinny, ever the savior. Seeming relieved by the distraction, Kenzie moved from her seat on the stairs to a chair near Dinny.

Wanting Kenzie to have a happy Halloween, Imogen leaned over to offer an encouraging whisper. "I think your costume is exactly right. You're perfect!"

Accepting the compliment, Kenzie sinks down with a shy slump and a smile. "Thanks, Imogen."

Meanwhile, Jones had to keep on going. "I'm *road kill*," he corrected. "Stupid."

Dinny shrugged. "Like I said," and he turned back to offer both girls a mischievous wink.

Hollers and whines then promptly filled the kitchen as burnt cookies emerged from the oven. The parents rushed to let kids take turns stirring the cauldron, hoping it would help calm them down, and the Big Kids took the commotion as a signal to be getting on their way. Imogen practically vibrated in her dead-man-walking boots.

**

Having to walk a fair distance to the nearest neighborhood, Imogen found it was well worth it once she saw the size of the homes. These people were *rich*.

Costumed children sauntered along the street with heavy plastic pumpkins and pillowcases filled with king-sized candy bars and festive tricks and treats. Front yards flashed spooky lights, stank of sweet smoke, and echoed of animatronic spooks and shrieks. Darkness was interrupted by dimly lit windows and the purple hues of black lights. Imogen had spent hours imagining what trick-or-treating would be like, and this was more incredible than anything her little mind could have conjured. It was the epitome of a trick-or-treater's dream.

It seemed to take no time at all to make it down a street, and their sacks filled with candy entire handfuls at a time. Within their costumed clan, Imogen was the youngest, but her strong legs carried her just as quickly as the rest. As if running through the trees with Dinny was preparing her for this moment, she relished being a Big Kid and savored every second.

Distracted by her candy count, she looked up to find Dinny ahead, under the streetlight, distracted as well, though by something else altogether.

"Dinny, what are you looking at?"

Following his line of sight, she assessed the grand house on the corner, towering with pillars and high windows and throbbing with a dance beat that slipped through crevices and slid through cracks.

"Oh, wow," she breathed, scanning the windows that tickled senses with the tease of luxury. The exterior could only be dubbed a mansion, with seasonal flora decorating the windows and a manicured lawn that saw nothing but loveliness every which way it faced.

Being the single night when walking onto stranger's porches was not only acceptable but encouraged, the two nodded in agreement and zipped up the walkway, eager to try and peek inside.

"Dang, the curtains are too thick," Dinny whined, but Imogen was mesmerized by them all the same.

"They're so pretty and fancy," she breathed, wondering what it would be like to touch such extravagance.

As the door began to open, their startled selves ducked behind a pile of pumpkins-and-haystack display, hoping they'd not been caught. A tipsy spider swayed out the door and stepped precariously down the steps as the light from inside washed over them and then shut them out. Several fake legs flopped about with every wavering footfall, making for a rather silly image that sent two costumed creepers giggling in their hiding spots.

"Do you smell that?" Dinny asked, as he took a deep breath.

Imogen's eyes grew as wide as the moon. "Cinnamon." She sighed in delight. "I can almost *taste* it!"

"Almost?" Dinny teased, as he licked the air and smacked his lips in mock satisfaction. "Well, it's delicious." He finished with a chef's kiss at his fingertips.

Dipping into their candy, the two resumed their admiration of the home, finding no need to do anything else than exactly this with only each other.

"Imagine living in a place like this," he mused.

Looking to his meager sheet, he crunched on a candy bar beneath his sheet and sat a moment, thinking.

"When I die, I'm going to haunt a home like this." Imogen giggled, but he continued with certainty.

"I'm going to live there, and relax, and not have to worry about anything. I'll do what I want when I want. I'll taste the best food, and take big bubble baths, and watch any movie I want. I'm going to finally live a dream life… even if it has to be as a ghost."

Bothered by any concept of him dying, Imogen grabbed his hand through the fabric. "Quit that," she ordered. "I don't want to think about that."

Catching the sadness in her eyes, Dinny chuckled with sympathy and pulled her into his side, surprising her with a sheet tossed overhead to join the two together.

"Obviously, we'd be together, Mo," he assured, as he squeezed her tiny body against his. "You know where I go, you go. So, you better not leave me behind, either."

With a quivering lip, she squeezed him back, surprised by the emotion but needing the embrace.

"Promise?"

"Swear."

Comforted, she then joined in the daydreaming. "You could have a whole *room* be a bubble bath. And you could eat as many cookies as you want all day long." After a pause, she considered that and sighed. "I wonder what rich-people cookies taste like."

With a glance to Imogen and then a quick kiss-tap goodbye, Dinny gave her hand a parting squeeze and then traipsed into the yard and around the side of the home. The gestures made her heart squeeze, and his leaving made a knot form in both her shoulders.

"What are you doing!" she whined. "Dinny! Don't get in trouble!"

She didn't mean it for the sake of avoiding punishment; she warned him for the sake of keeping placement. More than one kid had "disrupted" before, and they were removed and sent to another foster home. Or a shelter. She didn't want him sent away. Foster kids are expendable.

The side window illuminated the creeping ghost in the yard, though it seemed no one inside paid attention. A party was being enjoyed, and Dinny had set his sights on joining.

As Imogen watched from the porch, a chill swept across the neighborhood and shook the large Oak that loomed overhead, reaching out wide every which way to enclose them both within its canopy. The scenery's palette shimmered with color as the leaves of the tree shimmied and rained down, swimming through the air in the same way a ghost surely would.

"Jones, *stop!*"

On the sidewalk, a terrorized Kenzie tried to evade Jones and his heel-kicking offenses.

"I don't wanna," the bully laughed. "Just convince yourself you like it, *M&M*. Pick up the pace."

Imogen didn't know why he mocked Kenzie with that name. All the bullies did. Jones started the trend and others followed. It seemed to have stuck.

With a belly already jumbled with nerves, insides went taut as Imogen watched Kenzie turn around with shaking fists.

"I said STOP!" she screamed, shoving him back through tears. "I wish you *were* roadkill!"

"Kenzie!" Imogen hollered, hoping to help. Running to the group—bullies and Kenzie—Imogen grabbed her hand and pulled her over, back to the porch. Back to wait for Dinny.

After a moment, Imogen expected Kenzie to drop her hand, but she didn't. And with a glance to check on her—the only other person tolerable in their crazy home—Imogen caught two tears streaming down hot, angry cheeks.

"They don't know anything, Kenzie," she tried. Twisting to make sure they were staying away, Kenzie squeezed her hand tighter, as if asking her to stay. Stay still. Stay steady.

Imogen squeezed back, fine with the same.

Returning her focus to Dinny, a slow panic whispered in her chest and fluttered down, like leaves of what-ifs piling in her gut—because he was gone.

"Oh, no."

In sudden need of information, anxious feet ran before logic could catch up, and she followed in his footsteps to the looming window.

He was there, inside with a parade of people in colors and costumes, and he swam through the bodies in a dip-and-dodge manner. For a moment, he'd be gone, and then he'd emerge, and with every second of wondering and worrying, Imogen was ready to go home.

It wasn't until the spooking ghost got caught that Imogen's chest altogether imploded.

Just as the front door opened to flood the walkway with light and sound, Imogen met the troublemaker on the porch, likewise greeting a costumed adult who seemed rather annoyed.

Dinny acknowledged his best friend with a whine as he hung limp in the grip of the grownup.

"The bogeyman got me."

"What?" The man balked as he set Dinny down. "No, I'm not… ugh, hold on."

Kenzie joined them on the porch, clearly angsty from Jones' antagonizing, and the man in the doorway situated a wig onto his head in clarification.

"I'm a Mad Scientist, see?" He gestured his fingers to provide a heebie-jeebies vibe around his proclamation.

"Chuckles?"

Everyone looked to Kenzie, who looked to the Mad Scientist with excitement. Then everyone looked to the Mad Scientist, wondering of his true identity—if it was, in fact, their beloved case worker.

"Kenzie? Hey, what— ha! Hey, guys, what are you doing here?"

Realizing he was still clutching onto Dinny, Chuckles set him down and gave his head an awkward and apologetic pat. Dinny straightened the wrinkles with a few swipes of his hand and jiggled himself into a more natural stance.

"Do you *live* here?" Imogen wondered, flabbergasted to know someone so wealthy.

Chuckles looked to the home as if seeking assistance with the answer.

"Uh, no, just partaking in festivities." Looking back to the kids, he assessed in greater calculation and decided to join them. "I'll walk with you all a bit. Hey, Kenzie, our costumes! They could go together, like we paired up! Not too shabby, huh, Ms. Malloy?"

154

Beaming, Kenzie attached herself to Chuckles' side in answer and seemed entirely content. Chuckles always knew how to boost Kenzie's spirits; he knew the right things to say to the odd kid out.

"Much better than an old hag," Dinny encouraged with an eye-roll offered up for Jones.

It didn't matter, though; Kenzie barely seemed to hear him. She was too delighted to have her friend for the evening.

Imogen had noticed the way Kenzie always perked up when Chuckles made his monthly check-ins, clearly having found a comrade in the personable case worker. She wondered sometimes what they talked about, knowing Chuckles to have been a foster kid himself. Apparently, that's where he got his nickname—something about giggling in his sleep. So, one of his foster homes branded him from a "Chuck" to a "Chuckles." Imogen has had other case workers come and go, but no one had taken an interest in them like him. He showed up and he stuck around. He cared. He paid attention.

"We're the same."

Kenzie had once said that when Lottie had asked if she liked the caseworker. The odd girl had answered with relief in her shoulders, and Imogen liked him even more because of it. He knew how to make kids feel seen.

"I'm sorry you feel like you're so different," *Imogen had responded. "But I'm glad you found a* *friend. And anyway, different is good. You're much* *more fascinating than the others." She'd leaned in to* *whisper, "Jones is nothing special."*

Her efforts were rewarded with a giggle.

"You're different too, Imogen," Kenzie had insisted. "Different from the others. Better."

It had been a genuine moment of friendship, and Imogen hoped Kenzie thought so too.

"So, you're a scientist?" Kenzie bounced atop the décor-riddled walkway as she chucked an empty soda can into the street and gave it a hearty stomp. "You know, I was reading about psychological phenomena in one of the books at the house, and the brain is *so* crazy. Have you heard of the Thatcher Effect? Or Stroop Effect? Or Capgras Syndrome? Or Cotard's Syndrome?"

"Oh, man, *yes*! I think you were reading *my* book. I accidentally left it behind after my last visit. I'm in this Psychology class, and we were reading case studies on these, and how the brain is essentially psychologically malleable, and—"

Imogen followed and listened, smiling as the two fully embraced their "inner nerds," as Dinny would say. She embraced her inner nerd with Dinny, and it was one of her favorite things.

Turning to her best friend, Imogen pinched the gut of the ghost at her side, teasing with a tickle. "Want to race?"

In answer, Dinny launched for takeoff, but with a quick hand, Chuckles stopped him.

"Hold on, hold on. What were you doing, Dinny?" Chuckles gave him the single-raised-brow look but smirked through it; he could never seem too serious. "That wasn't very wise, you know… going into a place you don't know. You could have been hurt."

Dinny shrugged, and like always, Imogen could hear the grin in his voice. "It's Halloween! Trick and treat, right?"

Chuckles chuckled. "It's trick *OR* treat."

"Ah, that's no fun! Besides," Dinny insisted, as he began to jog backwards with readied legs, "sometimes I think they're the same thing!"

CHAPTER 22

A clouded night sky coils above a blackened sea, where the eastern shoreline stands firm in its battle with the waters. Scribbled with pivots and dips, the Cape Ann coastline twinkles muted winks, warning seafaring ships and sailors of its jagged edges.

Upon the land, plagued by a wind that is wet and raucous, Imogen scales a slick incline of jetting rocks, ignoring the protests of pained knees and bare toes. Despite a secured wreath about her head, the whipping wind struggles to free it, stealing away petals with its efforts. Likewise, the wintry fingers of the gale creep into her new gown, tormenting the delicate fabric like a ghost with jealous fists. Already tired, she tries to go faster, knowing her Task to be far from complete.

Though the night is thick in its darkness, filled with storm clouds that forebode as they billow, her way is clear and she finishes the trek with an earnest certainty. Upon her ascent, a lighthouse promises sanctuary.

Snaking about the sea, a sinuous fog curls its fingers in expectation, reminding of the swamp witch's readied hand. It beckons, dancing in invitation, asking to be joined. Imogen nearly follows, as if entranced by the rhythm of the mist, easily pulled in and pushed out by the soothing motion, lulled into submission like a sleeping ship at sea.

The spray from a violent wave at war with the rocks stuns her sober. The whip of an icy wind slaps at her cheeks.

Now vexed, Imogen hurries to prepare, seeking a spot to settle as she does so. Finding a nearby patch of wet but plush grasses, her trusty pack reveals objects ready to rally. The jar from the swamp witch glares in its container. An empty vial rests, ready to be filled. Words sit sung upon a scroll, ribboned until ready. And this Task's letter lies ready and waiting, with its counterpart reminder to "Do well."

She tries not to think about the dedication to the ghosts.

Though having read and reread it dozens of times, Imogen glances once again upon the Task's page of instructions.

To be someone who seeks the secrets of the world,
you must also seek the otherworldly.

Take the Witch's trade,
but be wary of its innards.
Within the jar, there sits a Spell—
be warned of likely tremors.

Use the Spell to lure a ship,
though be mindful of your mission.
The vessel you seek is quite unwell—
lonely in its condition.

'Tis a Ghost Ship, lost at sea,
aimless as the souls who steer.
Sing the Song of a Siren strong
to bring and beckon it near.

With sky water added from a fresh rain of fall,
Cast your voice with poise,
seeking shadows through the squall.

Taking the script line by line, Imogen settles on the most tangible instruction.

"Sky water," she acknowledges, and she snatches the empty vial, hurried by the havoc of the wind. Spotting a puddle of rainwater at her side, deep and fresh, she twists to face it, bending over the pool with angst.

Her reflection greets her, filling the wet canvas with color from her crown.

Again, the echo of herself is a surprise, akin to the dress shop's mirror, and she blinks away the fog that seems to fill the inside of her head at the sight. Slowly, as if sluggish—the way one feels weighted in a dream—she tries once again to focus on the Task before her and fills the vial with a dip.

Now targeting the witch's jar, her fearful fingers tremble. *Be warned of likely tremors*, the letter says.

"The effects of a Curse," she worries to the wind, thinking of the tendrils she traded.

With the lid freed and the vial ready, sky water rains down upon the objects in the jar, dousing them in a slight shower of nature's magic. Quickly closed, Imogen brings the Spell near to study. Odd things exist

160

inside, reminiscent of aged pipes, salt of the sea, and herbal ingredients that bother Imogen with their spikes and curls. The things give her pause, as an ancient sensation nips at her neck with a reminder. Reminding her of what, though, she cannot recall, so she shoves the jar aside and sends the nipping into a stifle, bothered by its bitterness.

With heavy breath, she stands to sing her Song, taking careful steps to close the space between where she stands and the roaring waters. Surely, like the ghosts she regrettably seeks, the vision of her seems to mourn with the wind, as her wild tendrils twist in the air with an ethereal gown that trails, soft in its fabric and extravagant against the backdrop of the night. She walks with tenacity and also fragility, passing the Eastern Point Lighthouse, pursuing the catwalk that sits of stone but seems to waver precariously within its oceanic cradle.

Upon the path of rocks, with arms outstretched in surrender, Imogen pours the Spell into the sea, and she sings her Siren's song.

"Hear my words, dear sailor's soul,
Follow my voice to find your dole,
Be lost no longer,
Become found this night,
Find solace and safety and blissful delight.
Hum, come,
Hum, come,
Hum.... Come..."

Her voice quivers and shakes like the waters that splash and spray in the storm. Now complete, she waits, suffering in strained silence and wondering what frightful mare of the night may come now. The snaking smoke upon the waters snatches at her ankles, fluid and sleuthing. As it reaches, the vision of grabbing hands attached to undead sailors drowns out reality as imagined phantoms emerge from below and climb upon the rocks to retrieve this makeshift mermaid.

The shallow breath that accompanies such grave uncertainty chokes her lungs. She falters.

Is it worth it?

With incredible will, Imogen steadies herself and summons a deep breath. The bitterness returns as the song's melody settles in her mind. It's familiar but also somehow foreign, and she tries to resurrect buried memories in hopes of revealing why the nipping has returned. She is frightened of the prospect of ghosts, indeed… but it's something else that steals her resolve. Some forgotten moment is trying to rise to the surface of her awareness, and her insides seem to know enough to warn with churning bile.

Triggered by the lighthouse, Imogen looks back to the ocean. The beacon's lulling shine dances over a spectral ship in the distance. And then she remembers.

**

A Memory:

It was fresh after her birthday.

She was a glowing nine-year-old, with ringlets as riotous as ever and a face full of freckles that danced in chaos across her nose. Dinny was twelve, his smile still timeless, and their friendship had morphed and evolved from childhood whimsy to truly belonging to one another.

Roused by a singsong whisper, she awoke to his gentle nudge and bright eyes.

"'Morning, Mo," he greeted, as he hummed some ditty about daffodils. He gave her a kiss-tap and tucked a yellow flower behind her sleepy ear. "Come on, get dressed." Pausing for theatrics, he wiggled his brows. "I found something."

Never calloused to the exhilaration she'd feel when invited into Dinny's adventures, Imogen launched from her bed in obedience and intrigue. And they were off.

A heavy autumn moisture weighed upon the morning, as if the heat was too heavy for the chilled earth upon which it lay. Bugs whistled and the occasional critter skittered into view, but mostly the morning was eerily quiet, only adding to the mystery that beckoned.

"Do you believe in magick, Mo?"

He smiled, but his eyes were serious as they studied hers, seeming to hope.

Unexpectedly nervous by the question, she shrugged. "I don't know. What do you mean?"

"I mean *real* magick. Like witches and spells and… unexplainable things."

Slowing to study him in turn, Imogen watched with inquisitive caution, witnessing her best friend filled up with this unexpected curiosity. There was an urgency about him. Almost an uneasiness.

"I've not thought about it, I guess," she finally answered. "Do you?"

He took a breath and his smile never faltered. "I never had either," he assured. "But then something happened."

Now startled, she pressed. "Well, tell me." Feeling odd, she pinched him playfully for good measure, striving for normalcy and banter.

"I'll show you. We're almost there."

In the distance, she spotted an unfamiliar Spanish Moss, and she only then realized he'd led her through a new route once again, somehow always able to find another despite their years of exploration.

"What is that?" she questioned with a giggle, as she spotted a very special kind of Swamp Sunflower decorating its trunk.

Upon arrival, she inspected it and nearly swooned. A peculiar carving ornamented the bark, etched to make a bouquet of her favorite yellow flower and then painted to bring out its brilliance.

"This is surprise number one," Dinny announced happily, clearly excited by the morning's agenda. "This is where I was when I found, well... the thing that I'm going to show you next. I think this is a *magic* tree, Mo. And you're magic, so it made me think of you."

She reached out to touch the painted petals, brushing her fingertips in a careful caress across the beautiful bouquet.

"Now, no matter what, you'll have flowers forever," he beamed. "Magical ones, just like you."

Bothered by his insinuation, she paused to correct him. "I'll already have flowers forever, Dinny." She forced a smile to cover her fear. "Or were you planning on moving into a rich home without me sometime soon?"

With a reassuring eye-roll and a kiss-tap, he pulled her in for a startling embrace, and she melted into him, fully aware his touch was a remedy she required.

"Don't be silly, Mo," he sang into her hair. Then, after a soft squeeze, he pulled her back to soothe with a sober stare. "You know you're stuck with me."

Fighting a knot from forming in her throat, she nodded and turned away, surprised to find his gentleness somehow summoned even more emotions to the surface.

"Good," she concluded. "And thank you. I absolutely love them."

Shuffling around the roots where they stood, Dinny sought something and then retrieved it, having tucked it away for safekeeping.

"You'll love this more," he swore.

Unwrapping the loose folds of a canvas cloth, his swift and careful fingers soon revealed a heavy book that exuded enchantment. Leather-bound and authoritative in its markings, one could expect it to belong to a witch or a troop of fairies, evident of magick, as if a spell protected it even in this moment.

Just as she had touched the carving upon the tree, Imogen now stroked the face of the tome, prompted by disbelief.

Inviting her to sit, Dinny leaned into the tree and readied his words. "I read some of it yesterday." He was breathless with enthrallment as he remembered the contents and their impact upon his soul. "It's like a textbook for *real* magick. For anyone. For *me*." He shook his head and laughed. "It tells you *everything*. Things to use for magick, things to use in spells, things that are simple for everyday and things that are bigger. Things you should do and things you shouldn't do. History pages. It even talks about when you might be affected by a spell. I mean—" He paused in his passion, sweetly staggered by this new reality. "To think that magick is not only real, but that it could be used by ordinary people like you and me."

She watched him with a mixture of fascination and melancholy. He was her best friend, so the sight of his euphoria made her glad… but she'd grown to be content with only needing him. In a way, it was as if the allure he felt for this bigger world meant that she was not enough for him, despite the fact that he was more than enough for her. He'd always protected her, and comforted her, and loved her. But today, there was a spark in his eye she hadn't ever seen before, and noticing it sent a pain through her stomach, raw and gnawing.

As this pain brought back the fear she'd felt earlier, her words rang of doubt instead of joining in excitement.

"How do you know it's real, though?" she challenged. "What if it's just... words?"

Never one to falter so easily, Dinny grinned. "Because I tested it, Mo. And it *worked.*"

In a quick flutter of pages, he flipped through and studied as he neared the page he sought. Chapters flashed before their eyes in a whirlwind of calligraphy and color. Imogen spotted summaries on Water Magick, noting differences between dew water, rain water, river water, and so on. Flora and Fauna covered large portions of the book, with color specifications and symbolism. Manifestation. Materials and textiles, even. Moon Phases and Stages of the Year.

Captivated, her instincts betrayed her, as they wandered away into the whims of the book and left her aching gut unprotected.

"Here it is!" Dinny's shoulders squared as he offered his proof. The page dazzled in the sun spots that filtered through the canopy and through the clouds, littering the forest floor with bright fragments that mimicked the very freckles on Imogen's nose. Illuminating the open-faced opus, the light caught a luminescence about the pages, as if it might capture the magick the shimmering sheets promised by merely forcing it to be revealed to the eye of the beholder. "*Detect & Discover,*" he read. "It tells you how to determine if there is magick near you—things that are naturally magical, or magick being cast by another, or even leftover magick—and it tells you what to do to find it."

Won over by his vigor, Imogen leaned into Dinny in anticipation. "And what did you find?"

Pausing to appreciate her interest, Dinny slowed his spiel and offered a honeyed side smile to his best friend. Then, preferring to show her instead, he grabbed her hand and tucked the book back into its secret spot. "The book was surprise number two. Now it's time for number three—the finale."

Hand-in-hand, they followed the path he'd taken the day prior, led by nothing other than mystical notions. The world still seemed to exist in a whisper, as the typical white noise that came from the ever-symphonic cicadas had been hushed to a dull decibel. It made their friend the forest seem less welcoming, somehow; like coming home to an expected sanctuary only to find it had been touched by a stranger. The alteration felt alien.

Imogen's ears primed with every discernible clang or call, now, as the little clamor that did exist felt eerily insufficient. Their scuffling feet cracked sticks and shuffled through grass. Creaking limbs snapped and popped under the summer heat that stretched and swayed with the breeze that blew through the sea of trees. Through their leaves, Imogen could see the sky was an odd one, today, as the color took on a sickly yellow.

Dinny mirrored her watchful eye, and he slowed their steps to a halt in response. "Storm's coming," he breathed, as he matched the hushed tone that surrounded them. "Hear that?"

Imogen waited, feeling she heard everything and nothing all at once. "What?"

That timeless smile shone bright with a wink of mischief. "The calm before the storm."

168

Relaxing from her efforts to listen, she released an eyeroll that spoke loud and clear. "Dork."

"Guess we better hurry." He squeezed her hand before releasing. "Race ya!"

He took off in a sprint, but she'd learned his tells over the years and held close to his heels. Now aware of the weather, Imogen endeavored to study the sky, noting its sour color to be tainting the air all around them with hues of toxins and bile. In her glances, though, she also sought to memorize their route, as every which way remained foreign and puzzling. The combination played upon her senses and made her question if she were actually dreaming; against the oddity of the day, it all felt so surreal.

Taking to the north, they traveled a bending path until they couldn't. Standing at the edge of the trees, they faced the front door of a structure that welcomed no words… because it was nothing like either of them had ever ventured to describe.

"What is it?" she whispered, careful not to wake any sinister thing that may have been sleeping inside.

Dark in color, the structure swayed like the cloaked ghost of a reaper, unsteady against the backdrop of strong trees that enclosed it, as their weather-withstanding bodies towered over a shape that suggested a quivering skeletal infrastructure. Similar to circus tents, fabrics dipped and then darted, as ropes wrapped around poles and tied to stakes rattled in the wind from the growing gale.

"I don't know," Dinny shrugged. "This is as far as I made it yesterday."

Leaning in, they both acknowledged the distant music with perked ears and wide eyes. Slow and seafaring. Oceanic in its ebbing. Akin to a sailor's mourning or a siren's song.

Struggling to swallow, she allowed an overflow of her worries to spill out of her mouth before she could cork it. "What about Jones?"

Dinny paused and looked at her. "What? What do you mean?"

Trying to form a full sentence, she gulped and took another go at it. "They said Jones was making trouble, and now he's gone. What if this is making trouble? What if we shouldn't do this?"

In reassurance, he grabbed for her hand and laced their fingers together as if a promise of protection could be whispered within their touch.

"No one's making trouble, Mo. We're just two curious kids." He emphasized his point with a batting of eyes and a flutter of lashes.

She watched him scan the dilapidated assembly of cloth and cables. That twinkle of intrigue that made her innards cower had returned, and she tried to push down the feeling that something was wrong. There was no reason to worry; quite literally, there was no evidence to suggest cause for her illogical dread. So, she pushed down the gall that rose like the blustering winds that whipped at her hair, and she suffered a smile for her best friend despite a yearning to be anywhere but here.

With that dazzling smirk of his, he invited her into his adventure. "Shall we?"

She followed him inside that day, and then she never saw him again.

**

Now she realizes: The trees didn't snatch up Dinny and steal him away… the bone bothy did.

CHAPTER 23

THE BONE BOTHY

As a deep gray swallowed the sky and sent a digestive rumble into the earth, Dinny and Imogen pursued exploration as a pair of pioneers. In contrast to the soldiering trees, the two dipped into the entrails of the eerie shack like angsty cats, arched with caution.

Under the cover of the wavering fabrics that rattled upon their posts, strings of lights swung about, echoing the curves of the canvas coverings. The darkness of the hour allowed for the glow of a dreamer's mystique. The dwelling seemed to breathe as it swayed with the whims of the weather. Trinkets and curios sat scattered all about, suggestive of a grand curiosity. And to Imogen's surprise and Dinny's delight, a tangible enchantment beckoned.

It sat in a chilling silence like a living secret.

Turning to his best friend, he flashed that famous smile that made her feel at ease, before chasing after the sorcery he sought and proceeded into the bowels of this beast.

The angles of the interior were much like those of the outside, with no seeming rhyme or reason. As her eyes settled and studied the eerie chaos, Imogen quickly wondered if they were wandering through a hackneyed witch hut.

A bundle of twigs and sticks lay scattered beside a miniature museum of birds' feathers and flying things. Luminescent wings stared back at her, as pins held them captured in a collage of categories and groupings. Around a corner, stones and pebbles trailed like footprints. Following their path, she ventured upon a section of jars that caused her a fright, as human teeth and creature fangs nipped and bit at her reality. Neighboring the incisors were labeled canisters of herbs and spices, though their names read more like potions than mere salt or pepper. Vials of the earth's remnants sat in unassuming rows. Flowers and foliage hovered near her head, gathered and tied for later use. Crystals seemed to cry out in the dark space as if stifled and desperate to be unstuck. Foraged mushrooms sat in various stages of dissection, opened and offended by knives and utensils. Whittled wood shavings littered the ground. Bones tied to string rattled like wind chimes.

Still faraway, the muted melody droned through the border of fabric and cloth, bleeding into the air from somewhere in the dark. It rose in waves like water of the ocean and beckoned in its depths. As she searched for the maker of the music, a hurried Dinny sniggered near her back as he rounded a corner.

"What'd you find?" she whispered after him, afraid of disturbing the creeping things that surely lurked in the deepest shadows. "Dinny?"

Now, in pursuit of his giggles, Imogen weaved through the hazy makeshift shack in obscurity. Though she tried to swallow her dread, her efforts failed, feeling stuck in her gut. Every step further into the unknown felt like being swallowed and followed all at once.

"Dinny?" she tried again, jumping as the storm grew all around them. "Dinny!"

With angst in her chest, she figured he was waiting around the next corner, teasing her and ready to scare. The moment of pause filled the immediate silence with the noises of the world as the hanging bones rattled with their clicks and the wind from the storm threatened the cloaked structure in which she stood.

Momentarily dulled, the world hushed, and the storm rested, and an audible call came from outside.

"Hello!"

Imogen startled at the voice, as it was familiar but unexpected.

"Hellooo!" it came again.

Uncertain what to do, she hurried back out the way she had entered, following the voice that howled. Away from the hut and back into the trees, a wandering Kenzie could be spotted, swiping windblown remnants of the forest from her rain-soaked cheeks and struggling to see through the lenses of her glasses. As she spotted Imogen in return, her shoulders tensed and then relaxed in relief.

"There you are, Imogen," she whined with a slump. "What are you doing all the way out here?"

Fighting the urge to look wistfully toward the direction of the shack where Dinny still dallied, the nervous nine-year-old swallowed apologetically and joined Kenzie's side.

"Got lost," she said, aided by the quiver in her words that made her seem afraid. There was no act at play, though; she was terrified. With every further step that separated her from the mysteries of that foreboding hovel, her chest screamed for merciful surrender. But she didn't want to get Dinny in trouble. Logic told her there was nothing to fear except "disruption," so it made more sense to follow Kenzie home than to risk the future stability of her best friend. So, she said nothing. She left him.

The seconds of that afternoon stretched into the evening with a painful, bitter languor. As the moments passed, Imogen sat by her window, watching for a mischievous boy to dart through the rain and soon greet her with a smile. The storm showered their forested world steadily, and there was no telling what hours had passed by looking at the gray sky alone. It was only when everywhere went dark that the nonsensical fear she had forbidden to fester was finally allowed to swell up and attempt its mission to destroy her from the inside.

He didn't come home by bedtime.

He didn't tap at the window before dawn.

He didn't tiptoe across her floor to comfort her upon crawling into a bed that barely fit their tangle of cozied limbs.

He didn't wake her up with a flower in hand.

It was the first night in years she spent alone… and she didn't sleep a wink.

Wounded and raw, Imogen ruminated, and the festering ate away at her insides, leaving what felt like a gaping hole in her chest that flamed at the edges. It burned; with every thought of "what if," worry seared like salt on a wound. Unable to sit still or wait any longer, Imogen rose the moment the sun suggested the daylight of dawn. Her legs pained to sprint, but the unfamiliar path Dinny had taken her on required a slower pace for the sake of recall. But she hurried, nonetheless.

The forest was louder now as the storm had passed, and the critters began to wake for the day. It almost reassured her, the noisiness. It was as if the normalcy of the forest she knew could also bring with it the normalcy of any other day… and she held onto that feeling like a promise.

In odd relief, she relaxed at the sight of the painted tree, its bark engraved with flowers just for her. The touch of the careful carvings filled her chest with distressed hope, reminding her that yesterday was very much real… but so was Dinny's love for his best friend.

Moving on, Imogen went by memory, taking the path of the day prior, and she readied her insides to prepare for the unexpected—to see a real witch, or to find a clue to follow, or to see a grinning boy who'd lost track of the time—but what she found couldn't have been predicted.

There was nothing.

The evidence of the eerie hut was gone. There were no posts or fabrics left to flap or creak. There were no remaining pebbles, or remnants of wood shavings, or forgotten strings for bones or flowers. There was no Dinny.

Try as she might—and she dared a dozen times over—Imogen couldn't find the witch hut. Convinced she'd not gone far enough, she trekked for hours in circles of certainty, then incredulity, having nothing else to figure aside from the thing that had brought her there in the first place:

It must have been magick.

Back at the tree, there was no tucked-away book bound in leather and cloth for her to find. There was no message left by a mischievous best friend. There were only the flowers that remained true to their promise, as she finally cried the tears that had been swelling up inside her. No other flowers ever needed to be picked, and she rightfully feared that none ever would be.

Dinny never returned, but that wasn't the worst of it. The loss of her best friend wasn't the single thing that made her sore all over with a sadness that ached with every breath. The missing of his presence every day wasn't the reason she screamed inside her skull. No. The thing that rattled her core like the bones in that bothy were the words he'd said in his promise to take her with him if he ever chose to leave. She had believed him then, and she believed him still... so the worry wasn't in the wondering of why he went; it was in the wondering of where.

The fear was in the gut-kicking question of where he could have taken her with him if the world was suddenly one that no longer had him in it.

PART THREE

CHAPTER 24
LOTTIE

Just as a banshee wails her warning upon unsuspecting windows, Lottie moans at the sight of her hovel of a home, covering its quiet corner of the forest in pained, frantic gasps. Desperate for its haven, she lunges past the wavering brick of her footpath and through the front door with such force that she collapses, relieved by its reality and praising the familiar floor.

With paranoia gripping her shoulders, she locks herself in and stills, deafened by her hurried heart. Struggling breaths beat at her chest, and her eyes search the darkness, cautious of the shadows.

"*Sleepwalking*?" She questions herself. "I don't sleepwalk."

Her thoughts riot to make sense of her soaking nakedness. They trace back to waking up within a rushing river stream, heavy from a fresh rain. Had she fallen in? Had her sleeping subconscious sought out the chilled waters?

Catching a breath, Lottie straightens, remembering the dream… remembering a face.

"Who are *you*… "

Like a florist at a bouquet, Lottie sifts through the images of her dream the way one fiddles through flowered stems, straightening and adjusting just so. Finding a vision of a freckled face beneath vibrant florals, Lottie grabs at it, holding it close. However, as dreams go, the memory is wavering, like petals in wind or water. Focusing on details is as sensible as trying to count the seeds of a Dandelion caught in a breeze.

What she does catch, though, is a quick detail of color—and it sends her searching through her home for a token from her recent soirée.

In a bag of favors from the Secret Garden dinner, Lottie had slipped in a completed crown from the dozens piled upon the dining table where patrons crafted their own to take home. Far from uniform, every flowered wreath of plants and ribbon smiled with a soft confidence, aware of their beauty, both as a whole and individually. Now in her hands, Lottie assesses the one bestowed her, noting the classic fillers of Baby's Breath and Eucalyptus and also spotting the selected beauties of deep Roses, the shades of wine, and accents of Lilies and Forget-Me-Nots. Specifically, however, is the hue of Hydrangea flowers that enlarges the bouquet with full-bodied charm. Knowing flowers, she knew this fashioning of the petals must have taken great care by its maker, and the colors were of a unique shade with which she had yet become familiar. All in all, it had intrigued her—especially paired with the rest in their funeral fashion—and it was pleasing to assess and smell.

And now, as she stares at it, remembering the many faces of lovely flowers that smiled upon that table, she also remembers the crown worn by the girl in her dream, decorated with the similar lot of Eucalyptus, Roses, and uniquely hued Hydrangeas.

Deciding what she'll do next, she plucks one.

**

Any grand research requires meticulous note-taking, and any such notes must live in a worthy space. Once upon a time, Lottie's scribbled thoughts existed in her special notebook—where nightmares were captured, inspiration soared, and stories weaved. Where Muses danced onto pages from dream-riddled routes that trailed along the mountains of her mind. She hasn't written down much of anything since she closed that chapter of her life, though unwillingly. Until recently, that is.

With her jotted notes before her - the bulleted list of attempted recall upon the outset of her quest for magickal understandings; *honey, mint, lavender, roses*—Lottie designates the otherwise empty journal as her new pet.

"Welcome to the world of Wonder," she congratulates to the blank pages, ready to fill them. And, so, she does.

Pen and ink slide across the bound sheets, as mementos are tucked inside fixated pockets, and floral evidence is flattened and taped. She notes everything - spilling her thoughts, and memories, and visions, and questions onto the paper that delights in her over-pour. Hydrangea petals neighbor Foxglove memories, and the reminder of poisonous postcards point to the question of death and at whose hand. Mugwort sticks to a page, sealed with a wax stamp, dripping with inquiries of spells, and sleep, and visions. Sketches of dreams range from muddy to miraculous, as memories of flowers and then of faces fill Lottie's mind and therefore her markings. The gaps of forgotten moments are attempted capture, and the fears that follow a sleepwalker's steps trail into her final pages.

At last, her mind feels cleared, emptied of its contents, and also somehow not yet ready to be once more filled. With a sigh, she stares at her studies and seems nearly numb—perhaps afraid to feel, for then more thoughts might follow.

Looking to the windows, the bright haze of the day refuses to be reminded of the frights in the night, as it now washes over the kitchen with the promise of peace and declaring to banish whatever silly worries linger. Having rained, Lottie instinctively itches to breathe in the green of the world in which she hides, finding it wet, and vibrant, and lush. Timidly, she rises to do so, still rattled by her nighttime wandering but aching to be comforted by the spaces she's grown to rely on, as one does a friend.

Opening the door, the moist air greets Lottie first, and she steps outside to smile at it. Still emptied of the thoughts that crazed her in the night, she stills where she stands, breathing in the fresh air, allowing it to rejuvenate a fatigued mind. In her best moments, there would be no hesitation to take this opportunity; it's the ideal day for foraging.

CHAPTER 25
LOTTIE

"Never be too picky for your pickings," Dottie would say. *"It's up to the mushrooms, not up to your mood."*

Today, surely, there will be a mighty number of mushrooms, spotting the forest floor and climbing up twisting trees. Waiting. Ready for her pickings.

Ignoring a tugging hesitation to stay inside, Lottie prepares to leave and turns for the door, finding the basket beside it seeming to smile in its wide wicker bend as it sits with an opened mouth, eager to be filled. It makes her think of a baby bird begging for worms from its mother.

"Ready for your worms, are you?" she chimes as boots get donned and the basket goes dangling upon the crook of her arm. "Me, too. Let's go."

Lottie does, indeed, find that the world is wild with mushrooms.

Delighted, the favorites are quickly found— Chicken of the Woods, Chanterelles, and Reishi—and, quite happy with any fungal friend, she follows her fillings with Wine Caps, Velvet Foot, and Black Trumpet. Also finding Inky Caps, Lottie harvests a handful for ink-making to sell at markets.

Finally looking up, now fairly deep into the forest, she lightens with a happy heart, relieved by her choice to explore. The day is chilly, and it nips at her nose, but walking has kept nervous legs warm and quenched the need to be normal and moving. So she walks on, wanting only to love these trees that have always protected her and not to fear the memory of their presence in the night.

Footsteps halt at the sight of deathly fingers that seem to claw out from the cold ground.

First rattled, Lottie's mind is flushed with the memory of a phantom hand reaching out of the creek, outstretched and expectant. Shaking away the disturbing daydream, she focuses on the fingers before her, dark like death and just as dormant.

"Dead Man's Fingers," she remembers. "Just like from Dottie's book."

**

"Like just here, inside this cover, there's a message to 'the reader who's lucky enough to find this next: read it while alone in the woods near Dead Men's Fingers.'"

After Dottie had shown her the magic of the bookshop, Lottie awaited the decoding of this "secret" message with a thrill in her chest that fluttered like a wheat field in the wind. Upon rushing back to the cottage, the two hurried to put on their proper boots and gather a basket, just in case. Then, they set off, and Lottie followed with thoughts that dizzied her, wondering where they'd find dead men's fingers, and what that meant, and if she should fear them.

That day, near the creek by the Red Fern, Dottie slowed and smiled.

"Little Lottie," she cooed with a twinkling eye, *"I present to you,"*—with a grand sweep of her ever-fluttering hands—*"Dead Man's Fingers."*

At the base of the tree, sickly twisting fingers sprouted from the dirt, black and eerie.

"It's a type of fungus," Dottie assured. *"During part of its life, it looks like this—and, understandably, it's been given the appropriate nickname of 'Dead Man's Fingers.'"* She smiled with a tongue between her teeth, tickled by the morbidity and surely amused by Lottie's hesitant assessing.

"They're quite ugly," Lottie had whined. "What do we do with them?"

"Ah," Dottie began, with the coded book in her hands, kneeling to sit and stay a while. *"We follow the instructions. We read this near these, and we see what happens."*

Upon joining her grandmother, Lottie listened intently, curious of what secrets would be shared in this shaded space where fingers grew. Dottie then whispered her following words.

"'Death awaits us all, though what of it?

Some things die, but they lead to new life—the way dead wood may ripen with spores of active fungi. Other things perish, and they may wander in the wind, or they may sink into the sea or be eaten by the earth. Should our deaths be significant so as to live on after

we die? Should we be selfish? Should we be giving?
Should we be hidden, to be a mystery eventually
forgotten or possibly uncovered? Should we be martyrs
to die with intention? Should we bask in the knowledge
of the secrets we leave behind—forever to remain as
such?

Death awaits us all, though what of it?'"

The words seemed to settle on Dottie with a
wisdom, though Lottie was too young to appreciate it.
Death was something she feared. It was an open
Unknown. An unquantifiable Abyss filled with
questions.

**

Lottie ponders the fingers and feels a cold touch
at her back.

Death still scares her, she decides, though not
necessarily in the same way as when she was a girl.
Now, it's another's death that haunts her, with
questions unanswered and the wonderings of *How* and
Why.

Stunned straight, she holds an epiphany, not
having made the connection before.

The girl. The Hydrangea flowers. The Foxglove.

Somehow, these things are connected. The floral
head wreaths and the forgotten Foxglove that found its
way from her purse to a postcard—their common
denominator is the Secret Garden dinner. Perhaps, if

she can find this girl, she reasons, then she can find answers to all of it.

The dreams, the death, the sleepwalking.

This conclusion scares her—the endeavors to understand what's going on have led to distressing endings—but such attempts have at least gotten her this far. Somehow.

"What's the worst that could happen?" She asks the eerie fingers, finding this Other to be just as unnerving as the curled fingers that reached up from the creek. Narrowing in on the fungi before her, she is reminded once more that *death awaits us all*.

"Well," she sighs, feeling resolved, "what of it?"

CHAPTER 26
LOTTIE

Magick got her this far, so Lottie settles to seek more of it.

Heading back into town, she hits both tourist shops and local spots, seeking ideas and options. Is it a ritual spell that's needed? A simple cocktail casting? A sleep satchel for more dreams?

In one shop, there is a Magick Tub Tea, meant to be performed when the moon is high. "Nope." She's staying away from the combination of tubs and teas for the foreseeable future.

Onto the next, with her notebook ready for comparison and review, she scans unfamiliar herbs and unique crystals, curious as to their background stories and noted histories of both magickal and medicinal uses.

"Lottie!"

Startled from concentration, she looks up to find Verdilla in the nearby corner, eyeing the gemstone jewelry.

Always pleased to see the sweet friend, Lottie smiles and greets. "Hello, Verdilla. Nice to see you."

"It's such a surprise to see you out before the weekend. I almost thought I had my days confused, thinking it was already tomorrow!"

Her friend laughs and Lottie's stomach dips as she is reminded that it's already Friday.

"I just felt like getting out." A heat travels to her cheeks. "Oh, and Verdilla, thank you for your sweet gift. I love it."

With a flap of her hand, Verdilla insists nothing of it. "My pleasure, Sweet. I'll see you at tomorrow's, too, yes?"

A second dip twists in her stomach as Lottie remembers another soirée is Saturday night. She'd miss the entire day of events if she could... but that's not an option. "Yes, absolutely."

"Marvelous," Verdilla sings. "I'll stop by your booth in the morning." Leaning in, she gives a quick kiss on the cheek. "Bye, Sweet."

Left to resume perusing, Lottie argues with herself internally whether or not she can skip Saturday altogether. She tries to convince herself she can, but her body won't accept it. Some part of her—maybe the responsible one—refuses to take the easy way out.

The market is her main source of income, and this is the final weekend of the season—making it one of the biggest. As for the soirée, a childish ploy in her belly wants to blame a sudden sickness, but another more persistent tugging insists she simply *must* go. It's an odd sensation. Something that pushes in the pit of her gut.

Stopping at a corner café in the center of the tourist district of Salem off Essex Street, Lottie situates into a small table in the belly of the restaurant. A wall of windows washes the room in an early-evening light—warm and weightless - and café chatter echoes through the chamber of high ceilings and cozy acoustics.

Upon ordering a black tea, she sneaks a dash of Star Anise into the steeping drink, stirring the spice clockwise and then counter as she summons the herb's assistance with psychic visions. Saying a simple spell into the steam—and feeling batty all the while—Lottie takes a sip and sinks into her seat, savoring the warmth of the cup in her hands and a quieting of her thoughts.

Basking in the moment of mindlessness, she stares idly out the windows, only vaguely coherent of the busy world, peppered with passersby and the commotion of traffic. It's funny, she often finds, how a simple sip can send a crazed mind quiet.

Like one grows aware of a dream—as if caught in its middle and unaware of when it began—Lottie registers a world of wild waves. Turbulent beneath a maddened nighttime sky.

A lone sailboat can be spotted, suffering in the downpour. Struggling to reach the harbor's refuge.

Despite the storm, warmth seems to permeate and exist more intimately than the rain. Quickly, Lottie realizes glass separates the watched from the watcher. It is through a large window that this storm is witnessed, with décor upon wood beams framing the picturesque tempest.

Back to the present, reality returns to the café once more, with only people and cars outside the windows and not the unruly ocean.

Excited to believe the Star Anise worked its charm, she takes another hurried swallow, hoping to see more.

In desperation, Lottie waits—and in defeat, all visions evade her. Frustrated, she tries to focus on what she can, struggling to remember the elusive details of the already-fading daydream. The view of the world under the storm is fogged, with a thick rain and the haze of a secondhand memory. Life exists within the harbor, but neither store signs nor building shapes are clear. Something within the recall is familiar, though. She sits on it, wondering if it will show itself.

Subtly, having been in view all the while, a tickling familiarity hovers over the décor upon the wall. In euphoric relief, Lottie realizes she has seen it before. Though in the peripheral and out of focus, its color, shape, and location send her stomach into an upset.

It's a mounted blue mermaid.

She knows where to go next.

CHAPTER 27
IMOGEN

Back within the woods, alone and watched by the trees once more, Imogen surrounds herself with a loot that sits rusted of age and enchantment. Elderly bottles of rum lie filled, ready for drinking. Blemished silverware sleep in sets, wrapped in antique ribbons and lace. Scrimshaw jewelry sings of old memories and promised moments.

She scans the contents with a faraway mind, as if her fingers seek the long-lost friend within the items themselves. In recalling her night as a Siren, memories had led Imogen to wonder if a mischievous boy might be greeting her in the form of a ghost, as she's always wondered of his fate. That had been his wish, after all. His plan.

It was as if her memories had gone dormant, though; the fresh recall had plummeted through her body like a wave in the storm, chilling her to the bone. Part of her had hoped to see him, in his full ghastly glory—prepared to roam through homes of riches at last. Of course, she had also pled with pursed lips that he be far from where she stood as she summoned with her song. Willing him to be busy exploring a far-off place. His cheeks flushed. His heart beating.

A crisp wind rallies the present and carries away the reveries. Finally, with a final dip into the sailor's bag, a traditional gown emerges, redolent of the 18th century and crimson in color, like the wax seal upon the letter pairing it.

This letter is weathered, as if it wandered into the same fates as the souls upon the ship, only now having been found and made known. Inside, though, it still holds the coiling script like all the others before it, with a new Task just the same.

The sailors upon this ship met their demise by the presence of a woman, snuck aboard and hidden in secrecy. Superstition prevailed, as bad luck cursed them to be lost at sea.

Now, it is up to you to find better luck on the Other Side. May you find favor with these souls whose fabled fates were ruined by the wearer of this dress.

They await your presence under the full moon.

The Coterie

CHAPTER 28
LOTTIE

Lottie watches as the vibrant world of evening turns black upon approaching the seaside city of Gloucester, closing in as the sun bids its final farewell over the horizon. For the first time in a long time, she itches to speed; however, she's stuck in the back, at the mercy of the driver she's rented to get her to where she must go.

The hotel restaurant.

Once upon a time, she had sought it out in solace, finding it offered inspiration for her stories, including that fateful afternoon she was served a Muse on a metaphorical platter. But now, it only avails of gut-twisting memories... ever reminding of the wrong *him*.

A Memory:

It was a few weeks after the initial rejection.

Wells' letters had become insufferable, and she needed a day off. She needed an excuse to avoid the office, to be rid of the drama. The appeal of a Wells-free setting—of a familiar comfort—lured Lottie up to the restaurant for a midweek respite. She looked forward to her favorite seat by the window, to the cozy charm of the wooden beams and adjacent lobby fireplace, to the wall of glass that beheld the harbor.

Settling in, the expectation to merely sit was invigorating—the anticipation of enjoying some peace, and being invisible, and having no immediate to-dos demanding all her energy.

And then, two drinks arrived at her table, and an unwelcomed face slid into the second seat. As if he were expected.

"Hello, beautiful," he cooed. "So happy to see you."

Lottie's head turned heavy, and her mind dizzied with the burden of having to understand any single part of what was happening. Only able to afford an expression, she glared at him with incredulity, questioning his presence, and his audacity, and whether he might actually be insane.

"You look so pretty," he continued, as he bit into the fresh bread. "I can't wait to tell you about the family drama. You'll cry, it's so funny. I'm actually inheriting a house, and my dad is beside himself, and—"

"What are you doing?" Dumbfounded, she attempted to sear him with glaring eyes, though that was only wishful thinking. "Why are you here?"

Chuckling, as if he was in on some joke, he laughed into his liquor and shook his head.

"Come on, I *know*," he swore. "It's just like your book. You know. The part where the two lovers are feverish with lust and have to handle their urges by sneaking into a guest's hotel room?"

Mortified, Lottie watches him glance to the door, spotting the hotel hallway—the hotel rooms.

"I know you were expecting me. I know what you're *planning*."

The wicked desire in his smile sent her legs sleeping, numb beneath the table. This was going to turn into a nightmare—the kind where the dreamer can't get away fast enough.

Falling into a fight-or-flight mode, Lottie raced to stand, to get away and report him. But though he was clearly inebriated, his reflexes were quick; he snatched her wrist, restricting her movement and likewise her plans.

"I need help," she hollered toward the bar. Panicked eyes grabbed the attention of the man at the taps nearby, pulling him over with the need for rescue.

It was the same bartender she'd noticed before, the friend talking to Brooks.

"What are you doing here?" He was talking to Wells. "You know you're not welcome here." Spotting the drink in the drunkard's hand, he added, "Especially not when you're sauced."

Challenged, Wells stood up in protest. "What's *wrong* with everyone, huh? My brother has poisoned *everyone* against me."

"You're a paranoid drunk who's a liability and violent, and you need to leave."

Chugging down his bottle, the drunkard smiled a sickly grin and reached for Lottie's elbow. "I have some business to attend to, anyhow," he slurred. Then, turning to Lottie, "Shall we?"

Heightened by the nerve of him, she barked back. "Don't touch me."

Shifting once more into a murderous glare, his threatening eyes bore into hers as he seethed. "Everyone prefers the 'perfect' twin brother... even though *I'm* the better one. The better *choice*."

Seeming to take on a knowing glance, Lottie watched the bartender process Wells' words, and she fled in shame, shoving her way past and fleeing for the lower lobby's bathroom.

She hid for an hour, fearing the asshole to be lurking all the while. Part of her worried he'd have the drunken whim to seek her for himself, despite labeled doorways restricting male access. At the time, she didn't truly believe him to be a threat of actual violence; she only feared such. But, then again, she didn't yet realize what he was capable of.

**

Here she is again, seeming to ever walk in repeated footsteps.

Just in time for the dinner rush, Lottie groans at the number of people bustling through the popular hotel doors and surely up to the top floor's restaurant. Against the growing angst that she might see a familiar bartender, though, the rush of a dinner crowd could be a comfort. The last time she was here, the humiliation that followed with Wells as a shadow was too much; she doesn't think she can face him—the friend of Brooks. Not when he's really *seen* her. Not now, so close to Wells' death, when her sudden showing-up could be seen as suspicious.

Thanking her driver, she pays him to wait and then hurries out as the valets open the door and usher her in. Quickly to the elevators, the heavy doors close and then open to a cozy lounge space, inviting anyone to be comforted by the glowing fireplace. Across the way, the entrance to the restaurant echoes of company chatter and dishes, and Lottie's mouth waters at the thought of her favorite meal.

Being a single diner, she accepts an open seat at the bar with a bead of sweat at her brow, having no logical reason to request otherwise. In keeping a low gaze, a menu slides to stare back, and the décor from the vision glares back in all its familiar glory. Jolted by the reminder of why she's here, Lottie spins with a jerk to take in the rest of the mermaids, echoing sporadically throughout the restaurant, mounted at intervals upon the walls and columns. A blue mermaid, stylized and iconic. The logo for this oyster bar.

"What can I get you to drink, Miss?" With a thrumming heart, Lottie turns back with a startle, fearing who she might find across the bar. It's not him; it's just a man. An average Joe. Relief couldn't be more apparent.

"A Sazerac," she answers, realizing her need for a drink is a desperate one and also remembering Dottie enjoyed the classic cocktail. "And whatever is the catch of the day." Her jacket goes shrugging off in preparation to stay awhile. "And, please tell me you have some clam chowder?"

"Yes, ma'am, will do. Let me know if you need anything else."

"Actually," she says with a raised finger, "just one more thing. Um…" She tries to decipher what to say, not certain how to present the things in her head that will surely sound insane out loud. "Were you working last night?" It was the night she dreamt of another's face and the night her legs went wandering whilst asleep, though she's otherwise uncertain of the timeline. Maybe it's the night that same storm had befallen Gloucester.

"Yes, ma'am."

Lottie takes a breath, hopeful. "I'm trying to find a girl, and I think she came here last night. Maybe during the storm."

The man shrugs. "Maybe. We had a few guests in and out, and it wasn't otherwise too crowded, being a week night and with the rain."

Already embarrassed, she asks for the only clarifying detail she can think of, crossing her fingers and hoping it lands. "She may have been wearing… a flower crown?"

Recognition paints his face. "Oh! Yes, ma'am, I do remember her."

Tickled to her depths, Lottie leans forward for more. "What else? Was she with anyone?"

Looking to the ceiling, he tries to recall. "Yes, she was… but I didn't get a good look at them. And, actually, the odder thing I remember about her were her legs—they seemed injured. She seemed sort of… in a daze. I remember thinking she seemed off compared to everything going on with her appearance. She was very dressed up."

Lottie sits back, processing the new information. "Did you talk to either at all? Do you know where they were coming from or where they were heading?"

With a tight line at his lips, a small head shake is afforded. "Sorry, Miss. They didn't sit at the bar."

"Is their waiter here tonight?"

The man looks around, notes the time on the large wall clock, and then glances back to the floor. "I think it was Anna." He ushers toward a young waitress with his chin. "Good luck, Miss."

Like a sailor lost at sea, Lottie advances toward this woman as if she is the final lingering lifeboat. Nearly causing two accidents in the process, she bumps into waitstaff with platters of dishes clattering unsteadily.

"I haven't even had a drink yet," she mutters to herself, unamused.

Finally, making it to Anna, Lottie stands and smiles awkwardly.

"Hi. Anna?"

The girl gives a hesitant smile back. "Yes?"

"I'm told you might have waited on a girl last night that I'm looking for—she was wearing a flower crown?"

Polite, the girl nods. "Oh, yes, ma'am."

"Wonderful. Um…" Lottie fiddles with her shirt hem. "Can you tell me anything about her? Do you know where she had been or where she was going?"

Very aware of their out-in-the-open location, Anna nods to the table at her side and excuses herself as she walks off to a corner, expecting Lottie to follow. Turning back and resuming the conversation, Lottie notes how the waitress's eyes have grown big.

"Is that woman all right?"

Lottie tilts her head. "Why do you ask?"

Notably looking through her memories of the day before, Anna's eyes are evident of recall. "She seemed so... silent. Or, *silenced*, even. The whole time I waited on them, she just sat there, staring out the window. Something seemed wrong, but... I wasn't in a position to report anything. It was just an odd gut feeling, you know?"

Eager for more, Lottie pushes. "What about the person she was with?"

Anna gives a sigh with less confidence. "They weren't in the state she was, but I didn't get a very good look at them either. They checked their watch a lot... seemed inpatient, maybe."

"Were they wearing anything... memorable?"

With a shrug, Anna answers easily. "A patterned raincoat. Typical for the weather."

"Was it a man? Was he old, young?"

"I couldn't say for certain; their hood was up— it had been pouring. I'm sorry."

Grateful but unsatisfied, Lottie heaves a long breath with a glance back to the bar. He's there. *The* bartender. He's there.

Twisting around Anna to keep her back to the bar, Lottie speaks quickly now. "Thank you. And no idea where they'd been? Or their plans?"

Trying to be helpful, Anna searches her memories once more, biting her lip in struggle. "No, I'm sorry."

Finding the time and remembering, once again, the market is in the morning, Lottie tips the waitress for her help, most grateful.

Eyeing the bar with what feels like a knife in her gut, she takes a breath to release the pent-up tension— but a frigid pair of eyes glares back.

Her knees buckle under a wave of nausea as that knife seems to twist.

The room shifts. Because he sees her—the bartender. He seems to have found her. Or, more so, he seems to have found her *out*. That face held no question of whether he knew her; that was a knowing stare.

An accusation.

A suspicious dread unfurls itself in Lottie's gut, threatening with rising bile.

He thinks she did something to Wells. And she did.

The savory smell of clam chowder passes through with the arrival of dinner. A plume of steam tantalizes as the poised water dips around the balking woman who stands in the middle of their busiest rush. But she can't move because he's still standing there, glaring at her from behind the bar, towering over her seat. Only now, he holds a phone to his ear.

"No." Her paling face goes white. "The police?"

Numb but not stupid, Lottie recognizes the need to move. The need to leave.

Avoiding further eye contact and keeping her head down, she grabs her coat and makes for the door.

One foot in front of the other. *Just get to the door. Then to the elevator. Then outside.*

"Miss."

She nearly vomits right there, mid stride.

"Miss, wait," he nearly barks. The bartender. The one who knows.

Practically running but stifled by so many bodies, Lottie pushes her way through the crowd and makes for the open elevator as those arriving file out. Making herself small, she slides in sideways to hide at the back. And right as the doors begin to close, she spots a ghost.

Wells.

He's there, closing in on the restaurant. His curly hair. His dark lashes. *Him.*

Now in overwhelm, nerves nearly give in; she feels faint.

As if feeling eyes at his back, Wells turns, finding Lottie. Their eyes meet, and her breath hitches. This place. That person. Flesh and bone. Caffeinating. Devastating.

It's Brooks.

CHAPTER 29
LOTTIE

Walking without pause, paranoid legs take Lottie nearly two miles before the hope of enough distance sat between the restaurant and her new status as a person of interest. Also, she couldn't think straight. Not with the fear of police. Not with the fear of having been found out. And not with Brooks.

Brooks.

She literally kicks herself at the way her heart flaps for him. "Idiot." The word gets tangled against the knot in her throat. "You don't *know* him, Lottie," she tries to reason to the part of her that refuses to listen. The part that has always refused. "You DON'T KNOW HIM." The memory of Wells berating her for the same beats at her chest like a hostage in a cage. "You've never met him. You were delusional then. Don't be delusional now."

Also, you slept with his brother. Thinking it was him. And then his brother almost killed you. And then you actually killed him.

The absurdity of it fights against anything sensible inside her crazed mind and sends a chuckle into the crisp night.

"You're fucking terrifying." She feels cracked. "I'm fucking terrifying."

206

With stinging eyes, her feet keep walking, and then a siren sounds around the bend ahead. She stills. Flashing lights paint the darkness with their red and blue as the siren grows louder. Now facing her, the blaring alarm screams out, slicing the night with its warning. But then it passes, and her pent-up bile finally releases, sending her sideways onto the pavement.

The release is clarifying. A weakness cast out.

A realization settles as she considers what's happened and what may be to come. What she's already done. What unknown awaits.

"I am terrifying." A strength oozes into her bones. "I am fucking terrifying."

**

That night, once locked inside and barricaded within her cottage, Lottie hopes, prays, and whispers spells she decides are no longer silly, intent to stay away from sleepwalking trips through the trees and also to avoid certain memories that refuse to be ignored.

For the remaining hours of the evening and into the late hours of the night, she works through fatigue to be ready for the market. Thankfully, being one to typically fiddle and craft for fun, an assortment of just-for-fun crafts and knickknacks have steadily continued to pile inside the hall closet, made for no one specific and no occasion in particular. Several land themselves inside bags and boxes of goods for selling, and she forces time to add Inky Cap ink from freshly foraged mushrooms and more fresh-flower pickings to decorate the booth with vibrance and texture.

As sleep forebodes, warning of its looming presence with a head that fogs and lashes that grow heavy, Lottie sips on a simple Chamomile tea whilst she works upon the couch and readies a sachet of Lavender to slide beneath her pillow. It's a silent, steady sleep she seeks tonight.

When consciousness does begin to drift - comforted by the view of a barricaded front door and windows cluttered of breakables to warn of any endeavors—Lottie finds she feels heavy. As if weighed down by rocks again, mutedly recalling the sensation once before, the awareness of helplessness begins to creep over her. Slowly, her head feels as if it might slide off the cushion, pulled, uncontrolled and careless. Quickly afraid of the sensations, magnified by the inability to stir or scream, desperate thoughts beg for eyes to open, finding that small movement to be most difficult.

Through exhaustion, internal efforts struggle on, and tired lashes rise ever so slightly. As if finding the reflection of a mirror against the wall, she registers her face, staring back at her, lying limp in near lifelessness. Then, in frantic recognition, she understands the face is not hers at all, but the same girl from before… who'd worn the flower crown.

CHAPTER 30
LOTTIE

The morning of the market is cheery and pleasant, and Lottie struggles through every hour. Irritable from a restless sleep and confused by the disturbing dream, she sifts through emotions, from angry to confused to worried to distressed.

She can't help but think this girl is in trouble, and the more clarity she seeks, the more troubled Lottie grows. It's no longer a question of what's happening to herself; it's now a concern of how to save this girl to whom she's somehow connected.

And how, exactly, are *we connected?*

Deep in her wonderings, she thinks these things, as she idly fiddles with the locket at her neck.

Suddenly, in the woman's typical whirlwind, Verdilla arrives with a spastic energy and a bright smile. "My little Lottie!" she sings, eager to hug and accepting no refusals. "My Sweet, I have a gift for you." With earnestness, Verdilla extends a bow-wrapped box, nearly bouncing.

Wading through a head of fog, Lottie smiles softly and peers at her friend, surprised to see a foreign image flash through her thoughts, sudden and interrupting. An invasive déjà vu sneaks in, and she spots a stranger's face whose hands hold out a box in similar fashion, surrounded by dresses and a soft light. There's a vision of lipstick. After a blink, it vanishes, and Lottie once again faces her friend.

"Oh," she acknowledges, hurrying through her muddled mind to accept the gift. "Verdilla!"

Inside, a classic gown beams, long and luxurious, with rich hues of a twilight velvet and dazzling in beaded detail.

"I saw it, and I couldn't help myself. It's *extra* special."

Lottie looks back to Verdilla, curious. "How so?"

Grinning ear to ear, the excited woman tells her tale. "That dress was your grandmother's. Check the tag."

And, so, it was. "D.C.D.," Lottie breathes. *Dorothy Charlotte Dutton.* "Oh, wow. How?"

"Fate," Verdilla shrugs happily. "I've taken donations of different things over the years, and we had a need for prom dresses, once upon a time. I'm sure she must have donated it, then. And I just happened to be looking through donations, and somehow, this one stayed as safe as a secret."

Lottie smiles at the wording. *Safe as a secret.* So very Dottie.

"This is *so* wonderful. Thank you."

"My pleasure, Sweet. Wear it tonight—you'll be perfectly fancy and formal."

"Definitely."

"Now I must do the final touch-ups, as they say! The silent auction is being set up today, and I'm going to put your donated gift basket front and center. The things your mind conjures and your fingers create are amazing, sweet Lottie."

Waving goodbye with blushing cheeks as her comrade prepares to stroll on, Lottie looks to the locket that she now habitually grabs and an epiphany swells through her, mighty as a wave. "Oh, Verdilla!"

"Yes?"

Hurriedly, fingers fiddle to free the necklace. "I was just wondering," she says, as the locket pops open for reading, "if you could look at this one more time. You had interpreted it to be, 'Think of me,' I think. I'm curious—is that the verbatim translation?"

Not as spazzed as she'd been in the gardens, with no patrons to please or hurry to host, Verdilla pauses to better assess the script, studying with held breath.

"Specifically, I suppose, it says, 'Bear in mind.'"

"Huh." The words settle upon Lottie with an ominous air. "Okay, thank you."

"Latin is such a rich language," Verdilla adds, with reveries playing behind her vision as she looks up at nothing but with eyes that flit and dance. "You know," she singsongs, "it's often used in spells!" Her face seems to glitter with pleasure at the concept. "Because the language itself is believed to hold so much power, it seems the Dead Language is actually very much alive, wouldn't you say?"

The mentioned trifecta of "spells", "power", and "dead" ignite Lottie's stomach with a heat that threatens to boil.

"Latin is considered powerful? What do you mean?" She tries for nonchalance but there's no telling what her facial features give away.

With a cocked head, Verdilla nods simply. "Oh, yes, Deary. If you *believe* in anything holding power, then it only makes sense for a language like Latin to be among the most powerful—a language that is rooted in history, has transcended civilizations for centuries, holds academic prestige and religious significance, and is *given* power by those who use it for things like spells and prayers…" She trails off, mesmerized by the significance. "Well, it's just all fascinating to me, but I'm a sucker for things like that." Now, a chuckle as a new memory is found. "Your grandmother, too. She and I would have such a hoot of a time, going all a-giggle with talks of things that made us giddy… but also sips of things that did the same." A cheeky wink.

The boiling in Lottie's gut simmers down as the image of Verdilla and Dottie pulls her in, like the current of her favorite forest stream, greeting her with sweet relief. "I wish I had sat in on one of those nights."

Fingers strum along a beaded neck, as Verdilla takes a grounding breath and noticeably reminds herself to get back to the present. "It would have been the best of parties, no doubt."

Back to the locket, Lottie clasps it and nods, grateful. "Well, thank you, again, Verdilla. Always love seeing you."

Verdilla gives another hug. "Oh, anytime, Deary. You look a little tired, you should go home and rest."

Amused, Lottie laughs. "Will do." Then a sudden prickle of a thought jitters to the forefront of her memory. "Hey, as a thank you, and if you're interested, I got a *glamorous* haul of fresh mushrooms yesterday after the rain. Lions Mane, even. Pairs perfectly with seafood. Would you like any for tonight? I know it's short notice –"

"Oh, yes!" Her eyes brighten as if aflame. "That's *perfect* for the event. I'll let the caterer know, and they can plan accordingly. An extra dish or something." She smiles with fluttering fingers. "You make magic for me, little Lottie. See you tonight."

CHAPTER 31
LOTTIE

The unboxed gown trails past her torso into a pool like black ink, fluid as liquid swimming over the floor. In the mirror, it's like a young Dottie stares back, smiling with a wink of encouragement. Lottie wonders where Dottie wore this dress—a soiree like this, or a New Year's Eve ball, or off to some foreign land to meet a prince, or simply to peruse a museum in luxury. The silly woman did all sorts of things like that—being anything and everything.

Wearing it now and breathing her in, Lottie almost feels different. Confident. Strong.

She hasn't felt strong in a long time.

Immediately tipsy with the sensation, Lottie hurries to silence the mouth that giggles in the mirror— only to a pause when a crinkling sound catches her attention.

The crinkling culprit whispers from near her wrist.

Inspecting the left sleeve, a secret-something crumples from inside the sewn-shut hem. Hardly thwarted by the challenge of having to resew the stitching, Lottie gently rips at the seam, finding the secret-something teasing at the edge with the promise of ink on paper.

"What are you?" She whispers to the thing.

Crisp with age, it unfolds easily as she works it open, crease by crease. Dottie's handwriting leaps from the page, and Lottie catches it with an embrace, holding tightly to each and every word like an embrace.

Made with magick. Sewn with Love. Wreak some Havoc. Best of Luck.

A message. A mantra. …A lifeline.

So many emotions whirl within her, but a single thing stands out with an assurance Lottie hadn't realized she requires:

Dottie *was* a witch. And Lottie knew it.

**

That evening, feeling quite like the undead but dressed rather snazzily, Lottie suffers her way to the event.

Though exhausted, she imagines the essence of Dottie entangles with her own tonight, and that—along with the fact that tonight's soiree is at Hammond Castle—urges her to hurry. Because she's back in Gloucester.

Now, with Dottie's magick bit of luck on her side—literally—Lottie hopes these things might coincide to her benefit. That they'll somehow assist Lottie in finding the mystery girl. Uncovering answers.

The hour of arrival welcomes the evening as the castle looms over the oceanside cliffs. Its façade is fantastical.

Though modest in structure, the detail is grand and the strongholds stand tall. Towering over trees and with a terrace that frames the ocean like a painting, the walk down the stone steps and into the gardens echoes of fairytales—promising intrigue and mystique at every turn. A drawbridge is lowered, assuring mysteries await inside. The surrounding gardens hide tucked-away benches and clandestine walkways for hushed exploration.

It's just as she remembers it; it's just as she had described in her book.

In the pages of her novel, one of the Lovers hid away in the gardens, wanting to start over—to grow anew, like the flowers and foliage. Feeling there to be no better backdrop than that of a seaside castle, they took root on a tucked-away bench, only to be surprised by their stalker and then suffocated into silence. That chapter was a toxic whirlwind of desire, entitlement, and expectations, and the two Lovers spiraled until one of them caused the demise of the other.

Instinctively, and as expected, Lottie finds herself in the quiet isolation of the gardens, easily lured by the what-ifs that emanate from the shaded entrances.

Terrified by the idea of an uninvited Wells popping up to silence her—still finding it hard to believe he's truly gone—she hesitates in her wandering. But the mystery of things hidden is an alluring one, so she follows the pull, figuring that if secrets lie in wait near benches, perhaps answers lie in wait, as well.

Once finding the familiar bench, the charming seat welcomes her. Accepting easily, the quiet remoteness further fuels her desire to avoid the forced chatter on the terrace—where patrons are surely already sore by the elbow-rubbing and brown-nosing.

Peeking through leaves, Lottie can already see the expected pop-up bars and platters of champagne, ready for orders and easy sipping.

Still too content to emerge, she watches, noting the familiar faces and hiding from feared ghostly phantoms likewise.

A familiar handful of men guffaw over their liquor, already red-eyed and easily pleased. Doctors and psychologists and well-known philanthropists. Pockets of women stand about and chatter. Pairs of couples wander to and fro.

As the evening's dinner table is set up on the terrace with the ocean view—beautifully lit by twinkling lights and accented candlelit centerpieces— staff members fold blankets over each chair, and heaters stand ready like guards.

Curious about her assigned seat, she's finally drawn out of the foliage and seeks her name card. As final touches are perfected by the busied staff, she remembers the bag of mushrooms in her hand and hurries to follow a staff member into the kitchen.

An array of readied dishes greets her warmly, aromatic and colorful. A chart of patrons' names and numbers outlines dietary needs and restrictions. As individual staff members enter and exit in carousel fashion, Lottie offers her collection of fresh fungi to any who will take it. Meanwhile, the food's delicious scent swirls into her head like a dream, and she decides she's hungry, and tired, and already eager for the event to end.

Because she's got other things on her mind.

Eventually, as dinner is announced and all take to their seats, a co-host makes for the enchanting drawbridge, taking the stage.

Lottie leans into her glass, grateful for the blanket and wishing for her bed. The speaker, whom somehow seems familiar, sets attention to the ocean— the inspiration for the event; the theme being, *Out to Sea*—and encourages the pondering of deep secrets that lie below and beg to be discovered. To be explored.

"'It is not down on any map,'" the woman quotes, and Lottie's spine stiffens with realization. "'True places never are.'"

That quote.

Moby Dick.

That night with Wells. The shirt she wore, now realizing it was surely Brooks'. And now this woman.

There's a reason she seems familiar.

It's Mrs. Stacey. Their *mother*.

This is the charity dinner for the Maritime Museum. This is the event where Mrs. Stacey was pictured in articles, being an advocate for the cause.

Lottie curses internally, finding her tired mind to be more infuriating with every passing day. It's like the fatigue is making her braindead; she can't think logically. She can't see things clearly. She feels entranced.

How could she overlook that *this* is *that* event?

Thankfully, back-and-forth waitstaff divert from Lottie's physical reaction. With grumbling bellies, all patrons politely smile and nod, though delivered dishes distract with their sights and smells. Mrs. Stacey is offered applause following her introduction, and then she joins the table, greeted by the fresh hors d'oeuvres upon her plate—which sits directly across from Lottie's.

Shit.

"Verdilla, what did you put in that champagne?" Mrs. Stacey giggles behind dainty fingers. Her hazel hair shines under the lights, catching the glow in its soft waves. "I've barely had a sip and I feel tipsy already."

Lottie tries not to watch her, hoping to avoid eye contact. But she seems endearing, already; silly but warm.

Verdilla gives the woman a soft jab like they're good friends. "That's because it's the good stuff, hey, hey."

She winks. They both snicker. Lottie almost does, too.

"Well, I'm grateful. With everything going on..."

Lottie gulps. She's talking about Wells.

"Oh, I know, Dalene." Verdilla grabs her friend's hand, squeezing tight.

Lottie wonders how long they've known each other. How long they've enjoyed events together. If, in another life, Mrs. Stacey—*Dalene*—could have even been friends with her. With Lottie.

In a breath, she decides likely not and best not to ponder it.

"Well, Brooks just got back yesterday. I barely even got to see him before he got some phone call and ran off. I have a sneaking suspicion is has to do with a girl."

A strange ache twists inside Lottie's chest, but she tries to ignore it. To deny it. Because it shouldn't exist. Jealousy should *not* exist.

"Now you can get on with the funeral, then, yeah?"

The small woman sniffles a smile. "Yes. Is it terrible to say I'm relieved? My sweet boy, well…you know there's been so much strife the last few years. I'm just ready for closure."

"What are the details for it? I want to write them down and be there." Verdilla fiddles in the purse at her lap. "Do you need anything? Anything at all."

Blowing through a quick breath, Dalene clicks her tongue. "No, thank you, friend. You're so good to me." Another sniff. "We're going to have the viewing and ceremony at The Waterfront Room. Tomorrow at five o'clock."

The second course arrives and neither woman has eaten their first. Lottie goes red at the fact that she hasn't either. Efforts to remain invisible threaten to fail as she hurries to clear her plate and make room for the next, having no excuse for sitting there like a statue. In her peripheral, the feeling of eyes scan over her, but she orders her own not to look up.

"Shoot, love." Verdilla drums her fingers on the table. "I won't be able to be there tomorrow. Oh, I just hate that. I'm so sorry."

"I'll have lots of people to put on a face for. It's better that we get to have now, just like this." They share a smile. Each gives the other an endearing touch.

And then, just as Verdilla says, "Oh, sweet Lottie," all attention turns to a man at the end of the table, interrupting the event in its entirety. Because something is wrong:

His silence is deafening.

With a face transitioning from red to blue, hands signal a struggle to breathe as the man claws at his own neck. He gasps, though; he isn't choking. A hand clamps to his chest. Chairs scrape against the stone terrace as others rush to his aid. The whites of his eyes bulge out, now red and bloodshot.

Lottie recognizes him from other events, like at Ropes Mansion. He was the speaker there, advocating for supporting youths needing foster placements. He's one of the regulars. She can spot him easily, having stood near the bar, guffawing over his drink, already glassy-eyed. One of the regulars, yes, and also one of the regular drinkers.

In fact, he's one of the heaviest drinkers.

He's known as Dr. Craven, and in a final bluster, he falls into a merciless stillness from his pained fit.

With an odd inkling that tingles as senseless as intuition, Lottie looks down to her fingers and fears what she finds. As somehow suspected, they're dirty, inked with the residue of Inky Cap mushrooms.

To her own ears, she acknowledges the alarming truth. "Poisonous when mixed with alcohol."

Swallowing in dread, a glance back up reveals the Doctor to lie unconscious, with a commotion surrounding him and incoherent claims that warn of death and "not breathing!"

Having taken careful measure to avoid bringing these—wanting only to have made ink to sell at the market—she now watches everyone in horrid expectation. Wondering who will be the next victim to convulse and collapse over their dinner plate.

Oddly, despite nearly everyone drinking in merriment, he is the only sufferer.

Desperate for understanding, Lottie's breathing grows heavy and her eyes turn wild in their chase of elusive answers. And then, she catches one—a rain jacket slung over the Doctor's chair, muddled with a unique pattern.

Blinded by a memory that's not her own, Lottie sees this patterned coat in a vision. It's wet with rain, cloaking an outstretched arm that points to a structure in the shadowed distance. A lighthouse.

CHAPTER 32
LOTTIE

Dizzied by another death, Lottie leaves the dinner in haste and looks to her hands. Remembering the locket on her neck, and the shears in her purse. Now the mushrooms, singling out a stranger. One killing. Two killings.

What other crimes have you committed?

Because this death was her fault, too. This was a murder. She's certain of it.

In this moment, she realizes too many things seem coincidental—too many oddities have taken place at locations significant to Lottie and her past. The backdrops of places that have been markers for her life—in her book, in her memories, in her significant moments.

Instantly suspicious, her insides go stiff.

It is no unknown thing that *something* has been going on… but the What suddenly seems grave and intimate. This is not just about a connection with a faraway face that visits her mind in unsuspecting moments. Someone is playing with her. Something is happening.

A common denominator whips through her skull with a sickening crack. *Verdilla.* The host of The Secret Garden dinner. The host of tonight. The busybody friend who's been insistent on Lottie's presence in the places where unlikely things have happened and harmed.

Can it be so? She doesn't know. The effort to process anything in this moment makes Lottie woozy.

And the very thought of Verdilla's name alongside that suspicion makes Lottie's heart sad. It can't be.

Moreover, a new lead has summoned her, and there's no time to waste. Not with an unreliable memory and hands capable of murder.

It's the lighthouse. Her lighthouse. Eastern Point Lighthouse.

Lottie directs her taxi driver to continue through the winding roads of forestation and darkening canopies—still lush in the evening light but darkening with the setting sun. She avoids eye contact with the pond as they pass. It watches her, though; the memory of the day she was dragged and nearly drowned hovers above it like a presence. It calls to her in silent recognition. And then it disappears, left behind as they proceed around the curvature of the winding road.

Immediately, the canopy overhead opens up to the sky and she spots it. The lighthouse.

It is, indeed, a match.

Fumbling out of the car and over a rocky hill—trying to be cautious of her grandmother's precious gown—Lottie steadies upon flat land, where she scans slowly. The night in question—when she woke up in the river—had been a stormy night, and the mystery girl had been near this spot, sitting in the harbor restaurant. Now, the question nags:

"Where was she with calm waters?"

In the vision, the waters had been so still, they enabled a reflection. In looking to the sea, even this night—with no storm clouds and only a hint of wind—the waves still rush and the tide still pulls.

Discontent, Lottie paces, scanning her surroundings, searching for answers, and actively ignoring the sitting rock where she indulged in the false fantasy of hiked hems and flirtation. It, too, hovers like a presence, watching her like a ghost, waiting to be acknowledged. It's unnerving.

And distracting.

Intrusive thoughts crash against her concentration, overwhelming her focus like the waves overwhelm the rocks along the shore. Memories rush in, blocking out the reality before her and demanding to be revisited. That hazy day. Her dress and heels. The twisted ankle. His eyes scanning over her. The feeling of being desired. The absolute foolishness of it all.

Since the past demands to be remembered, Lottie pauses her investigation and gives the sitting rock her attention. The face of it stares back, and she matches it with a scowl. She gives *Wells*—and everything he's taken from her—a glower that drips of a concentrated loathing. Rooted in the deepest parts of her soul, it's grown over the past two years. Now it's bigger. Stronger.

"I wish you would just…" Her voice hitches. An ache forms at the back of her throat and she tries to clear it away. "I don't want to *think* about you." The power of the words rushes through her like a wind, giving oxygen to the blooming hate. "I didn't then," she begins to holler, "and I don't now!" The truth of the trauma bleeds through her like a poison. "I hate you!" She screams. "I'm glad you're dead!" And then her knees find the ground as everything becomes too heavy. "Now, I just want you to leave me alone. Just… finally… leave me alone."

She already felt cracked. Now, she wonders if she's broken. If she's been broken for two years. If she can ever feel whole again.

In that moment, she doesn't know how to make herself forget. But she swears she's going to try.

"Now, fucking focus, Lottie. Focus."

Resuming her search for calm waters with a cleared mind, a bloodied bandage waves to her in the wind, peeking out from a patch of tall grasses. Screaming of suspicion.

"…the odder thing I remember about her were her legs—they seemed injured."

At first, Lottie's limbs tingle in delight, certain she's found a clue. But then the reality of blood—of what it could mean—processes through, trickling into her veins with a sting of worry.

Bending down to retrieve the bandage, she spots her reflection in a nearby puddle, and she is all at once both euphoric and maddened. This is it, clear as the picture in her memory. She's found what she sought, and even a new clue… and yet, she's nowhere closer to knowing anything.

Something terrible seems to forebode, but it's out of reach. Perhaps it's demons of her own, or the monster of another, or a ghost that may follow at her heels.

226

A shiver quakes through, reminding that she's murdered a man—make that two.

Is that what she feels? A warning from her gut? She swallows down the bile that rises at the thought of another victim looming nearby.

CHAPTER 33
LOTTIE

With a head full of horror, Lottie hurries home. But then hesitates.

She cannot be trusted. Not awake. Not asleep.

Nightmares fill the dark hours while mysteries and murders have begun to occupy the days.

If she did, in fact, have a hand in either Dr. Craven's death or Wells', they were administered using things Lottie has access to at home: foraged flowers—Larkspur and Lilies—and poisonous mushrooms, like the unsuspecting Inky Cap.

Her home is dangerous. She can't go there now.

Pulling into Salem, she makes the quick decision to stay at whatever hotel is closest—dreading sleep but also fighting a body that begs for it—and settles for the Hawthorne, remembering they have a pub inside. She could use a drink. She could use three.

Once checked in, tired legs find refuge upon a stool inside the inner tavern. Shadows of the night creep in nearby corners, and dim lighting comforts the weary traveler.

Desperate for that drink, she orders a shot of tequila—and another. It seems to do the trick, so her rising inebriation encourages a third something to finish off the night.

"A Moscow Mule to go, please."

With a knowing smile, the bartender sends her off with a "Cheers," and a reminder not to let the ghosts keep her up.

Great, she thinks, grumbling over to the elevator. "I forgot this hotel was a *haunted* attraction."

A ding echoes as the doors open to her floor, and she scoots into the hallway. Mug still in hand, she grips it a bit more tightly. Her room sits at the end of the long, elegant corridor—narrow, eerie, and seemingly made for horror movies.

With every footfall, childhood fears tap at her shoulders and nag at her neck hairs—worries of basement-dwelling ghosts and closet monsters—forcing her feet to quicken. By the time she reaches her door, a tangible panic clings to her back. She tries to ignore it, but paranoia wins; she looks behind her, afraid not of a person, but of a phantom. A sneaking monster. A trailing shadow.

Just as a child does, Lottie finds relief at the empty hallway behind her—but her toes still scurry on tiptoes in case of hidden Things under the bed.

Growing irritated with the seeming nonsense, she strips and praises the supplied robe in the bathroom. Taking the drink to bed, Lottie nurses it steadily as she waits for her mind to drift off into the peaceful volume of Mute.

In the meantime—hoping to clear it of wonderings and questions that will keep her up if not emptied—she flips open the trusty notebook, and scribbles take over.

The lighthouse.
The bandage.
The restaurant.
Last night's dream.
The vision of a box in a dress shop.
...The dead man.

Without realizing it—as liquored sleep is slippery and thus quick—the brink of unconsciousness swallows her, numbing her mind for a few happy hours.

When the liquor leaves her system, Lottie comes to. But she's no longer in her hotel room.

The superstitious haunts and horrors that surely beckoned have morphed into something terrifying. Truly haunting.

A ghost is close.

She can feel it.

Lingering.

A dark ceiling stares down at her as Lottie lies unmoving, paralyzed. A mangled groan sounds nearby. Unnerved, panicked recognition wonders if it came from her.

All senses feel stifled. Heavy. Pinned down and gagged.

And she hurts.

Instant recall of being dragged to the pond blinds her thoughts, stifling with alarm. But somehow, her thoughts feel muted and not entirely her own; the reality of Wells is a blur. *Is he here?* Is she there? She can't move. *Is the water next?*

A shadow passes in her peripheral, hidden by dim lighting. The unsettling presence poisons the air, choking it. Choking her. She can't breathe.

"Tomorrow, you'll finally see…" the ghost warns in a close whisper, "with the moon watching you."

The words are barely audible over the terror reverberating in Lottie's ears.

Gasping, she lunges forward—back inside her hotel room.

It was a dream?

But the terror isn't gone yet. It still dissipates—slow and painstaking—just like all nightmares.

The feelings of being stuck and stifled still cling to her core. Lottie has to assure herself of what is—what's true: that Wells is gone, that she can move, that she is safe.

But something deadly looms.

The ghosts of her nightmares, she's grown used to… but this visit was nothing of the sort. This was darker. Truer.

She will never again question if ghosts or phantoms exist… for she surely was just visited by one.

CHAPTER 34
LOTTIE

Drugged by fatigue and tormented by a bothered mind, Lottie journeys home with one promise on her mind: *"Tomorrow, you'll finally see... with the moon watching you."*

Tomorrow is now today, and tonight is a full moon.

For better or for worse, tonight may bring clarity. Perhaps with relief... Or the literal worst might happen.

The monster of her nightmare—or vision, or whatever it was—claws at her insides with talons of dread. Wherever she'd been—in that dim room with a shadow presence—her sleeping mind found it familiar. And that familiarity has latched onto a bone-deep fear that steals her breath with every recall.

She keeps reaching. She keeps searching the recesses of her thoughts and memories for a match—for the reason it felt familiar—but her brain feels useless. The only thing the fingers of her thoughts drag up sends her spine pebbling with goosebumps. It oozes up through the mud of her thoughts like worms after rain. Squirming.

"*'The Little Lunatic learned the gift of escaping into her mind','*" Lottie whispers to herself, remembering the dinner card from the Ropes Mansion. The garden dinner initiated by Dr. Craven.

Terrorized by her own ghosts, the notion of voluntarily spending time in her nightmares sends an involuntary jerk to her chin. A frenzy to her bones.

The Little Lunatic found *"her own monsters to be the only company worth keeping.'"*

An unwelcome vision flits through Lottie's tired mind, conjuring the image of a tossed-aside child who greets her nightmares with a smile. Who delights in them.

Shivers take over, and Lottie lets them shake her awake.

"If I could convince myself to *enjoy* my nightmares," she whispers to her waning ears, feeling plenty nutty, "I'd be a bloody serial killer, given I can't seem to keep from death already." And then, bordering on a fatigued delirium, a giggle bubbles from her chest. "And this has all happened while I've been in *hiding*." Now, a snort. "Oh, Lottie, you're an absolute mess."

Delirium dances with lethargy and soon she can't decide if she might cry or fall into an outright fit of cackling. It's all too much—the deaths, the visions, the exhaustion, the mental mania. She doesn't think she can survive another night.

Across the footpath, her tired toes stumble over the wobbling brick. Cursing, she enters her cottage— still cloaked in a now-stolen hotel bathrobe—and she readies an eager cup of coffee with unsteady hands.

"Tonight," she assures herself, struggling to persevere.

"Full moon," she reminds, aware that full moons have been timelessly revered for their magnification of intentions and a time of transition. A time for things to be made known.

"Magick," she settles, refusing to forget the distance she's come. Despite obstacles. Despite doubting her abilities.

A ribbon of aroma curls under her nose, and she breathes in the coffee with a deep inhale, picturing the very essence of caffeine to surge through her. All she wants to do is sleep—deeply and soundly—but the worries of "what if" plague her peace.

What if I commit another crime?

What if I wake up inside a river?

What if I sleep the day away and lose my leverage?

...What if something happens to the girl with bloody knees?

Thinking of bloody knees, Lottie salvages the bandage from her small purse—only slightly humored by the odd things that have found their way into its belly: poisonous flowers, flower crowns from visions, bloodied dressings, etc.

Clearing her coffee table, the decision is made to simply "begin." Just as she had to push herself with that first tea spell beside the tub.

"Be a little wild," she orders with a whisper. And then, finding a slip of a smile at her lips: "Be fucking terrifying."

With journaled notes splayed out, neighbored by the bandage and locket, she ponders her process—at a loss for where to start.

"Oh, Dottie." Groaning through overwhelm, Lottie leans into the sofa and studies the walls of this quaint cottage, so heavily evident of her grandmother's whimsy. "I feel like a fraud. And also, a lost little kid. But you..."

Stumped, she could use her grandmother's inspiration. And that gives Lottie an idea.

Back to the kitchen, trusting tea to do the trick, she brews a new spell with high hopes.

"My dear little Chamomile, to make me receptive to whatever other magick is at work. A pinch of you, lovely Hibiscus, to bring me closer to my grandmother's energy. And Peppermint, you doll, to inspire creativity as daring as Dottie's."

With quick sips, she waits. Then slowly, she smiles.

"Dottie, you made savoring the world's magic a part of your everyday. You created it, and sought it, and..."

Spotting the twilight gown—its velvet fabric lying like a sigh upon the sofa—Lottie rushes over to, remembering.

"You even tucked it away, safe as a secret."

The zing of a revelation jolts her, and Lottie clutches the hem of the dress where the secret spell sleeps, heightened with a new energy.

"*Insist on sneakery...* "

It's been so obvious.

With eyes that now feel open, she scans the cottage anew, figuring the batty woman surely hid all kinds of things—just to tickle herself. *Maybe*, Lottie hopes, thoughtfully tingled by a notion, *even a thing of magick or two.*

Having existed in this home a thousand other moments before this one, Lottie now seeks out secrets like a child hunts for hiding playmates.

Facing the bookshelves, she scans them for the millionth time, having always wondered where the books of secret messages from the corner bookshop had been stowed. There are no spines suggesting wild ways or cozy curiosities—nothing fantastical or for the magick-minded—but she decides to look more closely, positive now she must surely be missing something.

Pulling out several at a time, she opens them up to peer inside, wondering if their contents match their covers.

Finding no leads, she checks for false shelves and taps on the backing, hoping a hidden passageway might pop up or a secret crevice is discovered.

Nothing. She falters, freshly stumped.

Despite the dead end, her gut kicks at her to continue, certain there are secrets to be shared.

In the kitchen, cupboards and cabinets get inspected. In the bedroom, floorboards suffer tappings and wall panels endure knocks. The bathroom tiles are tight; no flooring gives way to secrets beneath.

"I refuse to believe this," she whines at the wall. Sucking in a harried breath, she tries to think like a batty, old, wonderful woman. "Where would you hide something…"

Peering out the windows, it seems she erred in her initial hunches. Dottie loved books, indeed—but she loved the outside more.

236

Like a bee to the flowers, Lottie buzzes out the door and hovers above the planted beauties. The Lilies still smile and the Honeysuckle still smells sweet. A border of rocks lies playfully about the home, full of character, misshapen with stones and sticks. The short pathway of pebbles and bricks sways into an abyss of grasses and moss. Ivy climbs the confines of the cottage.

Lottie walks out upon the path, turning fully to take in the home, with its hushed and hidden things... and something stops her. The bricks that wobble, loose in their dirt, sing the song they've always sang—and, finally, she's listening.

Stooping down to wrangle a weathered stone free, the promise of intrigue glints from below. A stroke of sunshine gleams from below, as it catches the corner of a silver, buried thing.

Quick to free it, pebbles get swept away as dirt and dust form a cloud. The slight shine gives way to a solid, locked case. For the moment, exhaustion is a faraway feeling, replaced by a happy euphoria. At the found secret. At memories of Dottie. At the feeling she might be here now, proud and with a twinkle in her eye.

Lottie cries a happy tear. "I knew it."

Hugging it tightly, the seeker and the secret return to the cottage. At the box's entry, a keyhole sits, and she taps upon its face, curious of its required companion. The face is aged and dirtied with grime, but the detail and filigree are whimsical, seeming like something Dottie would cherish.

Delight in, even.

Maybe even display.

Lottie races to the bedroom, finding the strung key ready and waiting. It dangles as it always has, dipping as if to collect the dreams of a dreamer. She retrieves it readily, confident in its match.

It slides in easily and unlocks with a satisfying *click*!

Inside, a tangible energy emanates.

First, Lottie recognizes the book that had been read to her beside Dead Men's Fingers. A sweet nostalgia flurries in her torso. Flipping to the inside cover, she finds the handwritten dedication once read to her by Dottie, instructing the reader to enjoy the book beside the morbid fungus. But in a different ink, a familiar script grabs at Lottie's attention as she reads over the interlineation with a sharp inhale.

Put to Death—A Spell

With a swallow, Lottie drinks in every word, one by one.

> *To be rid of rotten musings,*
> *from this world or another,*
> *wrap a Finger, bound by Death,*
> *plucked from a head uncovered.*

Something deep inside Lottie accepts the words easily. Their meaning sends her relaxing back in relief.

It's a spell. And it's in Dottie's handwriting. And Lottie reads it with a sudden itch in her shoulders, pricking with ideas for what it might do for her.

Tucking the discovery under her arm for safekeeping, the pilfering resumes. There are odds and ends and knickknacks among an assortment of filled vials and a collection of curiosities.

At the bottom, a weathered notebook waits.

The exterior fabric sings of her grandmother, embroidered with a décor of their neighboring forest—detailed with flowers, and mushrooms, and ferns. Lottie touches it with a shallow breath, as her hunger to find more of her grandmother is both quenched and then altogether voracious and insatiable.

Without opening it, the pages are noticeably thick—worn and weathered by great use. Inside the front cover, the first page dazzles with illustrations of what's to come. Like an index collaged, pasted pictures hint at the subjects inside—with ribbon-tied images of recipes to flip through, a strand of mycological references, a fixated package of tea labeled to "sample," and a dozen other whimsical particulars.

Quite humored, Lottie guffaws. "I guess I get my journaling style from you."

Turning the page, and then another, the answer arrives—the insight to ease Lottie's desperation. The pages are not mere mementos of thoughts or ideas; this book is filled with magick.

Scrawled incantations surround images of recipes, and instructions suggestive of wild ways infuse the pages. They are not ancient castings but, like Lottie's own, they are Dottie's creative ideas and personal notions. Tinkered concepts of intention and expectations for mystical results. Fanciful ideas surrounding buried things that fester.

It's a grimoire. It's *Dottie's* grimoire.

Flicking through, familiarity covers the tone of every page, but Lottie can't put her finger as to why.

With titles like, "***The Ground & Being Grounded***," she reads, ravenous to greet the Unknown that fills these pages.

The ground is where everything begins and everything ends. It is literally the origin and the hereafter. It provides sustenance for life, allows our bones rest, and <u>aids us in between.</u> Magic is birthed from the ground, and so too are things in the ground magical.

Fascinated but likewise perplexed, Lottie continues her flicking, seeking something else—but uncertain as to what.

Inside the center pages, a fashioned envelope sits, secured to the paper and sealed shut with a medallion of wax. "Secret Ingredient" labels its top, and Lottie reads the following script with caution and resolve.

Warning (to my future self and all the batty I surely shall be): To unseal this envelope is to take the first step in the potential waste of its product. Do not do so lightly. The object sought is difficult to create and, therefore, worthwhile to use… so make it worth it.

Charmed and otherwise despairing, Lottie reasons if there ever was a worthy cause, the crimes and confusion perplexing her days should more than suffice. With determination, she opens the enclosure, and a small card inside carries her mind to memories in the forest—and her feet follow.

CHAPTER 35
LOTTIE

Back to the depths of the forest—passing the ever-familiar friends of Oak and Elm and ever-changing comrades of fungi and flowers—Lottie returns to the creek.

Still frightened by the nonsense from the last two times she visited—first the eerie hand, then the naked sleepwalking—she stands now with a shiver in her shoulders, wondering what spooky thing might hover nearby.

At this hour of day, with filtered sunlight and wakeful creatures cooing their songs and calls, the stream seems as steady as a childhood friend. Ready to play. Filled only with happy things. Nearby, the flourishing Monkshood can be spotted, and Lottie glances to the card that she carries.

"'It won't be that easy,'" she reads aloud, with a smirk. "'This secret is not meant for any old fool. It requires some seeking, and—if it's any good—some sneaking. Look between the blue royalty and the roots that are red, amongst all the green, and where fingers once spread.'"

She remembers again what Dottie had called the blue flowers. "The Queen of Poisons." Narrowing in on the wording of "royalty," she then scans the forest floor on her way to assess the Red Fern nearby, where she and her grandmother sat near the Dead Man's Fingers—that day they read of secrets and whispered of death.

Delighted to find it had been as treasured a memory to Dottie as it had been to her, Lottie fills with emotion. It rises her up and cascades over. It's as if her very truest friend is able to see her—right now, this very second—and it is both wonderful and entirely unbearable.

"I miss you, Dottie," she weeps. "I miss you so much."

Honing in on the space where they sat, the anticipation of deadly fingers clawing through the dirt should be sufficient to stifle a startle—but it isn't. The sight of the morbid stalks still gives her a start. She imagines the rest of the phantom they seem attached to—surely gray, decrepit, and decayed beneath the dirt, stuck in a struggle to escape. A dead man flailing in his grave.

The logic in her knows there is no such being beneath her feet, of course, but the fleeting image sends a ghostly finger tracing down her spine.

With a gentle hush, the afternoon breeze washes the world in a whisper.

"Dammit." She chuckles to herself. "It's just a mushroom. Get a grip." Humored by the pun, she does just that—entwining her own fingers with the Dead Man's—and gives a tug. And then another. "Stubborn little bastards."

If it were just the Secret Ingredient she sought, she'd leave the deadly fingers to their fate inside the forest floor. But she has bigger plans. Much bigger.

When they finally give, they're tossed into the foraging pack at her side. In exchange, a small gardening shovel takes their place within the dirt, beginning its descent.

Acting on a hunch—given Dottie's secretive style and her typical encouragement of insisting on sneaker—Lottie figures this Secret Ingredient is hidden in similar fashion. The grimoire was in the ground, so, why not this, too?

Having missed the dirt these last couple of days, she soon abandons the shovel and greets the moist earth like an old friend, leaning into it with a sigh.

The softness soothes her.

The cloying scent calms her thoughts.

With a deep breath, she imagines she could nearly fall into it as a pillow, with her heavy fatigue and its deep comfort.

With splaying fingers reaching deeper, pushing in, their tips meet something buried. Uncovering a tin canister, the contents seem to whisper as they clink.

Inside, a single vial sits, seemingly empty and alone. The only companion within the tin is another paper, cluttered with cursive.

Buried Secret - Do not open until ready to use.

CHAPTER 36
LOTTIE

Pouring over Dottie's grimoire and making notes within her own, Lottie endeavors to draft the strongest spell she can imagine. The product resounds with a disturbing boom inside her chest, like the thunder that accompanies a deadly storm. She had been intentionally avoidant of anything to do with the pairing of baths and teas, and now—as she circles the spell that's found its way onto her page—she glares at it with a seething betrayal.

Full Moon Water Ritual.

It stings her eyes with every syllable. But if she's going to put an end to whatever is going on, she has to commit. She has one shot, if that, and she has to get it right. So, she has to *do* it right.

But first, she has one more errand. With a check on the time, Lottie fills her pack, changes her clothes, and hurries out, wondering if she's actually gone insane as she sets out to The Waterfront Room.

She has a funeral to attend.

**

The Waterfront Room sits on a clifftop enshrouded in trees, leaving the ocean view to be exclusively savored by those inside. East-facing windows and glass doors welcome the majestic sights at all hours of the day and, likewise, the sea breeze when the weather affords. Like today.

From a hiding spot behind a nearby Pine, Lottie peeks around to assess her options. To be covert. To remain discreet.

Because she's not here to offer her condolences.

She's here to collect.

Retrieving Dottie's book, she rereads the scribbles inside the front cover for the hundredth time, locking into memory the *Put to Death* spell and what it requires. What it means.

If Lottie wants to get rid of the way Wells follows her—of the trauma that haunts, and the memories that refuse to be ignored, and the fear that constantly follows at her heels—she has a chance. With this spell, she has a chance.

But to do this spell, she needs to *"wrap a Finger, bound by death, plucked from a head uncovered."* She has to wrap one of the fungus fingers in death from a head. In hair. From a corpse.

She has to steal a lock of Wells' hair.

A shiver zips through her, and she slams the book shut with resolve.

She's here. It's time.

"Just do it."

Glancing back to the event center, she falters as fancily clad funeral-goers pepper inside. Formal wear to mourn the son of a rich family. Massachusetts royalty.

Looking down, a fresh assessment determines black leggings and a simple dark top pale in comparison.

Her efforts to be inconspicuous are going to end up making her stand out like a wound. And then Lottie remembers the girl, and the *actual* wound—with her bloody knees, and the grave nature of what tonight may entail—and she decides this is all so petty in contrast.

This is just a funeral. She just has to do it.

Sure, she assisted in the decedent's murder, but there should be no reason for anyone to suspect that...

"Right?" Looking to the Pine for emotional support, Lottie tries to convince them both. "Not *really...*"

With her first step, she pauses, remembering the glare of the bartender. "Shit."

It's now or never.

The nearest south door pushes open as a catering crew ushers in and out. She rushes inside like one who rallies to jump off a cliff; she stops thinking and just acts. She jumps.

The kitchen greets her first, with its many aromas and sounds. Platters sit readied with hors d'oeuvre and glasses with contents that bubble. The fleeting thought to grab one and pretend she is waitstaff passes, but she knows herself better than to risk that. She's much too clumsy.

In reaching swinging doors, a peek through reveals a gathering room where fancy people mingle near the bar at the back. A grip of nausea twists in her stomach as she spots him immediately:

Brooks.

And, just as immediately, the sight of him makes her sad. At the sparkle in his eye. At the delight in his smile. At that caffeinated charisma that stood out to her that very first day in the hotel restaurant.

It's like she misses him. And the reality of that makes her angry. At herself. At her nonsense.

You don't know him, she chastises.

Even still, it's hard to feel nothing at all when a beautiful girl at his side wraps her arms around him in a knowing embrace. An intimate one.

That kick of jealousy returns. *Lottie, get it together.*

Through burning eyes, she orders her brain to focus. With a scan of the room, another doorway leads to the next, and a propped sign foretells of the open casket inside. *Viewing Room*, it reads.

"Gotcha."

Refusing any more thoughts to clutter her processing, Lottie ducks behind a waitstaff as they enter the room with a platter raised high. Grabbing a glass of champagne as she continues on, it hides half her face while she stares out the windows, altogether avoiding the bar and anyone standing near it. But for the first time in her life, she finds she'd actually *prefer* to have dyed hair; she would love to be diluted right now. To be that much more invisible.

A whiff of the ocean brine drifts in through the open windows. She breathes it in, once, and then another, until it pulls back out to sea, following the waves that pushed it in.

And there he is.

Wells.

So many emotions swell inside her at once. Memories, both sweet and scary. Fear at her back. Nightmares. Hatred. Remembering the last time she was alone in a room with him.

Looking at him now, she does see an instantaneous similarity between them both—these twin brothers—but she also sees an immediate difference. Now that her thoughts have been taken up by the both of them, for one reason or another, it's easily noticed. Now that she's familiar, even if only *truly* with one of them, she struggles to accept that she ever thought they were the same.

But she had. She had fallen for the trick.

At the bottom of her bag, the trusty shears sit ready. With a peek over her shoulder, Lottie tiptoes to the head of the casket. One hand prepares the tool, and the other stretches in beside the resting Wells, trembling, reaching for his dark curls to give a quick snip. They rake through to gather a lock and she stills, as the memory of touching his hair on the beach assaults her. The rainy sky. The smell of him. The way he leaned into her and groaned with desire.

It was perfect. Until it wasn't.

And then it was horrible.

"It's you."

Oh, god.

Oh, no.

Oh, god.

Brooks stares at her and there's no telling what he's thinking. *God, he's beautiful.* But there are plenty of guilt-ridden guesses to choose from.

If it's the "her" from that first day they met, after she'd spent the night with his brother.

If it's the "her" who had something to do with the death of his twin.

If it's a question of what she's doing here, as she suspiciously stands over a corpse to steal a lock of hair.

"It's me?"

He steps forward with a mouth postured to speak, but then he pauses, and she sees his eyes catch the shine of the sheers. *Fuck.* Almost amusedly, he stops his advance and leans into the doorframe.

"What are you doing?" Muscled arms cross in assumed authority.

Struggling to breathe at all, much less *slowly,* Lottie tries to regulate. Between the spinning room and a storm of thoughts rioting in her head, fainting feels near. Panicked fingers grab hold of the casket's edge for support.

And then she decides she's over it. *Fuck this.*

Meeting his gaze, she finds her breath, and then she uses it.

"I'm taking something your brother owes me."

Keeping his eyes on hers, a dimple pulls at one corner of his mouth. "Oh?"

Her eyes narrow. Is he *mocking* her?

Enraged and exhausted, she steps forward, indignant.

"Your brother has taken things from me I can never get back." Her past life. A time before trauma. Years of safety. And then she considers the nightmares, and fear, and paranoia, and everything else. "And he's burdened me with things I can't get rid of."

Unmoving but softened, he blinks at her in question.

"So, yes," she continues, and she retreats back to the head of the casket. "I'm taking something he owes me. And, unfortunately, it's something he won't even miss."

Adrenaline accompanies her anger, and it sends a fearlessness through her veins for the first time in too long. Now, openly and undeniably, she pulls out the shears and cuts a curl from the resting Wells' head.

Turning back to Brooks, she quiets. Watching him, she realizes it is entirely possible that she hates this man whose death brings her relief—but is also altogether sorry that anyone has to suffer the loss of a brother. Of a twin.

With tears in her eyes—from anger, and sadness, and fatigue, and everything—she rallies a breath and wipes a tear. "I'm," she starts.

"My handsome boy!"

A singsong voice swims into the room before its speaker does, and Lottie goes stiff at the joining of another. And then the person enters, and she goes even stiffer.

"Hi, mom." They hug. Lottie swallows.

It's Dalene Stacey.

"Oh, I'm so glad you're back." Her eyes are glassy. Maybe from drink. Maybe from crying. Probably from both. "Where have you been since yesterday?" She looks from her live son to her dead one and downs the rest of her champagne. Eyes swimming.

Without answering, Brooks looks to Lottie, and Lottie looks to Brooks, and Mrs. Stacey looks back and forth between the two of them.

"Oh!" The small woman's eyes light up. "You're Lottie! From last night!" And then aghast. "Can you *believe* what happened? That poor Dr. Craven." She tries to take another sip, but meets an empty glass. "All this death." Her eyes swim again, brimming and wet.

Lottie's mouth goes dry and she has no words. Brooks is now the one to shift his glances between the two women, eyes wrought with questions.

"Brooksy!"

A fourth enters the room, and Lottie has to look away before the stupidity in her emotions shows itself. The girl wraps her arm through Brooks' with an easy confidence and a smile that lights up the room.

"Guys, the service is about to start. Dalene, do you need anything?" And then, noticing the tension in the room, the young woman shifts, trying to read what's untold. "Hi, there," she beams, and then looks to the others. "What's happening?"

A speaker in the other room signals attention and all turn to give it.

"I'm sorry for your family's loss," Lottie offers.

And then she walks out, back the way she came.

CHAPTER 37
LOTTIE

She heads for the wetlands.

Having grown accustomed to being without a car, Lottie knows how to gauge her time for travel. Where she ventures now requires a trek on foot, but she knows the way. She's been there before.

The sun has already set upon her arrival. Unobstructed by immediate trees, a slate blue expanse stretches overhead, casting the marshes and wet meadows in its sleepy glow as the sky greets twilight.

With a tuned ear, Lottie can hear the shrill thrum of cicadas in the nearest trees. Closing her eyes, individual chirps and trills of other winged solicitors join the melody. The hour buzzes of bugs and rousing nocturnes. The things of the day are winding down and the creatures of the dark are readying to play.

The day's sleepy energy is exchanged for a vibrant but eerie alternative—welcoming a flirtation with critters of the night and the death and slow-rot that beckon beneath still waters.

A smile tugs at Lottie's lip. "Hello, again."

Through the sloshing grasses—riddled with mud and patches of puddles—she stomps through, intent on reaching the trees.

Like falling asleep, twilight gives way to night, and the world goes dark. But she treks on, familiar enough with her route. Muck and mire squelch with each step and then smack upon release—like a sloppy kiss to the earth with every footfall. The chill splashes up her legs with a biting embrace.

That same slapping sound echoes from behind.

"Hello?"

Twisting to find who follows, it's hard to see anything but shadows. Darkness and then deeper darkness.

The moon hangs low, but the slight light stretches silhouettes into misshapen and looming beings. But no one emerges, and no more sounds alert of another. Then, just to be sure, she clicks on a flashlight and casts the beam over the bogs and marshes.

"Okay, then," she breathes to herself. "Just that trusty paranoia."

Gripping the bag more tightly, she comes upon the first tree at the start of a small wood and then hurries past. "Let's get on with this, then."

It won't be long, now. Around a few trees, avoiding deep puddles and sopping pools, Lottie tiptoes with ease. Sticky tendrils of grasses and reeds graze her passing fingertips. And then a pool winks from the base of a tree, mirroring filtered moonlight.

Enshrouded by undergrowth, the pool sits under a tree that twists in a trio of bark, eerily suggestive of conspiring gossipers.

"The Cauldron of the Swamp Sisters." She cackles at the sight of it. "You haven't changed one bit."

And, really, it hasn't. Not in the time between visiting as a young girl and then returning as a young adult seeking inspiration for a debut novel. And not in the three years since.

"You know," she starts, nearly giddy as she takes the pack from her back and begins her rummaging, "I named you that in a book that I wrote. I don't know if anyone else would agree, but you have a very witchy aesthetic."

One by one, she sets out ingredients: a candle, the bandage, a teacup, a mushroom, a lock of hair.

"And I know you're not actually a swamp. You're a natural spring. But," she shrugs, "a swamp worked better for the story. And now, here I am in poetic fashion, ready to join you in making magick." With a touch to her neck, she confirms the locket still dangles.

Though the yellow moon rises, a warm lantern gets situated on the bank as Lottie opens to the spell inside the book cover once more, joining it with a scribbled spell of her own.

"In my story," she starts again, looking to the wicked tree, "a woman goes to you asking for a favor. In bartering, you demand her clothing as payment, and she washes in your cauldron as you brew her in a potion, making her part of the spell."

Lottie wonders if that's what this spell might require—being one with it. Entirely and with abandon. Not just steeping… but *brewing*.

"So many things from my story seem to be playing tricks on me, these days." Her chin jerks away at a creeping hesitation. "Maybe I just have to lean into it. Maybe this is part of committing."

Past branches, the moon watches. At the sight of its face, Lottie is reminded of the need for urgency. It's already getting late. It's risky, she realizes, having waited to do this spell until the moon was in the sky— given the morbid vision and eerie clue on timing—but it also seemed a necessity. This is her one chance to know more. To end things. To be done.

Her spell has to work. The full moon will help.

Standing up to strip down, black clothing is tossed beside the lantern and timid toes step into the dark water. The depth is unknown, and her skin crawls with every inch further. A sharp sigh from the chill bleeds into the night, merging with the sounds of critters that watch.

Carefully, Lottie lowers to her hips, but her wandering toes still meet no bottom. "Dammit." Breathing through her angst, she lowers further, inch by inch as hands grip the grassy bank. As the icy water reaches her waist, her feet find the bottom—and the rough greeting of rocks and their jagged edges warrants a squeal.

"Focus." A slow breath.

She looks to her made-up witches, and she looks to herself—bathing naked in the moonlight like a proper maniac—and then she looks back to the entrance of trees as the paranoia returns. It's the feeling of being watched that further primes her already pebbled flesh.

But nothing can be seen. And, likely, she tells herself, nothing is even there. *It's just the paranoia.*

So, turning her intentions to the making of magick, she begins.

Leaning over to the notebook that lies open-faced nearby, the first task receives a mental *check.*

"Under the full moon, be washed in Moon Water."

With eyes closed and breathing slowed, she pictures a tangible energy. Just like from her forest. A creeping magic, ready and waiting. Conspiring with the moon.

"Charge me like you do the waters—rivers, and oceans, and lakes. Create in me a conduit for your Energy; from you to me, may magic take."

With the strike of a match, a black candlestick flickers. Lottie holds it in one hand as the locket lies in the other.

"Blaze to bond with the spell in this locket. May the black in you reverse it. May it bind to the person who owns it."

Leading first with a gulp, she dips the melting wax onto the necklace, flinching as its heat kisses her skin. Again, the task is ceremoniously checked off her list.

"Pair my sights with the owner of this blood," she starts, retrieving the bandage and placing it in a teacup. "My visions, may they flood." Spring water fills to the brim, tinged pink as it soaks. "Washed clean, free of mud." With only slight hesitation, fingers dip into the bloody tea, stirring clockwise, then counter, and

Lottie runs them over her body, bathing with the essence of the Other—the mystery woman.

Now, taking a single Dead Man's Finger, Lottie holds it in one hand with the lock of Wells' hair in the other.

"Put to death the musings," she starts, borrowing Dottie's words and following her instruction, "that haunt my mind like ghosts." Picturing Wells and her last visit to the lighthouse, her tone grows more certain. "Clear my mind of fear that follows." She thinks of the paranoia she feels now, and the reminder of being dragged during a nightmare, and the inability to separate one nightmare from another. "So that only the truth, I'll know." Enough with this nonsense taking up her mental energy; Lottie's ready to put the monsters of her mind to death, just like the real monster who's heading for his grave—if he's not already in it.

If there are more monsters to deal with, she tells herself, directing her intentions, *then add them to the death wish.*

With one final step, she marks her notebook and reaches for her grandmother's vial.

"May I see what I need and find answers with speed, and may this Buried Secret sharpen this spell to succeed."

Uncorking the top, she lights a match to burn within, twisting about as it turns to smoke and swirls around the unheard words. Like a bundle of Sage, it encircles in a wave with hands that dance and a smoke that seeps and creeps into the air, settling over her spell with an ethereal blessing.

Now still, she sits, quiet in her mind. Waiting for insight. Trusting the spell to work.

"Please," she adds, remembering her research:

"Spellcasting is putting an action behind your 'Please' and trusting that you've done your due diligence."

Something swims beside her.

Aghast, Lottie splashes back with a scream stuck in her throat as a curling hand rises from the water at her navel. In a flash of memory, recall swims before her as if to correct itself—as if to show the *truth*.

The eerie Other from the creek in the forest.

The summoning fingers.

The effort to rescue whomever swam beneath the surface, despite the impossibility of doing so.

Now, Lottie can see it properly, realizing it was a borrowed vision made murky by a similar but different setting. It was actually here, witnessed by the girl with the bloody knees.

The girl has been here.

Lottie should have figured as much.

In the corrected vision, Lottie can see what the young woman saw: a swamp that seemed alive, with an ethereal commotion, and a witchy hand that reached up from its depths, all under the watch of a thick and hazy sky.

"Strange."

Lottie compares the borrowed memory to her immediate reality, noting that, even in the dim light of the moon, this water is clear and calm. Somehow, the memory presents the spring to *be* a swamp, surrounded by the very things described in Lottie's novel. It's as if the girl was seeing the actual *Cauldron of the Swamp Sisters*—as if Lottie's fiction had existed in her reality.

Watching the peaceful water as it is now, Lottie shivers and begins a retreat, wondering what fingers might soon emerge in *her* immediate reality. And curious about what the girl was doing. And what the witchy hand wanted. And who the hand belonged to. And what other terrifying things she's about to willingly confront.

With fear-ridden limbs, water slides off her slick and naked body as she hurries out of the spring. Like a child feeling followed by a monster in the dark, Lottie's chest beats with a rhythm of creeping footsteps as images of those reaching fingers terrorize. But she's out. She's safe.

Except now, the presence of another returns. Potent.

"Either the spell is working," she breathes, incredulous, "or I just cemented my own insanity and have fully lost it."

Putting out the lantern, Lottie grabs for her clothes and dresses. The locket returns to her neck. The pack slings over her shoulder. The spell is done, and time is of the essence, and she does not have enough of it to handle whatever lurker may or may not watch from the shadows. She just needs to get out of here.

"Well?" Offering a glare to the moon, she challenges, wanting to know what's next. The answer finds her like a dream, and it dances through her mind's eye like a film, clear as day under the irony of a full moon.

Eerie in its greeting, a cemetery's signpost
warns: "Old Burial Hill"

"Old Burial Hill," sings a cemetery's signpost.

Imogen stands before it like a peasant gawking upon a castle. Through the night's veil, her eyes sweep over the gravestones that lie scattered about a field, chipped and broken like a clutter of old teeth.

Distant branches whisper through leaves, tickled by light winds that shake their hands and settle. Shadows stoop behind stones as if cowering from the watchful eye of the moon. Wispy clouds flank the peering ball in the sky like ghostly comrades.

All is hushed, and Imogen waits, wondering what souls lie in expectation, buried in the ground. Soldiers, surely. And executed witches. And puritans from the past.

Though the night has grown cold, the gown from the ghost ship hugs her warmly, dripping down her legs in a fabric that bleeds crimson. In her grip, a bundled bag accompanies, awkward and precarious against her slim arms and nervous chest.

The initial step of this Task is simple enough:
Find first the oldest grave and seek its sleeper.

With a shovel ready, Imogen searches the haphazard rows of stones and structures, finding many to be illegible and warily weathered. Grateful for the light of the moon, a sad stone sits at the back, empty of any discernible words or markings—worn by time to its humbled beginnings.

Horrified but hurried, the bundle gets tossed and the edge of the shovel digs into the cold ground. Quickly, pained groans sound throughout the eerie graveyard as Imogen's frail arms weaken beneath the protest of the night's chill. The surface is solid. Her clutching fingers soon turn aching. But she's come for a purpose, so keeps on digging.

As the hours increase, so does the chill, and heavy breaths soon puff fleeting ghosts into the air. Nearly spent, she breaks to breathe, then hears a song much like the Siren Sonnet she sang.

It's a hummed tune that perks ears and hovers above her head.

Looking up, it seems Imogen must have unburied a soul, freeing it from a prison of grime and time—for at her nose, a long face looms.

Empty eyes study her own as if lost and wanting to be found. It's a gentleman from another time, and Imogen stares back at him, stunned into stillness.

With a slow smile, he gestures to the bundle and then to the land, acknowledging a party surely awaits. Through both surprise and fright, Imogen's understanding moves slowly, but she nods. Offering a trembling spoon to this new acquaintance, she follows the Task's instruction.

One by one, phantoms emerge from their silent sleeps, and the borrowed loot from their ghoulish sailor counterparts is offered to resolve the conflict brought on by the Woman's Curse.

The wearer of this gown caused aimless fates and sorrow.

Now bring it purpose to break the curse by 'morrow.

Prompted by the loot within the bundle and the gown in which she's dressed, Imogen rushes to pass out party favors of utensils and rum and jewelry, seeking to make this night a memorable one for these souls who've long been waiting. Effortlessly, merriment commences, and the soft song evolves from a single hum into an eerie chorus, empty as a whisper and slow as a wail. Ghostly partners take to pairing, and the long-faced ghoul offers his hand.

Easily, Imogen accepts it, wondering of this world and of this hour and of what's next. Quickly, her thoughts follow her footsteps, turning from questions of reason to accepting the push and pull of nonsense— twirling in submission until she's dancing with full abandon.

Her laugh pierces the whispering song, loud in the otherwise silent night, and the smiles of the souls gleam back at her, happy to be merry above the ground instead of six feet under it.

CHAPTER 39
LOTTIE

Lottie runs without stopping.

Past hovering spooks in the trees and critters of the night, she sprints to the entrance of the wetlands and heads south, having no idea if she's going to make it in time—to whatever "it" is. She's going in blind, but she's going.

Rounding a neighborhood block, she takes to a side boulevard, hoping to spot a bike or scooter. In luck, a freestanding cruiser leans against a mailbox, begging to be borrowed.

"Thanks!" she whispers to the yellow home behind her, but she's already down the street and out of sight before the next breath, pedaling until her calves burn.

She knows nothing of what's to come, but the concept of a cemetery under a full moon sends the feeling of phantoms clawing at her back. So, she tries to mentally prepare. For anything.

As she pedals, the world shifts to sleep. Dark back streets hum empty, and lulled houses line blocks with window lights that have been hushed. All the while, the moon watches her, staring at her with its downcast grin.

Considering the Moon's governing position over the dozing sky, more of the Lunatic parable flits through Lottie's recall—reminding that the monsters of the night can be one and the same as the monsters of the mind.

"*Under his gaze,*" the dinner card had read, referencing the Man in the Moon, "*monsters of the night became bearable, and foes in the shadows became playmates.*"

A chilling trickle travels down her spine as if a monster lurks just behind, teasing her with its ethereal fingers. Shaking away the sensation, Lottie considers this Man in the Moon, suddenly wondering which side he is on.

"I hope you did your job," she whispers to him as her pedaling legs waver. "I'm not feeling very 'powerful.'" With this acknowledgment, she sits up a bit straighter and stands with a surge, forcing the opposite to be true. *But I intend to be* fucking terrifying.

She arrives at a neighboring road, familiar with the area and attempting discretion. All seems quiet. Nothing's amiss.

Seeking intel, ears perk to listen and eyes squint through the darkness. Movement catches her eye.

Or, rather… dancing.

Inside the cemetery, within the gallery of gravestones, a lone woman wanders. She sways… as if a lost soul herself.

Mesmerized, Lottie watches, curious of this woman she recognizes only by nightmare and vision.

It's her.

It's the woman from the reflection with the flower crown. The one who stared back in the mirror from inside a nightmare. Who's known for her bloody knees.

Here, she seems to dance, pale as the moon and in a dress that screams of murder. If it weren't for the noticeable accents of lace, Lottie would wonder if she'd bathed in blood—the red runs so deep.

The swaying settles upon Lottie like a song, harmonizing with her own heartbeats. For a moment, she forgets the need to rush, or stay alert, or remain suspicious... Then the girl falters.

Freezing in her movements above a staggered stone, the gowned girl hunkers over as if gasping to breathe.

Reflexively, Lottie takes off in pursuit, recognizing someone in need—just as she had that day with the eerie curling fingers in the creek. An instinctive reaction. But her frantic steps fumble at the sight of another—a second who watches from the shadows.

They're closing in on the girl with distinct intention. A black hood hides their face. Before they can reach her, a crimson gown goes flying, trailing behind the young woman as she runs toward the pond.

It's difficult to tell whether or not she *sees* the pond. Or if she merely runs blind. Because if she does see the sitting water, her movements suggest sacrifice. As if she were fleeing life itself. Or, perhaps, a Death at her heels.

With prepared interruption, the hooded figure stops her somehow. Easily, the girl collapses into them, quickly and with surrender. She neither wavers nor wails. She merely melts.

Tenderly, they hoist the woman over their shoulder and carry her away.

And just as easily, Lottie follows.

CHAPTER 40
LOTTIE

Deep within the trees, and tightly tucked away within a swamp conservation, the careless footsteps of the one she follows silence Lottie's own footfalls. Swift crunching fills the wooded world as brittle leaves surrender.

They soon come upon a small home, enclosed by the canopy of towering trees, much like Lottie's own cozy cottage. The similarities end there, though; this boarded structure is nothing like her home. It's a shed. Weathered and rusted. Perhaps it was once a proper house, but now it threatens of death and decomposition, surely infested with termites and secrets in the walls. Festering.

The figure in the hood walks on as the girl lies limp over their shoulder, flung like hunted game—a wrangled rabbit ready for its dressing.

Without hesitation, they enter the precarious structure of boards and shingles, and Lottie dares herself to follow, feeling unable to turn back now. She's come this far, and now she's seen too much; if she were to walk away this moment, what would she be deserting? Or *who*?

But advancing is easier than it should be, somehow. And Lottie pictures magic once more— giving it a face. A tangible presence. One that seems to carry her now, pushing her forward. Answering her requests.

Because answers *are* near. She can feel it.

"Ready or not," she whispers to her legs and to the locket in her grasp.

Nearing the doorway, Lottie chances a peek inside through the weathered boards, bent and warped and shining of a seeping dim light in the otherwise wooded world. Under a single bulb, a dirty room sits, with desks and tabletops braced against walls and a limp body sprawled in the center, haphazardly tossed upon a weathered operating table—the young woman.

Her dress lies hiked to her thighs, baring bloodied knees.

With a sobering gulp, Lottie pushes through the threshold with a focused silence in her step. Upon the wall-lined tabletops lies evidence of experimental endeavors: bottles of liquids and vials of labeled herbs; texts on flowers and toxicology; pages and notes interrupt the monotony of colors with tabs of bright orange, pink, and yellow.

Lottie's eyes widen as suspicious nomenclatures scream at her upon their stickered pages—like Foxglove... and Larkspur.

Additionally, Roses are tabbed, and scribbles of emotions and corresponding colors outline principles from floral texts, citing *The Language of the Flowers*. That book sits open-faced just beside it.

More texts and journals exist in lopsided piles and disheveled arrangements. A binder of faces and profiles warns of distressing contents. Photos and identifiers are pasted beside listed vulnerabilities and locations—age, sex, city, state, trauma histories, mental health instabilities, triggers. One after another, finalizing notes are circled and underlined: Orphaned; No next of kin; Abandoned; Parental Rights Terminated.

The pages don't make sense to Lottie, but she understands enough to be scared.

A familiar face stares up at her from the bottom of the stack of journals and binders. Hurriedly sifting through to reach it, Lottie pulls it up and greets an image of the redheaded woman.

"Imogen," Lottie mouths, reading the binder's title, now having a name for this mysterious girl who's haunted her dreams and intruded her thoughts.

More scribbles line the interior, with handwriting that matches all the rest. Detailed accounts of moments and memories tell stories through the pages, and in her haste, Lottie is only able to make out that Imogen and the author spent time together in a shared foster home when they were children.

Unable to dwell, Lottie proceeds along the tables, peering with a bent neck and tense shoulders. A leather-bound manuscript that nearly vibrates with enchantment catches her attention and holds it, enthralling in its aura. Weathered but likewise beguiling, it seems to be a book of spells and charms.

The confirmation that magick has been involved since the beginning settles with a satisfying relief and a terrifying wonder.

"Who is doing this?" she whispers to the books. "And *what* is it that they're doing?"

In quiet answer, unfolded pages of elegant script and broken wax seals challenging of Tasks wave her over in a windless flutter. Signed by *The Coterie*, a dreamlike sensation of memory and mystification washes over her Lottie.

Looking to the woman on the table, she somehow understands the emotion is a borrowed one. And with it, she realizes the world may hold much more magick than she'd ever imagined. And that is absolutely terrifying.

Finally, the most ferocious of items yet glare from their metal tray, indicative of intrusive incisions and surgical inquiries. Syringes sit filled with a mysterious fluid. Knives glint with evil winks. Bloodied bandages scream in their soiled bundles.

Remembering the woman's bloodied knees, Lottie looks back to wonder of this Imogen. She recalls the stranger at the restaurant and his concern for her injuries the night of the storm. The same night Lottie woke up in a river. The same river where she saw a wicked hand reach for her.

An idea pushes into her mind from somewhere else—somewhere outside her native thoughts—as if the magic that carried her here is trying to feed her insight.

She and this Imogen have a connection, she reasons. She doesn't understand it, but she knows it exists. So she tries to reach back—to dip into Imogen's mind instead of waiting for borrowed images to bleed over.

A physical pain blasts through Lottie. Her head goes splitting with aches. Her body feels battered. And it works.

Flashes of new memories zip through her mind as they are simultaneously recalled by a waking Imogen.

Recognition of the room drips with a dread that oozes down their spines, slow and sickly. Blurred movements of a shadowed figure shift about as if evasive. The room spins, and the lights flicker—like racing through days and nights within seconds.

Feeling dizzied, Lottie looks to Imogen for understanding and realizes what the girl is seeing is not all an immediate reality—but it is to her. It is to Imogen.

Something has poisoned Imogen's mind; it's as if her memories have become monsters themselves, haunting her waking visions… and now, likewise, Lottie's.

Disturbed by the images wreaking havoc on her mind, Lottie steps toward Imogen to comfort and ease the girl's fears, hoping it will simultaneously ease her own. But the figure that steps toward Imogen is grotesque and blurred, mirroring the rest of the nightmares filtering through her thoughts.

To her—to Imogen—it's as if Death has come, ready to snatch the damsel away.

As Imogen imagines this, Lottie is blinded by the same, somehow existing as herself… but also stalled by the images she sees through Imogen's borrowed perspective. She is both outside herself and still in her own mind, and it sends her dizzy and to her knees—just as Imogen flees into the trees.

CHAPTER 41

Monsters close in on Imogen.

Inside the wooded world, faceless fiends seem to follow easily, like raw flesh pulled together by frantic stitches. With every step, a new stroke slashes at her mind with a sharp, painful image. At her back, violent beings threaten to catch her. From the sides, witchy hands summon with twisting fingers and long-faced ghouls moan after her with siren hums and empty eyes. Past the trees' canopy, high in the sky, a disapproving Moon frowns upon the world, cloaking the atmosphere in bitterness.

In pursuit of the woman, Lottie watches through the mind of another, struggling to make sense of their surroundings. Borrowed memories of rain-soaked bothies and shadowed halls warn of danger in the distance. Much like a haunted house attraction, every second promises further priming for a trouble that forebodes. Jump scares startle them. Beings dwell nearby. The Unknown awaits within the abyss of the dark, beckoning with an invisible leer.

Imogen stumbles. As she meets the embrace of a strong Oak tree, the world shifts.

Strokes of sunshine replace the shadows of night. No ghosts lurk and no monsters follow. It's daytime, smelling of the sweet summers from yesteryear, with echoes of the distant laughter that accompanied Imogen's childhood.

Seeing the same through the eyes of a Dreamer, Lottie bears witness to a foreign Florida world, forested with rich vegetation and heavy of moisture. She watches Imogen pause in the distance, startled by the moment.

The tree the young woman clutches is familiar—an old friend—and Imogen looks to it for direction, wondering about something of great importance.

The summer world shimmers surreally. As words slip out of Imogen's mouth, they seem to slur like they're underwater—swimming over Lottie's ears with a resounding murmur. It's a question that she asks, but Lottie can't make it out.

"Any?" is how the word sounds, swimming through the world washed in sunlight.

"Dinny?" Lottie finally hears, and there he is: a young boy with a timeless smile runs barefoot through these dreamy thoughts.

Dazzled by the memory that isn't hers but feels just as personal, Lottie turns to follow him, curious of this boy she suddenly knows through another. But with one step forward, following Imogen as she follows the boy, reality returns.

With disarming overwhelm, the night's shadows wash over the imagined sun, leaving only the moon in the sky.

And someone has found them. Someone else lurks close. Lottie can hear footsteps running toward her through the foliage. Toward Imogen.

"Mo!" the voice hollers, and the daylight daydream returns, promising a playful Dinny.

"Dinny!" Imogen cries, seeking her playmate in the sunny world. But Lottie sees through to reality:

The hooded figure is closing in.

With an invisible force propelling her forward, Lottie obeys and follows the direction, blind but ready.

She runs.

Clutching the spelled locket for strength, Lottie braces for impact as she launches toward the two others, causing a collision that makes everything go dark.

CHAPTER 42

Back inside the bone bothy, where flapping canvases warn of wicked witches, Imogen glances in fear at the familiar haunt—and Lottie watches from behind, quiet and curious.

Scurrying footsteps startle them, sending Imogen taking off in pursuit to follow a youthful Dinny, just as she had on that final day. Lottie does the same, though she's slowed by the realization that this is a distant memory of Imogen's... or maybe a dream.

Still gripping the locket, she repeats the spell spoken at the start of the night, as if in prayer that it might come true—or might be *coming* true.

Visually taking in the room, similar things to what she'd seen moments ago—back in the boarded shack—are strewn everywhere. Lottie recognizes the handwriting, too. The labels of pinned winged creatures and categorized critter bones hold the same scrawl from the journals she'd scanned.

A bitter twisting sensation felt by Imogen is shared by Lottie, as a black fear colors their insides with a knowing dread. Something is coming. And then Lottie realizes: something has *happened.*

And they're about to learn what.

The Imogen that Lottie follows can be heard trying to warn the curious boy who saunters deeper into the shadows, but the voice is silenced by the then-reality—for there was no one to warn at that time.

This is only a Sleeper's watch. So, they do. They watch.

They watch as he's lured away. They watch as he's swallowed by shadows. They watch as he's there… and then he's not.

He's below.

They don't follow yet; it's too frightening. Then a voice calls out, and a young Imogen runs by, racing out worriedly. She pauses in their line of sight, staring at the Dream lurkers through the shadows—as if she can sense them. Sense a wrong presence. Then she vanishes, disappearing into the storm that rattles the posts. The shack quivers like a grumbling belly, begging to digest the boy it just swallowed.

Inside that belly, at the bottom of a shallow pit, Dinny lies limp, still as Death. The feared thoughts Imogen held as a child swell up and pour over, wrenching her to weakened knees as she mourns over her best friend. Lottie watches with pain in her own soul, somehow feeling deeply for this boy she's never known—and for this girl.

A trap door snaps shut with a shriek, and they startle to a scene before a grand house that looms with pillars and high windows. Evening settles over the horizon with a gentle exhale, and the moment is calm and quiet. Soft music cascades through the open windows and slips through crevices and cracks. It is immediately familiar to Imogen, and thus it is simultaneously recognized by Lottie through their shared bond.

The conversation that took place near this home flutters through the air with a haunting whisper.

"When I die, I'm going to haunt a home like this... I'm going to finally live a dream life... even if it has to be as a ghost."

Imogen looks to the porch, finding where she was pulled into her costumed best friend's embrace, fully content. He had said he'd take her with him. He swore.

Alerted by someone at the house's front door, Lottie gasps. Imogen turns to her, confused by the presence of this woman in her memory—or dream. And then, as Dreamers do, Imogen accepts it, and she follows Lottie's glance toward the front door—where a young boy eerily stands with a horrid gash along his throat, murderous in its silence. A walking ghoul.

"No," Imogen whimpers, terrified for him.

He enters the home slowly—as if intentionally but without purpose—and they follow him. They watch as he meets himself at a mirror, and tired eyes seem to strain for understanding. He walks on—wandering the home as a ghost, just as he'd planned—but he doesn't do the things he'd promised. He doesn't linger to taste and savor the things that smell so sweetly. He doesn't sit to touch and stroke the gentle fibers of the bedroom throw. He doesn't slide down the railing of the winding staircase or swing with abandon from the chandelier.

He just walks.

Moving. Hopeless. Haunting.

But then he changes.

The women witness the evolution of passing years within a mere moment—catching the subtle shifts in his features that ultimately confirm an aging body. A body that's alive, pumping of blood and breath.

"You're alive?" Imogen begs, wishing her friend would answer.

Lottie nods to herself, figuring he must be. But within the passing time of seconds and years, his features don't only change from age... they wane.

Sweet, smiling Dinny is not playfully sneaking... he's existing in the darkness. From the grand house to darkened rooms to dilapidated shelters and shadowed woods, he wanders aimlessly and without rest. Like a true ghost—or a true lost soul—he seeks a home that never arrives. And every day, more darkness settles.

Weakened by what she sees, Imogen stumbles where she stands, grabbing for Lottie's hand. In odd relief, Lottie lets her, and both squeeze the other with a sad, sorry strength.

In a final structure of weathered wood, the three of them stand in a barren room as the final stretch of day darkens and all is silent—like a held breath. They wait, and the world turns cold, creeping its chill into their clothing alongside a morning dew. Their dream journey has taken them to the woods, where Dinny lies limp once more.

The black-hooded figure approaches, picking Dinny up and carrying him off... just as they had with Imogen at the cemetery.

They follow to a nearby country home, where a road sign suggests they may be in the state of Idaho.

Around the back and inside a covered porch, a metal operating table sits cluttered with menacing tools—syringes, knives, vials, texts.

"This one might be fried, now," the hooded figure says toward the opened backdoor as they plop Dinny onto the table with a careless abandon.

Imogen balks at the sight of her best friend's bullied body, and Lottie squeezes the hand she holds, trying to remind the both of them that this is in the past. It's done.

"Saw there's an opening in Tulsa, Oklahoma you could try," the cloaked one continues. "I've got some good leads on a few runaways, but there's also a promising seven-year-old who keeps self-mutilating. Her grandpa did some nasty work on her. She seems ripe for our purposes."

Now, it's Lottie who gasps. She has no words—not even silent ones to scream in her mind. She spits at the monster, knowing they can't appreciate her wrath but doing it anyhow. And then she does it again.

Because she better understands now. The vulnerable are being exploited.

As this obscure other continues fiddling with Dinny's body, the women watch in petrified awe, bewildered. Because it's false.

The wound is fake.

Gloved hands peel a prosthetic gash from the withered boy's neck. With ease—as if in routine—fingers retrieve a syringe and plunge an unknown drug into Imogen's best friend. Finished with that, a notebook is reviewed and a pen runs through checkmarks—and the two eager spectators hover close behind to read over the fiend's shoulder.

The notes are experimental, and the comments are studious—with notations on drugs, and medications, and hypotheses regarding mental states and hallucinations. Histories for this "subject" entail childhood wishes and fears, confirming Dinny's spoken desires of wanting to haunt the homes of the richest merely to enjoy the luxuries.

"Method of retrieval," reads the text "Hypnosis."

With a quick scan, other notes indicate "false wounds" and "intravenous."

With a turn of the journal page, they're back at the shack in the woods. Now, the page is titled, "Imogen." Though the location exists in the present, this moment is still in the past. Transported from one memory to another—like hopping from river rock to river rock.

At their sides, a redhead kneels in agony, silent but shaking. The witnessing Imogen—the Dreamer–watches herself in both fear and fascination as they continue to observe the ways of this wicked man.

On the page, notes include "bloodied knees," and "submission kneeling," and "injection avenue."

With a closer look, they both take notice of the planks of wood and bark beneath the kneeling form, with crusted powder gathered at the edges of her fresh wounds.

The drugs.

Reading on, scribbles list "memory retrieval," "childhood associations," "hallucinations," "pain," and "The Coterie."

Ginger in their approach, the black-hooded figure nears the suffering woman. "Asleep," they command, and the kneeling Imogen of the past wilts into a heap of limp limbs upon the floor.

Lottie thinks back to the cemetery—how the fleeing woman had collapsed into the other's arms instantly.

In scanning the doll-like damsel on the table, Lottie easily recalls the afternoon she had somehow glimpsed a moment of this suffering. The moment where she awoke to feel weighted, with a need to fight and resist but an inability to do so... and a final effort to open her eyes, only to find the reflection of Imogen staring back. Was it a shared experience of this *exact* moment? She's not sure. But something tells her there were many other moments like this. Trials. Experiments.

As if she were a plaything, the unconscious Imogen is hoisted and maneuvered this way and that as a delicate dress is situated upon her figure. The ethereal fabric catches a shine from the dirtied bulb above of the room, illuminating the redhead in a soft glow— reminiscent of a holy innocence. The contrast of the angelic presence against the grimy room only harshens the appearance of her bloodied knees and pained body.

It's unignorable.

This is noticed by the hooded culprit likewise, for the site of her injury causes pause—a desire to peer closer into her wounds. As the maniac endeavors to inspect more closely, their hood goes falling back, shoved away in annoyance—revealing a woman's face.

Both Dreamers gasp, jarred. Surprised to find a female behind such grotesque brutality. And surprised to recognize her.

Imogen recalls her face-of-only-lipstick from the flower shop. Her kind eyes and amicable presence.

"Mac," she whispers, remembering.

Similarly, Lottie can picture the woman holding out a package, having caught a fleeting image once upon an afternoon when her features shone over Verdilla's—that day Verdilla gifted Dottie's forgotten gown.

With a glance to her watch, this madwoman rummages through an assortment of fresh bandages and ointments as she huffs at the time and wipes a line of sweat from her brow. Not having worn glasses in the flower shop but sporting a pair now, the two Dreamers watch as her frames turn slick upon moistened skin. A hurried panic sets into her shoulders.

"Quite the bleeder these days, aren't we?" she questions the unconscious body on the table. "We can't have you bleeding out all the good stuff before it's time, Mo. We've got work to do."

Hearing that childhood nickname—that name only Dinny ever called her—sends Dreamer Imogen to her knees, feeling as if a ghost had just sauntered by and kicked her in the gut.

Reaching for a nearby desktop, she struggles to steady herself, only to be knocked over again. Because she's breathless. Because she can't believe her eyes.

There on the desk sits the never-forgotten textbook. It's the magick book Dinny showed her. After all these years.

In a final whirlwind of movements, the woman—Mac—retrieves a box from nearby and pulls out a familiar floral head wreath. Into a bag she tosses nonsensical things, like a glass jar, a sealed envelope, and more bandages. And finally, as a rolling thunder threatens in the distance, she hollers toward the rest of the shack—as if there might be someone sitting on the other side of the door at the back. "I'm taking your coat!" And she does, retrieving a patterned raincoat identical to that of the now-deceased Dr. Craven.

They wait and watch as she wheels the unconscious Imogen away in a wagon, left to stand there and wonder what's next—what other truths are coming for them? A shared knowledge settles as the unspoken understanding of *which* night they just witnessed is felt. It was the night of the lighthouse. The night of the storm. The night Lottie woke up in the river. That first night of a shared peek into another's life through the reflection of a puddle.

A movement shifts from behind them, alerting they are not alone.

"You're not the first Flower," an unexpected voice whispers from the shadows.

As if Death himself just stroked a fatal finger down their backs, the two women twist in dread, finding a third observer to be partaking in this shared Dream. A third Dreamer. Out of the shadows she emerges, taking form like blood that pools.

The hooded one.

Mac.

The one of this night. The Other who hunted for Imogen, and ran through the woods, and collided with the women upon Lottie's attempt at rescue.

"You're just the first Rose," she continues. "He gets all his victims from the system, but I was the beginning. I was targeted before anyone."

Again, the world shifts.

They greet the tree with painted flowers—the tree where Dinny showed Imogen the magick book.

Storm clouds stir above their heads as thunder claps through sheets of rain. Realizing the day, Imogen looks toward the direction of the bone bothy, still half expecting to see a traipsing Dinny sauntering away with a mischievous smile. She doesn't, of course—but she does see a cloaked figure in that godforsaken patterned raincoat. Stalking toward the tree, scooping up the book, and continuing on.

Through the torrent, the three Dreamers follow the figure all the way back to the foster home. As they arrive, Imogen spots a lonely Kenzie sitting outside, aged as they were then—young and awkward. She wonders why she's sitting there, wet and all alone.

"Kenzie," Imogen sighs with relief, finding an odd hope blooming in her chest at the familiar face of another childhood comrade. Without thought— forgetting this is not the present—she hurries to hug her, but the young Kenzie looks toward Lottie in accusation.

"You're not supposed to be here."

Stunned, Lottie looks to Imogen for understanding, and Imogen nods with wide eyes toward the cloaked individual holding the book, standing at Lottie's back. A man.

He's the one being scorched by Kenzie's glare. Not Lottie.

"You were supposed to meet me," Kenzie continues, angry at the man. "We almost got caught."

The memory of Kenzie hollering for her outside the bone bothy floods Imogen's mind like the rain floods the sewer, recalling the way she thought Kenzie had been searching for her.

"There you are, Imogen," Kenzie had said. "What are you doing all the way out here?"

Imogen now swallows an unsettling sensation of embarrassment with a sickening understanding:

Kenzie was never searching for her. Imogen was never close to being discovered the way she thought she'd been... Kenzie was hollering to meet up with this man.

And Imogen left Dinny that day because of her stupid fear of getting caught.

The cloaked man chuckles with a glimmer in his eye, and he takes off his raincoat's hood with a sobering stare.

"Chuckles...," Imogen whispers, audibly assisting herself as she tries to process a whirlwind of thoughts. In borrowed recognition, Lottie likewise understands this man to be the child welfare caseworker, and both women look to the hovering Mac now partaking in this dream, curious of this stranger and how she fits into this puzzle.

"Sorry, champ, I, ah… I got caught up."
Chuckles pauses, clearly recalling whatever it was that
delayed him. Imogen's gut churns, thinking of Dinny.
"I think you'll forgive me, though. I've got some big
news. You ready?"

With heavy shoulders Kenzie sighs, as if having
learned to grow tired of these "surprises."

"I finally finished. I got my degree. So, I'm
going to move… and I want to take you with me."

Feeling wanted, Kenzie perks up in question.
"What do you mean?"

"Well, I want to adopt you, squirt." The man
grins, showing too many teeth. "We're a great team."

Again, a sigh. "I don't know," Kenzie fusses.
With an exhale toward the house, she glances up to a
window, spotting a young, wistful Imogen. The
memories of that day swell up with the rest of the water
that attacks the world, brimming at Imogen's eyes and
flowing over, making her cheeks hot.

She had been waiting for Dinny. And even then,
she somehow knew he was already gone.

Seeming exasperated, Chuckles takes a breath
and leans down to meet Kenzie's eyes.

"What do you mean? I got that bully Jones
moved from this home, didn't I? I did that for you,
yeah?"

"Yeah, but—"

"You gave me a name, and I took care of it,
yeah?" Then, under his breath, "And I fucking torched
my hand while doing it."

Another sigh before a slow nod from the tired child. "Yeah, but *how* did you take care of it? Where did Jones go?"

"Pfft." The man clicks his tongue. "I gave you the magick book, you know there are different ways to do things. We can Manifest what we want, especially with the help of the things *you* brought me. Right? We can wish for things that come true. We can make things happen. The flowers, the dirt, the wings, the bones... all of them have uses. So, it's not what *I* did, it's what *we* did."

"You know what I mean," Kenzie whines. "Where did he end up? After he left?"

Deciding to pause, the caseworker studies Kenzie as they enter a battle of silence. A staring contest ensues, but Kenzie's shyness pulls her away in surrender.

"Don't you want to never have to deal with foster homes again?" he asks the young girl gingerly. "To never be bullied or knocked around? To never have to be on the outside looking in, like a pitiful wallflower? Things can be better. It'll just be you and me."

Once more toward the window, Kenzie watches Imogen and seems to consider the offer. Beside Lottie, this Imogen watches curiously, trying to understand what she's seeing. She never knew Kenzie watched her; she never thought she watched anyone. She just... did her own things. She just did her Kenzie doings.

Finally, Kenzie agrees, and the two shake hands, as if entering into a partnership.

"No more 'M&M' name-calling. No more Mackenzie Malloy... From now on, you'll be Mackenzie Craven—maybe even Mac," Chuckles assures with a grin. "And I'll finally be 'Doctor.'"

The mention of his name transports them to the scene of Dr. Craven's death, back upon the stone and pebbled terrace of Hammond Castle. Like a film in reverse, the events unfold and rewind to reveal the things Lottie had suspected and feared.

Her hands were at fault, indeed, for the Inky Cap mushrooms that made their way into his dish, evident by her leisure stroll into the kitchen and their sneakery into his stew. As if indicative of magick and the results of a spell, a visual glimmer illustrates her sorcery-induced actions, confirming she operated under the agency of a charm.

The scene continues on its path of reversal, pausing for the Dreamers to watch as Lottie is spelled to ensure the mushrooms make their way to the event. She catches Verdilla and encourages her "glamorous haul" of mushrooms, easily accepted for the night by the dizzying coordinator.

Continuing on as if in rewind once more, the magick reminds her to go foraging after the rainstorm, gathering the mushrooms that stain her fiddling fingers.

Breathless by the rapid display, Lottie falters where she stands, but the realities continue.

There she exists in a daze within a coatroom, that night of The Secret Garden event at the Ropes Mansion. Unaware, the spelled Lottie slips familiar flowers into the pocket of a patterned raincoat—

Craven's raincoat—and the conscious Lottie conjures the recollection of petals peeking up at her from the bottom of her purse. Following her trail in reverse that led up to that point, she cuts Foxglove from the flowers in the garden, just as had been suspected.

Finally, it's the day when it all began, as Lottie watches herself sitting at the bustling Saturday morning market. She'd watched others, and she'd felt watched too, now realizing it was this Mackenzie all along.

Not Wells.

Mackenzie had slipped a vial's worth of Mugwort into her tea, and she slid the spelled locket onto Lottie's table for quick finding.

"I knew it," Lottie breathes, recalling that Mugwort surprise. "I knew it."

And lastly, with the air of a grand finale— though it was actually the beginning of it all—Lottie watches as a poked and prodded Imogen lies upon the table. Standing over her, Mac—*Mackenzie*—holds Lottie's published novel between them, forcing the entranced Imogen to stare into the eyes of the author on the back cover. Lottie.

"*Ferre in mente,*" Mackenzie chants into Imogen's ears as the battered victim wears a special locket. "*Ferre in mente.*"

CHAPTER 43

In a wash, the visions evaporate, and the three wake to the present.

Lottie first, clinging to the strength of the spelled locket at her neck. Then Imogen, surging in fear. And finally, Mackenzie, confused and rattled... and caught.

As the others try to gain their footing, Lottie catches a gleam of the syringe Mackenzie wields, given away by the moonlight, and Lottie's instincts—paired with a heightened awareness—act to snatch it from Mackenzie's grip. Figuring the madwoman brought it to victimize Imogen once again, Lottie spits on the perp reflexively as she yanks it from clenched fingers.

Then she spits on Mackenzie again—just as Imogen had tried earlier—and it lands with rapt surprise. A small satisfaction twitches at Lottie's lip.

Imogen tries to steady herself as she comes to from a slumber that's been much longer than their shared Dream. Just as a Dreamer emerges from the stories of one's sleep, Imogen's awareness floats to the surface slowly, passing by moments of memories as it rises—suffering with each and every retrieved recall.

For a moment, The Coterie takes the spotlight. The question of Tasks and her status come into focus—as if by habit. But then new memories follow, and the sobering truth rushes through her with an onslaught of nausea.

She can remember the way the mere name made her insides churn and twist, with both fascination and fear, as if she had always been so familiar with this legendary club of sorts. As if she truly had always hoped for Their approval, like she had been coerced to believe. As if she had ever once in her sane reality cared about joining the ranks of an esteemed secret society.

No.

The promise of such a society was a prop—a tool to encourage a false reality. To encourage wishful thinking, and a malleable mind. She now recognizes it was only something her thoughts accepted within a dreaming state and nothing more. It's nothing powerful. Nothing true.

The nausea overwhelms a second time, making her sick, as Imogen looks into the darkness that surrounds her and finds the face of her perpetrator—the quiet childhood acquaintance she assumed was her friend—who's bloodied her body and broken her heart.

"No, no, no," Imogen whimpers, frightened by the images that race through her memory. She is frightened for herself from the pain she's endured. She is frightened for this strange woman at her side and their odd bond. But then she remembers Dinny, and Mackenzie hovering over his poor, limp figure, and Imogen wishes she could kill this woman with her screams and wails because that's all she can muster.

She screams.

She wails.

She mourns.

And then she screams again. *"MONSTER!"* Only... she didn't.

Both Lottie and Mackenzie go still, startled to have heard the proclamation only in their minds. Like the audio of a dream.

"Kenzie?" Imogen now begs through straining gasps. "How could—" she chokes.

With high brows and high hands, the caught woman begs for mercy, swearing she's innocent.

"You don't understand!" she yells. "I'm not the bad guy! I got *rid* of him!" Looking to Lottie, she nods ever so slightly. *"Well, you did,"* she says, though somehow silently. Back to Imogen, she pleads. "I've been doing everything in my power to help you, Mo." She goes to her knees. "Please. I can explain *everything.*"

As Lottie watches, she struggles to keep straight all the things she needs to be explained. "Wait," she barks to the pleading maniac. "Did you just... *think* something to me?"

With shifting eyes, the pleading Mackenzie looks to Imogen, remembering her internal screams and wondering the same. She says nothing at all, but her thoughts speak in answer. *"Did I?"*

"Oh, God," Lottie thinks in response, dreading the familiarity of this mental invasion. She recalls the scene of *"ferre en mente,"* and intrusive notions rain over her. Her mind is open. And the monster is inside of it.

This woman had spelled Lottie and Imogen first, and tonight, Lottie's spell has bound them all. Now, here they are… at the mercy of each other's minds.

The spark of an epiphany ignites in the depths of Lottie's skull.

This woman had a grip on her mind and on Imogen's, and she's wreaked hell and havoc as she has pleased… but now, maybe they can grab *back*.

"Imogen, look at me," Lottie orders, soft but stern. The shaking woman glances toward this stranger, and Lottie thinks a sentence for her to receive. *"Nod if you can understand that I'm speaking to you."*

A small gasp whispers past her lips, and Imogen nods obediently.

Turning to Mackenzie, Lottie prepares for battle using a strength she knows she possesses:

Ingenuity.

"If you're not the threat, then prove it. While you explain yourself, we're going to leave your sight, and you're going to let us. Then we'll decide if we can trust you."

Taken aback, Mackenzie looks to Imogen, and Lottie catches a sense of entitlement. Of ownership.

"I don't know what this is," Lottie asserts with a step closer, wielding the stolen syringe, *"but seeing as how you were prepared to use it on* her*, I am more than willing to try my best at landing it in* your *neck until one of us ends up stabbed, meanwhile giving her time to flee."* She chooses the mental language on purpose; if she were to try and threaten this verbally, Mackenzie might just catch a quiver in her voice. *"Either way, she is not going back to your operating table. Your choice."*

She's not bluffing, but she is fibbing; Lottie would rather avoid any hint of violence because she's almost certain she would lose. Mackenzie's not particularly burly, but… Lottie's not particularly strong. Unfortunately, that's already been proven.

But she's almost died before, and with no choice in the matter. At least now, should tonight end with her own demise, it'll be for the sake of another.

Death awaits us all, she remembers, summoning the wisdom of Dottie's notated book and its reflection of death. *What of it?*

"Of course," Mackenzie tries with wide eyes. *"Imogen, I was always protecting you. I would never… Just, please, believe me."*

Stepping between them, Lottie takes control. "Turn around. You're going to answer *out loud*, so that we can hear you are staying put. We'll ask the questions with… our minds." *Weird to say.* "Understood?"

Though clearly hesitant, Mackenzie gives a hard nod and settles her gaze on the thick forestation under the moon. "Fine."

Feeling closer to an impossible safety, Lottie wanes internally and meets the wide eyes of Imogen's fearful stare. With an outheld hand, she tries to offer even a slight sense of security for the terrorized woman, and Imogen accepts the invitation eagerly—like a lost child found.

Now touching, something feels different as they look back to Mackenzie. In submitting a question to be answered, Lottie tests their mental boundaries and wonders if her forming theory holds true.

"First, I want to know: why Imogen?"

They pause, not leaving just yet, and both hold their breath as they wait for the answer, though for different reasons. For Lottie, she thinks her theory is right; she reckons the strength of her spell, paired with their physical collision, has somehow bonded them all together via their minds. She bets the channel of their communication closes off to the third if two of them touch. Somehow, she can *feel* it—like an energy that takes up space in her thoughts. It's as if the three of them exist within the movie theater of her mind, having watched the visions play together from spots within the gallery.

And Mackenzie was an intruder. And is. She came in unwelcomed, and she held Imogen hostage all the while.

And, now, she's shut out—allowing Lottie and Imogen to share the space anew, likeminded. And safe.

"She can't hear us when we touch," Lottie thinks to Imogen. With a smile and a quick squeeze of her hand, she let's go, so they can resume their interrogation.

For Imogen, she's barely caught her breath.

With a mind that feels beaten and bruised and a body that echoes the same, she had succumbed to the haven of this stranger's hand with a swelling of tears.

Because when was the last time she had received a loving touch?

When had she shared in a genuine laugh?

When had she been comforted to subside her cries?

…She can't remember. The only memories that manage to be summoned are the falsities of forced dreams and fake realities. There are no memories of years spent, or of people met, or of days lived. She can remember Dinny… and that final day. And nothing else.

All reality that follows? It doesn't exist in her head… and she wonders if she may have lost her mind—or had it stolen from her.

"No," she begs as she grabs for Lottie's hand. *"Don't leave me."*

Startled and softened, Lottie sees the pain in her eyes and aches for this woman who's been through literal hell.

"I can't hear if you're asking me anything," Mackenzie offers over her shoulder.

Hurried, Lottie retorts aloud. "Wait."

With quick thinking, Lottie gathers fabric from the skirt of Imogen's dress and puts it between their hands, allowing their grip to remain but to keep their skin from touching. Imogen relaxes with a nod, and Lottie squeezes assuredly, genuinely happy to have been able to provide any sense of comfort at all.

Turning back to Mackenzie, Lottie tests their channels. *"Why Imogen?"*

A deep inhale signals a weighted answer, and the two women begin their backward advance as they seek a swift but cautious departure.

"What you saw is true," Mackenzie begins, "but it's not the whole story."

"Louder," Lottie demands as they pass by shadowed trees and secrets of the dark. She wants to

298

ensure Mackenzie shouts as needed, but somehow it's still audible within their minds, too. As if her intentional projection crosses through a megaphone, they can hear both her true-voice and her thought-voice simultaneously.

"Craven always had his eye on Imogen. Just like Dinny. Ever since we were kids." At the mention of her best friend's name, Imogen squeezes Lottie's hand in distress. But they continue in their steps as the perp continues in her answer. "When Mo popped up on his radar—becoming one of his Flowers—I knew I had to keep her safe."

"Liar!" Imogen wails, crying both internally and aloud.

Lottie rushes to stifle her sounds, desperate not to have their position given away as they seek safety.

"If *I* hadn't experimented on you *for* him, he would have done it himself!"

Both women shudder at her meaning.

"How long has she been your plaything," Lottie challenges, buying time as she spots the shack. Conflicted by the need for safety for Imogen and desperate to understand what exactly is going on—for something much larger is happening here, that is certain—Lottie hurries them both to the shack for a quick pause to plan.

"I resent that," Mackenzie seethes, "but the answer you're looking for is: when we moved here. The beginning of the summer."

Imogen listens with a brain that feels stupefied. She can't remember much of anything, real or fake. Childhood reveries sift by in the background, but everything else up to now is like a wasteland of sadness. Somehow, she feels weathered but also empty, like a soda can that's been poured out, wasted, and then stomped upon and kicked aside.

"I didn't want what happened to Dinny to happen to Mo…," the explanation continues.

In heated anger, Imogen backfires. *"Don't call me that,"* she rages. *"What happened to Dinny? Where is he?"*

"And why Imogen?" Lottie throws. *"Why protect Imogen but not Dinny?"*

A weighted silence passes, and Lottie can see Imogen wondering the same—wondering what it is that's worth saving in her when Dinny *was* the best of her.

Within the shack, Lottie searches for a way to keep their channel open but also to communicate with Imogen. Finding one of the journals and a nearby pen, she scratches a message onto a sheet.

"He didn't die on that table," Mackenzie swears as she hollers, selective in her answer. "What you saw happened years ago… and I never wanted to be a—"

"Murderer," Lottie interrupts.

The sigh is notable. "Right. Once he was… in the state that you saw… we admitted him into a facility."

Holding up a message to the disbelieving Imogen, Lottie motions for her to flee.

RUN TO CEMETERY—HIDE—WAIT FOR ME

Pointing with an urgent finger, Lottie begs with her eyes, wanting to keep Imogen safe. But something bigger than both of them keeps Lottie there in the shack, as much as she wishes otherwise.

Imogen's expression screams back in horrified refusal, desperate to stay. Thinking of walking alone through the dark trees maddens her with the borrowed sensation of walking alone in that bone bothy—and the childhood horrors that haunted those shadows—and realizing that one of those horrors has grown up to lurk nearby this moment.

Taking a quick touch to the chilled skin of her cheek, Lottie caresses Imogen to allow for a moment of silent words between them. *"For Dinny,"* she urges, as she circles the word Hide with her finger three times.

Letting go of one another, Imogen cries muted tears as she obeys, and Lottie resumes with her questions, intent on getting answers—through Mackenzie and through her own means in this demented room.

"How many have there been?" The binder with the faces looks at her, screaming of voices that have been silenced.

"Craven was building himself a Bouquet. At least a dozen." Mackenzie pauses. "I swear I hated working on every one of them."

As she flips through, Lottie finds more time to dwell on the details. These are children of all ages and all trauma histories, preyed upon and exploited. Categorized and labeled with nomenclatures to the doctor's pleasure.

"That's why I had him killed," Mackenzie volunteers. "By you."

"Explain," Lottie orders, ready for these answers.

"Imogen was the conduit to get to you, to control your subconscious actions through magick. It kept my hands clean, and kept Craven from ever suspecting it."

Looking to the large leather-bound tome, Lottie reviews its pages anew, now having an eye of understanding. Tabbed pages of spells stand out to her, and an odd sense of closure releases a tension from her chest as she understands just how deeply magick has been involved since the beginning. A section on *"Manifestation"* catches her eye and pulls her in, quick to scan. The introduction is, in itself, resounding.

Due to the nature of Magic being an energy, it, like all energies, can be controlled and directed to do work.

When paired with Mental Energy, like intention, and Physical Energy, like spell-casting, the trifecta allows for the power of Manifestation. Specifically, the trifecta is most powerful when all three energies target a singular outcome.

Depending on the amount of energy provided, the outcomes will vary.

It reads like an actual textbook but speaks of such mysteries as magick. Lottie is spellbound, having dove into the deep end of a concept and is now drowning in the realization.

"I figured there was going to be some mental debris on your side," Mackenzie continues.

Lottie is pulled back to listen. To remember. The spelled locket, a spelled girl, two spelled minds... Though disturbing, her hunch was right—and that is its own relief.

"Deja vu, odd dreams, some fatigue—but... I must say, I'm impressed."

Questions pile and pound at the door of Lottie's mouth, but only one stands out above the rest and pushes through.

"*Why me?*"

As if she can hear the smile in Mackenzie's words, the woman answers deviously. "I read your book. You actually taught me a thing or two."

With a sinking stomach, Lottie's sights land on her own face as her published book glares at her from its spot within a pile of binders and texts. Retrieving it, she swallows the bile that rises in correlation with the number of tabs counted within its bound pages.

"Your story showed me the depths of your mind," Mackenzie explains. "How you can see and create a world that does not exist. You basically *showed* me what I wanted to be able to do. Plus, the connection of utilizing places close to you allowed the bond to be that much stronger between you and Imogen, which was essential to being able to handle the dirty work with Wells and Craven." Like the closing of a cage, Mackenzie's fingers fold in over the subject and lock it shut. "Then, once I got a look into your actual mind, I mean…"

She trails off as if mesmerized, and Lottie flips through the pages with frightened fingers. Paragraphs are circled, and sentences are notated. The ways her characters stalked are highlighted. The watching but not being seen. The locations that were inspired are underlined and scribbled—though some of them were from her own memories, not the book…

The hotel restaurant. The Ropes Mansion. Hammond Castle. The Lighthouse.

"What do you mean, my actual mind?" She swallows.

"I mean, you're impressive. I've tried my hand at Manifestation. Plenty of times, in fact. But to literally summon a stalker by stalking… and then to have been almost *killed* because you didn't realize what you were even doing. You weren't *careful*. And the way you got away, that day he nearly drowned you…"

"But I didn't know I was Manifesting," she pushes back, defensive and desperate to understand. She had been humored by such a notion in the beginning and during the daydreams, but that was over an inconsequential concept of wishful thinking. Meager manifestation. Not *magick* Manifestation. *"So how did I?"*

"Your *book*," Mackenzie stresses, as if bored. "Your wishing was your intention. And then you wrote your wish down, just like one does in a grimoire—in a spell. As far as the third ingredient—magick—well, maybe you're just one of the lucky ones. Maybe it just listens to you." Lottie doesn't miss the mark of jealousy in Mackenzie's tone. "And since I was using you to do me a favor, I did one for you. I saw the way Wells' mere existence still threatened you... so, I killed him for you."

"But..." Lottie tries to comprehend, pressured by the gravity of the moment. *"What would have been more careful, if I—"*

"You didn't use grounding rituals, or directive measures like crystals or herbs, or *clarifying* your intentions with *who* you were wanting."

With a jolt in her gut, Lottie recalls the way Wells had blamed her... that final night. *"This is all your fault."*

It seems Mackenzie remembers the same, from rifling through Lottie's mind.

"It really actually *is* your fault, if you think about it."

Now Lottie's being taunted.

"It's actually a pretty sad story for Wells, don't you think?" The tyrant continues.

"I have no shed of remorse for that bastard," Lottie tries to emphasize steadily.

"Well, maybe you should," Mackenzie retorts. "Turns out, he wasn't actually trying to murder you that day at the pond."

Lottie balks. *"...Why do you say that?"*

"Because I read the letters. He wrote to you nearly twice a week for those two years, and boy, was he *desperate* to be rid of you. But, no... he wasn't trying to kill you. He was trying to wake you up."

Forced memories that are not her own find their way into Lottie's thoughts, evident to be the intentions of Mackenzie. Recall of frantic letters crammed into her vacant home's mailbox, weighted with pleadings for absolved guilt and forgiveness. Script that swore Lottie had accidentally fallen into her bookcase and gone unconscious—that Wells had been trying to force her to listen to him, but the result was terrible and unintentional. Underlined promises that the pond was the only thing he could imagine would wake her up because nothing else had worked. Assurances that he never meant to hurt her and that he understood she wanted to be rid of him. But that he was sorry.

"I never meant to hurt you."

"I can't stop thinking about you, PLEASE RELEASE ME..."

"I am not a murderer, I was trying to wake you!"

"I miss you."

"You haunt my dreams."

Lottie shudders. How ironic that the ghost of her own nightmares found Lottie to be the ghost of his.

In the same fashion of shared insight, Mackenzie sends new thoughts through: infusing an expensive liquor with the poisonous flowers; propping up postcards for a tongue-in-cheek clue; leaving it on his doorstep because a drunkard asks no questions when free drinks arrive without fuss.

Mackenzie is blaming Lottie for the stalker *and* his death.

"I even stole his Wellies as a souvenir," Mackenzie jests devilishly, and a present viewing of her person pushes through into their shared mental movie, Wellington boots and all.

Lottie remembers trying to grab them that night Wells attacked her. She hadn't been quick enough to make her escape.

Inspired by the tool of the mind, Lottie looks back to the many questions that lie sprawled about before her and then retrieves the many others that have festered within her mind for a week now—and she dares them to be answered.

"What was real?" she demands, forcing her own memories through of reaching fingers, and flower-crown reflections, and Mackenzie holding a package.

Spurred to question the recall shared by Lottie, Imogen begins to collect pieces of her own memories.

"Dress shop," she remembers, and her own depictions process through as if on a film reel, reliving that day in the dress shop, recalling the fabrics, and the texts on a desk, and the back door. All together, the three acknowledge what was true all along:

The dress shop was a façade; it's the same room where Lottie now stands in secret. The shack.

"It all felt so real," Imogen whines, though seemingly far away. *"And now it just... hurts."*

Noting the texts recalled and simultaneously sifting through others, Lottie hurries, certain there's more to see, more to discover. Tossing aside loose papers, a packet labeled "Imogen" sits beside her respective binder, and inside are photographs of the redhead that date back more than a decade.

"That was the point," Mackenzie insists. "Doc wanted to explore the minds of those who've endured trauma, figuring he could eventually rewire their memories and help them *believe* they were happy, or excited, or so on." By force once more, the image of the card that accompanied the charity dinner at the Ropes Mansion flits through their shared view, reminding Lottie of the tragic story she'd read—*The Little Lunatic.*

"That *was* Doc. He found his greatest solace to be in the relief of his imagination. Even his nightmares."

Confused, Lottie challenges. *"That story was about a little girl,"* she fumes.

"No. People assumed he was a girl," Mackenzie reasons. "His hair was so long from neglect, and he was so dirty and small… there was no way to tell otherwise." One could hear a shame in her voice. "It's something we had in common—others failing to see us, *really*. To appreciate us."

A memory discerned as Imogen's enters their three-way channel, and Lottie watches a shared reverie involving Imogen and Mackenzie, some Halloween years ago when they were small. Boys made fun of Mackenzie, teasing her about being an old hag. About lipstick. And then Imogen rescued her. Her friend. Offering her hand as a lifeline.

"I don't understand," Imogen cries quietly, having only thought she was helping.

But then the young Imogen let go, as soon as her best friend was back at her side. She didn't choose her friend Kenzie. She chose Dinny.

Bothered by the petty specifics, Lottie mentally spits at Mackenzie, ignited. *"You were torturing her, you louse."*

"Trauma, at times, requires trauma. To work, the brain has to be opened, and pain, well... it's an effective tool."

More images. Memories. Mackenzie's recall while working with Doc—their once-beloved Chuckles—watching as he'd stress his medical theory, over, and over, and over again. Experimenting with magick and herbs and medications, researching dreams and hallucinations and hypnosis. Justifying their experiments by convincing himself their victims were being helped.

It didn't matter what pain they endured if they didn't actually feel it in their minds. If they believed they were happy—fulfilled wishes, hope, desires. Better lives were lived, even if only in their heads.

"The mind wants to enjoy a treat, even if it's only a trick. Sometimes, they're the same thing."

Sifting through the images of Imogen on the table, Lottie eerily notes the oddity in her clothes within every one—frilly, frolic-like dresses. Eager and fumbling, she searches for any hint at a memory she may have glimpsed over the past week, pairing her shared memories against the photos at her fingers, and then she realizes: these are commemorated experiments documented as keepsakes... and Mackenzie is in them all, hovering, seemingly a friend to this dreamy out-of-her-mind damsel.

Dresses.

The ripping of Lottie's own, instigated by Wells' violence. It summons an epiphany. An understanding. A knowing.

In the childhood memories of Imogen—the day of the bone bothy—she sported play clothes that were well worn of youth, and dirty knees, and sun-filled hours, and reckless fun. This, to Lottie, is significant.

So as not to give herself away, she stays calm and pushes for more.

"So, how is it you kept Imogen safe, then? What is it that you *controlled that would have been worse if you hadn't?"*

"I got to be in charge of her story contexts. I got to come up with things I figured she would enjoy."

Alarm creeps into Lottie's shoulders. She doesn't know when Mackenzie stopped shouting, but Lottie only now realizes she's only mentally speaking… not audibly, like they agreed. Now, there's no telling where the fiend is. Hunting Imogen… Hunting her.

"How are you supposed to know what she enjoys?" Lottie challenges. *"You said you only knew her as a child."*

"I do know her," Mackenzie fumes, *"and also, yes, I explored her mind."* She now whispers, quiet and slow. *"I tapped into her trauma—that part of the mind that festers like an opened wound—and I planted my workings there. My methods of magick, and medicine, and hypnosis. It spreads through her bloodstream, through her nervous system, her person."*

"Like a disease," Lottie insists.

"Or like the cure," Mackenzie retorts back.

"Imogen," Lottie starts, risking her input to ensure she's still safe… unsilenced. *"Do you prefer dresses?"*

The photographs in Lottie's hands practically burn at her fingertips as she waits for the expected response.

Too far away to suggest she's in the safe watch of Lottie, Imogen answers, *"No..."* The exhaustion and fear within her are audible in their minds and notably distant. *"I never have. Why?"*

Delighted to reveal this Mackenzie for the liar she is, Lottie utilizes a borrowed strategy from earlier—forcing her current perspective into their three-way mental dialogue. One by one and all at once, the photographs prove the deceits Mackenzie has tried to hide behind. The history. The manipulation. The selfishness.

She's been in Imogen's life for years, operating as an infatuated sadist for every moment of it.

As if their very emotions are shared, Imogen's dismay is tangible, and Lottie's sorry to cause it. But now she knows...

"You have to stay away from her, Imogen."

The sight of this damsel in distress flits through their thoughts with a blip and Lottie freezes at the realization. Mackenzie sees her. Whether that information was shared by accident or on purpose, Lottie's unsure—but Mackenzie is out there, watching her victim, stalking Imogen like prey... and Lottie doesn't know if she'll make it.

"Run, Imogen! She sees you, run!"

Knowing only the direction she had sent her, Lottie takes off for the cemetery to find Imogen and runs like two lives depend on it.

312

CHAPTER 44

Behind a lonely tree, a quaking Imogen hides.

She saw herself—in the image shared by Mackenzie—and she fled, led only by the strength of despair. Still in the shadows, she knows her enemy sits, waiting. Mackenzie is hiding, too, and Imogen wishes the night would end and the sun would steal away the monsters of the dark.

Something darts in the distance, veiled in a hood and cloaked in the darkness. The sight of it startles Imogen, and she swallows to stifle a scream. Mackenzie waits behind the stone, squatting as if in play.

A giggle rises as if from the dead, echoing over the graves. Imogen spots the one she dug and considers its haven. Would Mackenzie dare join her, with another chasing her, too? Would Mackenzie harm her once together? Would Imogen be silenced if she screamed?

Does Imogen have any energy left to care?

Fear and fatigue seep into Imogen like death as if the very graves themselves could suck the life force from her shaking limbs. She's so tired. She's so lost.

Choking on her thoughts, she catches sight of another dashing shadow taunting her.

"Just like when we were kids," Mackenzie encourages. *"You always loved playing. We can play now."*

In reflection, Imogen feels dizzy as she shakes away false memories and tries to restore true ones. Kenzie didn't have an interest in playing when they were kids; it was always just her and Dinny.

"*What?*" she begs silently, wishing for relief.

"*You love playing,*" Mackenzie reminds with a snap. "*You always had time for Dinny. Let's play together. Now. You and me.*"

"*I needed Dinny!*" Imogen mentally hollers. Spent.

"*You needed a friend you could rely on,*" Mackenzie barks back. "*Dinny left you that night. He left you alone on the porch. And then he left you alone in the bothy.*"

Imogen falls over in surrender. Not to Mackenzie. But to the sadness that eats away at her, feasting upon her soul. *No*, she wants to shout back. *You stole him*, she wants to scream. But it doesn't matter. Because he's not here. And it's her own fault, too. He may have left her to explore the bone bothy... but then she left him. And then he was gone.

Somehow, in her falling, her body found the grave she sought. The one she dug. She lies in it now— feeling like a hollow person. A likewise corpse. A bag of bones and nothing else.

Lottie catches up in time to watch the delusion.

The demented perp peeks about and giggles as if the sweet bliss of childhood could be enjoyed for so cheap. Scanning the scattering of stones, Lottie begs for a glimpse of Imogen, wondering where she could be hiding.

Then she's reminded of the needle she wields and decides it only matters that Imogen is out of Mackenzie's reach.

Quickly, Lottie realizes Mackenzie has distracted herself with a childhood fantasy of friendship—as it seems she has altogether forgotten that Lottie is a problem to be concerned with. Or, perhaps she's crazy enough not to care.

But she should.

With a final creeping skitter across the cold ground and planting a seat behind a nearby grave, Lottie can see her. Can reach her.

Mackenzie nearly welcomes Lottie's borrowed weapon as she's stabbed in the neck with her own syringe.

Does it hurt anyone else? Dottie used to ask. *Ought it to?*

"Imogen" Lottie mentally hollers, not wanting to stir the sleeping homes nearby. She has plans for Mackenzie before she wants others snooping at the mess the devil has made.

"Lottie," Imogen sobs from behind, and she finds the terrified girl in a freshly dug grave. Crawling out and stumbling over, the two strangers collapse into one another in relief. In shared fear. In mirrored understanding. In *truly* being known.

"I'm going to handle Mackenzie, and I want you to get out of here. Okay?"

Imogen heaves with an exhausted wail. "No, I don't want to be alone. No."

Touching her face with tender fingers, Lottie gives her a sobering stare and a silencing announcement. *"I'm going to make sure she never bothers you again, Imogen. Do you understand?"*

Looking to the entrance of the cemetery, Lottie ushers her. "My bike is over there. I *promise* I will come right over."

Sobered by the statement, Imogen summons the last of her energy and first goes over to Mackenzie in closure. The woman lies like a ragdoll—crazed but conscious. Imogen knows the feeling, reminded that not every syringe promised a sedative. Some were just paralytics. Used on her to keep her weak. Submissive.

Now, Mackenzie is the weak one. The victim.

Spitting into her stilled features, Imogen screams. "That's for Dinny!" And then she spits again. "And that's for ME." Then she leaves Lottie to the rest, just as the fiery peaks of dawn hint at the horizon.

Weighted with paralysis, the conscious corpse slides across the cold ground one yank at a time. Noting Redd's Pond just ahead, Lottie nearly laughs in her exhaustion, finding the promise of rest to be within reach. True rest. Mental rest. Emotional rest. Rest from crazy ones who manipulate, and coerce, and lie, and threaten.

"No!"

She drops the bobbing head in surprise, still able to hear Mackenzie.

"I'm sorry! I'm sorry! I'm sorry!"

Picking the figure back up, Lottie only pushes faster, ready to be done.

"You're not sorry," she scoffs, disturbed by the still-conscious thoughts of the body she grips but certain in her desire for it all to end. "You just regret you weren't quick enough." Tightening her fists, she tugs harder.

Nearing the glassy water, it beams red, reflective of the sky. Lottie looks to the fiery horizon, remembering—for the both of them.

"Red skies at night, sailors delight. Red skies at morning, sailors take warning."

A squishing of mud sounds in the stillness of the morning as Lottie's shoes upon the slopping bank warn of the watery threshold. A ripple of wind tosses water weeds with a shiver, and cattails bob low... as if they know what's coming.

"You've made me kill two people already," Lottie reasons. "I had a literal hand in two deaths." Appreciating her logic—and possibly bordering hysteria—she cackles at the ragdoll, now poetically claimed as the plaything of another. "At least this time, it's because the person *deserves it.*"

With a final tug, she sends Mackenzie's top half over the slope of the pond's shoulder, sloshing through and swallowed whole. Sharing in the experience—as the limp body retains a wild mind—Lottie can see the water wash over, and she can feel Mackenzie perceive the darkness that drifts across her stuck-open eyes, and they both endure the promise of a quiet oblivion that forebodes.

And then, as if once more assisted by a magic presence, Lottie reaches in and yanks the body back out, remembering and realizing all at once:

"Soil is to sweeten, as boot dirt is to cheapen. Dirt of bones brings cursing, and a bit o' mud's for sleepin."

It wasn't just a gardener's quip. It was a witch's. The page that Lottie has looked upon a thousand times, she sees now, is a page ripped out of Dottie's grimoire—from *The Ground & Being Grounded.* It's magick. It's a curse.

"'Dirt of bones,'" she quotes, looking to the cemetery at her back.

Still wielding the emptied syringe, she stuffs it with dirt from the bothered grave, tantalized by a buzzing in her veins and fingers. Mixing in pond water to allow for an effective plunge, she then pushes the needle into the maniac, packing her veins with the wicked muck.

Now, Mackenzie is cursed to be Lottie's secret, and she watches the sadist sink into the murky depths, mentally hollering for mercy until the water, at last, overwhelms.

CHAPTER 45

Imogen insists on returning to the shack.

After finding her safely cowering by the bike at the entrance of the cemetery, Lottie was prepared to take Imogen to the hospital. Or home. Or anywhere she wanted… And without hesitation, Imogen wanted to go back.

"I have to find out what happened to Dinny." She was wild-eyed and shaking. Sickly pale in her blood-red dress. Pleading.

There was no arguing with her, and Lottie didn't have a mind to. In the brief moments of shared memories, she got to peek into the friendship shared between these two tortured souls, and, somehow, she felt it: the aching for him. Perhaps borrowed, or perhaps genuine, she doesn't know, but she shares in it—fearing for this sweet Dinny—and she'd like to help find answers.

Now with time to find those answers—and no one bothering them with experiments, or spells, or trauma, or murder—they investigate.

Lottie returns to the texts and documents on the table from her prior inspection, and Imogen dares digging into unmarked boxes. There's no telling what might be found; there's no warning on how many

Flowers have wilted at the hands of Craven and Mackenzie.

Nothing can prepare either of them for the images of victims that have come and gone, with each of their stories ending at some point or another, evidenced by experiments that went too far.

And then there are the *binders* of photographs that document the one and only Rose—the Flower that has lasted through the years, with respites in hospitals and then trial, and trial again.

She was never going to be saved from Mackenzie; Imogen was only going to become the madwoman's full property instead of being shared with Craven.

The pictures and pages spell out every experiment. Each time, it seems Imogen's "story"— each respective trial—sent her on errands to collect things for her own torture.

Most recently, Mackenzie required ingredients like *"water from the ground"* and *"seaside sand,"* and Imogen collected them unknowingly as she completed what she thought were Tasks ordered by The Coterie.

The fake society.

Mackenzie's make-believe prop.

Used to abuse.

The collections were tossed into spells, or ground into hypnosis medications with a mortar and pestle, or set aside for future need.

Having been distracted by her own disgust, Lottie now looks to Imogen and her heart breaks.

The battered woman—still dirty, and exhausted, and bleeding, and raw… she sits on the floor of her literal torture chamber and flips through page after page—face after face—wondering who else was like her.

"I recognize some of them," she confesses, possibly to herself more than Lottie. To her own memory. "But I don't know *why*... I don't know how. I can't remember."

Easing closer, Lottie offers a gentle thought. "I'm sure you will soon. When your mind and body have had a chance to recover."

"And Dinny," Imogen whines, flipping faster, eyes swimming. "I don't see him in here."

A tangible panic courses through Imogen's body, so potent Lottie thinks she can feel it. That they're somehow still bonded.

"What if Mackenzie is lying?" Imogen cries. "What if they killed him?"

Everything inside Lottie wants to help, as the damsel on the floor begins to hyperventilate and weep. There is no helping, though. Not on this. So, Lottie lets her cry. Lets her mourn the lives that have been stolen from the both of them. Her and Dinny.

In heartbroken desperation, Imogen grabs Lottie's hand, needing relief. A steadying reality. A scrap of comfort.

And all at once, their bond proves intact—their magical tethering—as a flood of images and emotions drowns them both in a shared onslaught of Imogen's pain. Lottie can see so clearly the chaos that consumes her. Rioting. They flash through recall like a television changing stations with speed:

Being drugged into submission but still afraid.

321

The forced hypnosis and trauma tactics.

Bandaging her own knees with a madman's medicine.

Glitches of memories that may or may not be true.

False realities.

Real fear.

As they process together, silent but suffering, Lottie's memories swim into the shared reel of snapshots, showing Imogen what she saw in the graveyard. Offering the anchor of an outside point of view.

"It felt like waking up," Imogen whimpers. "I woke up from a dream but realized I was in a nightmare. A real one."

Recall displays the unburied souls she'd danced with—or thought she had. And the music she'd imagined. The woman's curse she'd believed was being broken by her courage to dance with the dead.

Then a dread took over.

"Something in me felt it first. Something in my bones… Like my body was screaming at me to be afraid." She swallows, eyes faraway. "That pain was coming. That it knew."

Lottie remembers the way Imogen had suddenly run for the water. How Lottie had wondered if the twirling woman knew where she was headed.

"I was so scared, I wanted to die. I didn't know why. I just knew I wanted to. I wanted to die instead of suffer."

The memory ends, and Imogen looks at Lottie with red-rimmed sockets. "It's like the drug—the dream drug—wore off and I woke up. But then he caught me somehow. He put me back to sleep. Just all the way under. Not just back to sleepwalking."

Feeling she knows why, Lottie scans Imogen's binders and finds an easy tell.

"They used trigger words," she says. "To control your state of consciousness." Lottie's own memory makes sense now.

The woman that danced.

The woman that ran.

The woman that collapsed only to be carried away by a hooded Mackenzie.

"I remember more, now." Imogen goes quiet, barely saying anything at all. "I do remember Mackenzie. Not just being afraid because of pain. I *remember*." Her chest heaves. "She was always watching. Always... *playing* with me."

"She's gone, now," Lottie soothes, pulling Imogen into her chest. "She can't hurt you anymore. And neither can the Doctor."

Imogen goes straight with a gasp.

"The Doctor." She looks to the scattered binders. "These are Mackenzie's notes..." Sprinting out of the room, she dares to look deeper. Reckless and eager.

And she finds them in a nearby room.

Dinny's binders.

In unsettling silence, they both notice the same thing: there are even more than hers. And they're thicker.

Turning to the back pages of the top file, Imogen searches for the most recent notes. Scribbles. Doodles. Anything.

She nearly faints from the angst.

It's all so much.

Lottie races through others, wondering if any have an indexed timeline. She finds something promising, with Dinny's name near the top—the beginning—right under the name of "Jones Smith."

Jones Smith: "Suicide Spell"
- *Ingredients: highway gravel, ill will, spittle, flame*
- *Result: stepped in front of truck*
- ***(Note: burned – wear gloves)***

Reading on, Dinny's name lists the first spell used on him—the one that sent him missing.

Dinny Walker: "Lure & Lull Spell"
- *Ingredients: earthworms, dirt, lullaby, curiosity*
- *Result: lured into secret and sent to sleep*
- ***(Note: use trap door and shallow crawl space)***

And then his name continues, on and on, interrupted by other victims—including Imogen—but always back again.

"Maybe he's in Oklahoma," Lottie says, trying to hurry as the frail young woman wobbles. Through their mental connection, she pushes through an image for understanding but feels it stop short. Blocked

324

somehow. Grabbing Imogen's hand, she tries again, discovering the physical conduit to be necessary now.

Must be an effect of killing Mackenzie, Lottie figures. *An effect on severing part of the original spell.*

Now linked, she replays the magick-made memory of Dinny wandering as an imagined ghost. In the vision, Mackenzie had said there was an opening in "Tulsa, Oklahoma." Dinny had been limp on the table… but not dead.

As she continues scanning through more binders, she realizes there are more players in this madman's game—of course there are. Someone has to send the demented duo updates.

There are pictures of Dinny asleep in a hospital bed… but the timing isn't clear. Photos aren't dated. The aging of his resting face is indiscernible, aside from aging in general.

How many people did Craven and Mackenzie have in their pockets? How many vulnerable kids have been doomed by communal corruption…

An otherworldly shriek pierces the silence of the eerie shack.

"Look!"

Imogen points with a trembling finger to a loose photo peeking through the back pages. It's Dinny:

Alive.

Alert.

…And smiling.

He faces the camera with a waving hand, as if saying *I see you* to whoever watches from the other side—hospital security, guards at an institution, whatever kind of facility he's in.

In the center of his palm, there's a tattoo. A drawing of lips.

A shared memory zooms through their minds, authored by Imogen, educating on the best friends' kiss-tap histories.

"That's… for me."

Imogen's wavers, stunned. By the relief that those distant memories were real. By the reality that he did, in fact, love her as much as she loves him. That he may be okay. That he may *still* love her. Belong to her.

Flipping the photograph over, an audible gasp hovers at two pairs of lips as they read the urgent warning:

MISSING!

**

With no reason to stay and every reason to go, Imogen insists on trying to find him. She has to.

And Lottie agrees.

She's certain it's dangerous, and Imogen surely needs to be medically examined, absolutely put into therapy, and probably placed in some sort of witness protection program… but she also needs this. Lottie believes that entirely:

Imogen needs to find Dinny. To at least try.

The market season is over, Lottie is literally connected to this young woman who has no home but a single hope, and there's nothing holding them back. Nothing to keep them from *trying*.

And so, they plan for their journey. They prepare for Oklahoma.

CHAPTER 46
LOTTIE

Lottie quickly realizes she is not well positioned for travel.

She has no car.

She has no credit card to rent a car.

She has no debit card.

She hasn't visited the bank in two years in fear of being discovered.

And now she's in a hurry, and the dilemmas are infuriating.

But she does have a P.O. box with checks to cash. So, she starts there.

For the first time in two years, Lottie arrives at the post office with a freedom in her stride and a weightlessness in her shoulders. The key vibrates in her fingers, alive with her pulse. It slides into the lock, and a smile likewise slides across Lottie's face.

"Finally."

Inside, a stack of envelopes sits packed tight, ready to overflow. Relief washes over as she retrieves the happy bundle, knowing every envelope should be a check with her name on it. Lottie Lockwood. The only reason she has this P.O. box was for those royalty checks and those alone.

So, it's an odd thing when she finds a nondescript envelope on top of the pile, addressed to *Lottie* in an unfamiliar scrawl.

A pit forms in her gut as she questions if it's from Wells. He may be dead, but had he done it—had he found her?

"He's gone, Lottie." She takes a breath. She shakes the fear. "He can't bother you."

Nearly tossing it aside, she goes ahead and rips it open, won over by morbid curiosity. Unfolding the page, her vision blurs at the message.

It's from Brooks.

I saw you last night. I need answers. Meet me at my boat—I think you know the one.

- Brooks

"No."

In a breath, she's on the floor as the reality of those words and what they mean roll over her and proceed to assault. Pummel. Overwhelm.

Like water.

She's drowning.

"Last night?" *Could it be?* There is no date on the letter. But it sits on the top. New. The date on the check behind it is from this week.

"Shit."

If Brooks had any suspicions of Lottie, last night would have sealed those down tight. The glare from the bartender tested the waters, and Lottie had to flee like the suspect she was. Is. The crashing of her victim's funeral didn't help. But this... there's no way to excuse dragging a body into a pond under the cover of night.

If Brooks figured Lottie had anything to do with the death of Wells... now he has no reason to doubt it. He just witnessed the extent of her capabilities in all their full-moon-shining glory.

She has to face him. She has to see what he wants. To find out, *exactly*, what he knows—and what he's planning to do about it.

Would he turn her in? Would he grieve her in the press as some twisted villain? Would anyone believe she'd only wanted to survive?

With stinging eyes, resolve settles on her like a weighted blanket, somehow anchoring her down before she spirals.

She'll go. Maybe, somehow, a part of her even wants to. To face the truth. To stop hiding. Once and for all.

CHAPTER 47
LOTTIE

The sight of the cozy trawler at its dock makes her legs weak.

It rocks upon the gentle waves, just like every other time before, and a hundred memories litter her mind in an instant—like rain at a window during a storm. A rumble in her heart echoes a distant growl from the sky as storm clouds coil in from the horizon. With a breath, she tries to dam up her memories, blocking them out and keeping the forefront of her cluttered skull cleared.

Because most of her memories are fantasy. Most of her memories shouldn't exist.

But then Brooks appears inside his cabin, grabbing a cold beer from his fridge, and some of those memories come thundering back.

It's a familiar scene, she realizes, as she thinks back to the dozens of other times she's admired from a distance and watched him entertain company with a bottle in hand. He didn't typically drink alone; he seemed to save that for shared moments with another. Used to, anyway.

It's another difference between Brooks and Wells. Wells didn't need a reason to drink. But Brooks did. He marked occasions with it—made the moment feel special. Lottie had convinced herself she loved that about him, even though she truly knew nothing of it.

Forced to pause before the chaos inside her head dredges up the person she used to be, she takes a breath. And another. The past claws at her, trying to drag her back to show she was:

Shy. Weak. Timid.

That's not her anymore. She's changed.

Knocking the wooden dock with each step, she arrives, and he spots her through the window.

The cabin door opens.

"You came."

The waft of the warmth from inside lays upon her like a blanket, wrapping her in his scent. Lottie tries not to let it knock her over.

The hesitation in his posture puts her on edge; she didn't know what to expect, but it wasn't this. She expected anger—some sort of vengeful fury, something that made sense with what he would have seen. What he must guess. But he just stands there, avoiding eye contact.

A twisted truth in all of this makes Lottie sad, winding itself into a choking ball of emotion inside her throat. The result sends her own words spilling out and tainted with annoyance. It's the only way to force them out of her mouth.

"I didn't think I had a choice." Notably irritated, she offers his letter for emphasis.

With a heavy sigh, Brooks doesn't answer. He just moves aside to make room.

Catching sight of the bed and feeling clouded from the way his scent swirls through her thoughts,

Lottie declines. "I'd actually prefer out here." *Please*, she thinks, but that word doesn't come out.

Accepting with a nod, he grabs two bottles from the counter and follows to stand portside. Some of that same warmth seems to linger, tugging at her insides with the notion of joining him for a drink.

Of all people. Of all scenarios. Here she is, drinking with him on his boat.

"Figured you might need one as much as me," he says, still not looking at her.

He isn't wrong.

She sips in agreement. "Thank you." The cold of it bites with a clearing effect. Its chill makes her insides cold.

Snaking closer, the winds of the storm warn of the looming clouds, and the waves grow choppy, causing the boat to jerk and pull at the ropes secured to the dock. Lottie shivers from all of it.

"So." Daring herself to find his eyes, she watches Brooks, waiting for him to meet hers. "What is it you need?" A swallow does little to help a dry mouth. "What is it you think you saw?"

With a readying inhale, he levels, looking at her through low lashes. "I saw you in the dark." Her gulp is audible. "I saw you at the water…" A shake in her legs threatens of collapse. "With…"

To her absolute agony, he pauses, returning to the cabin with his unfinished thought. Once back, a wadded towel accompanies his grip. Her insides fold, bracing to retch.

Oh, god, I left the syringe. He watched me paralyze Mackenzie before I pulled her into the pond to die.

"I can explain."

The words are barely audible to her own ears. But then he opens the towel, and all efforts to explain evaporate, because it's not the syringe. It's the Dead Man's Finger… wrapped in Wells' hair… that Brooks watched Lottie cut from his brother's corpse during the funeral.

"Oh." That's all she says. It's all she *can* say. *It was him. That's who was watching.* There's no explaining this.

In the silence, his words seep into her with new meaning. He didn't see her at the pond. He saw her at the spring. He watched her work her spell. He witnessed this lunatic playing with morbid fungus and his dead brother's hair while naked in the moonlight.

Mentally digging for any conceivable excuse or plausible justification that doesn't sound outright ludicrous, Lottie strategizes instead: she goes on the offensive.

"Did you enjoy the show, then?"

A quick blush reddens his cheeks, but then he meets her challenge and counters.

"That wasn't my intention. We had just had our interaction at the funeral." She gives him that point. Lottie would have done the same thing; she would have followed. And then, under his breath, "And it's not anything I haven't seen before."

"What did you just say?" Is she hallucinating? Has she officially gone mad? *This is Brooks, not*

Wells... I haven't... We... "What do you mean, 'seen before'?"

Without answering, he shifts the conversation. "You first." Stern. To the point. Warranted. "What were you doing?" He extends the hair-wrapped Finger. And then, when she doesn't give what he wants right away, his voice breaks. "I just need to know."

She hates that he deserves the truth. And she hates more that she has to be a part of the answer.

"I was taking care of a problem." He waits for more. Where does she even begin? "I've been having a pesky dream issue."

Searching her eyes, his own seem to struggle. First, they grow wide. "Oh?" Then they narrow in accusation. "Did it work?"

Remembering it did, indeed, she feels a smile stretching in relief. "Actually, yes."

Something in that answer sends him spiraling. Despite a steady hold on the gunwale, Brooks dips down and finds a seat on a nearby cooler, his expression distant.

"I've been having these *maddening* dreams." His eyes find hers, and a furrow finds his brow. "I can't shake them." Pulling away, his gaze scans over Lottie's everything—her eyes, her lips, her body. "I've been having them for over two years." And now, a whisper: "It's like I've been bewitched."

Mackenzie's statements echo through Lottie's memory. *You have been.*

And it seems he knows it.

But something in him is skeptical; he just stares at her, refusing to say the word out loud but remembering the things she did in the water under the full moon.

Witchcraft.

An alien emotion slides into Lottie's insides as she tries to follow what he's saying. She has also been having nightmares for two years—ever since her fantasies summoned the wrong twin. But it's Wells who haunted her nightmares. And now, it seems *this* twin feels haunted by her...

Brooks has been dreaming of me? For two *years?* The thought refuses to settle. It bubbles, fizzes—then sinks like stone. She can't fathom it.

"Try lavender satchels under your pillow," she tries, but the words seem stolen by the wind as a gale pulls across the sea. Now, louder, "I have to go."

Because this is too much. Too painful. Two years ago, the thought of this man dreaming about her would have been the most invigorating news. But now, after all that has happened, and knowing that his dreams are all false—all based on magick. It's devastating.

Magick. Manifestation. *Maddening.*

That's the worst of it. He's haunted by it. 'It's *maddening.*' He's not only been bewitched—he's been cursed.

Lottie is a curse. First, that curse ruined Wells. Now, that curse has come for Brooks.

Budding saltwater burns at her eyes as she turns toward the sea and then for the dock, cursing internally as it brims at the edges.

Oh, god, is that *what he meant about having seen me naked before?*

A cloud of shame darkens her mind as Lottie mulls over the insinuation. An unwelcomed humiliation sears through her thoughts like acid rain as she realizes: he's been dreaming of her *naked* and still hating every moment of it.

That's a hard truth to top, she berates herself. Feeling small.

Brooks stops her retreat. Grabbing for both wrists, he holds firm, pressing his calloused hands into the flesh at her palms.

"Wait."

Stepping around her path, a sweatered chest blocks any further retreat. A groan of frustration vibrates from his throat as he slides a hand through his lazy curls and over his face in angst. He seems tired.

"Hold on." He shifts on his feet. "I have something for you."

Dizzied by his touch and frazzled by the emotions that insist on zipping through her, Lottie nods—assuring she'll stay put while he fetches whatever it is. He hurries, seeming worried she'll disappear anyway. But she doesn't. And when he returns, he holds a green notebook.

As if he'd brought out a long-lost friend, Lottie gapes at the sight of it, finding clarity.

And then her face drops as she remembers what's written inside.

"Have you read it?" The question drips of ire.

"Just enough to know it belongs to you. After my mom recognized you and called you 'Lottie,' I made the connection. It's... it helped me find you."

This notebook belongs to Charlotte Lowe, Lottie remembers. That's what's on the inside page of her notebook.

A black ichor seeps into her gut, as she understands this must have been how Wells learned her true name. He must have snuck a peek between the canoodling, the lying, and the insufferable stalking.

Now, Brooks knows it, too.

As she considers what else Brooks could know— if he were to read a single page—the ichor thickens like a bleeding wound.

Have you deduced my delusion? Have you realized it's you who fills these pages? Who filled my fantasies? Who I thought I was with the last time I came here?

"Thank you," she says as she takes hold to accept it. But his grip holds.

"I was tempted to, though." His fingers tighten, forcing Lottie to stay put and listen. "Because I *do* have questions that I need answered." They both swallow. "And I wondered if any might be in here… but I don't *want* to pry."

But I will, his glare seems to promise.

Lottie now takes a seat on the cooler, hands in her hair. "Why? Why do you think I have answers?"

"I know you do. At least some." He watches her for a long moment, silent as the wind continues to whip around them. "And some part of me trusts you'll tell the truth. Even the hard truth."

That surprises her. "Oh?" An amused grunt fills her chest. "What makes you think that?"

With complete tranquility, he answers.

"Because of yesterday. At the funeral. I found you fucking terrifying…" It's easy to discern how his eyes find the memory of Lottie with scissors at his brother's casket. "But that's because everything you were doing was *real*. Not polite, or socially acceptable, or tiptoeing around those mourning."

Shame covers her face, but not for long—a clang from the sky startles her, jolting her body into his.

"Dammit." The pressure of the threatening storm and the desire to get away pull at her in a tug-of-war against his request. It doesn't help that everything about the man makes her knees weak. And the existence of *that* incessant fact irritates Lottie to no end.

"I don't…" Now she strokes her face, also feeling tired. "I really do have to go."

Back to face him, she hesitates before saying more but then figures to hell with it. She'll tell him what *she* wants.

"I have to take my sister to Oklahoma."

"What?" Though features still frown at her under a furrowed brow, his eyes dart between hers in a frantic search for insight. It's dizzying. "When?"

"*Now*," Lottie urges, gesturing to the present as she finds her breath. And then, without thinking, she adds, "Well, as soon as I can find a way to get there." Her mind races back to *no car, no credit card, no way to navigate.*

"Okay." The scent of him swims through her head once more as she finds Brooks right at her nose. Towering with resolve. He looks at her with a fervor. She can hardly breathe through his closeness. "I'll take you."

In the same breath that follows, the clouds open, and the rain pours.

CHAPTER 48
LOTTIE

Lottie couldn't say much—not with the storm interrupting. But Brooks refused to be left with nothing.

"Consider it," he ordered, refusing to loosen his grip as he held her gaze through the downpour. He was serious. "I want to."

So she nodded. "Okay." Serious, too.

She doesn't know what it means—if he hates her, if he pities her... if they might someday be friends.

But she would like that. To be friends.

Now, Lottie and Imogen pack what few things they can as they prepare for the unknown: essentials, binders from the shack, a blank journal for Imogen— for when memories come rushing back. And so on. They may be in over their heads, but they've made a plan. And they're following through.

But first, before they leave, Lottie has one final thing to do.

**

Under the cover of night—and the cover of a spell—Lottie returns to the pond that holds her secret.

In the sleeping darkness, the boding water whispers. Smokey wisps of clouds and steam slither across the surface.

Hesitant, Lottie looks into the murky depths below, remembering through spell-induced empathy what it felt like to drown with no way to convulse, or react, or fight it.

Her own battle with a pond slams into her. She shakes off the pain that follow. Then, before losing her nerve, she dives.

The panic in her chest sets in from the terror, not the chill.

Breathless, blind, and senseless, she aims for the spot where Mackenzie should be—existing as nothing more than a lifeless piece of décor for the fish and bottom feeders. Her arms grab, yank, jab, and reach in both hope of touching the sunken corpse and fear of the same.

For a moment, dread overwhelms Lottie—what if the curse she cast made Mackenzie unrecoverable? What if her own spell doomed the body to vanish forever, even to her?

Skimming a fleshy surface with a startle, Lottie's insides recoil and churn as she latches on. Anxious legs can't thrash fast enough. Her skin wants to crawl away and tuck itself under a nearby gravestone for safekeeping.

At last, the kiss of a crisp night embraces the tips of her fingers and slides over the rest of her as she flounders onto the bank.

Breathing is hard. Her chest is tight.

The gaping pond waits to swallow her again, but she fights the fear that swims through. Determined, her grip tightens on the morbid wrist she pulls.

With a heave and a yank, Lottie delivers the limp body from the water and meets the glare of eyes that still seem bright. The sight sends spiders all over her. Closing Mackenzie's lids with a quick swipe, Lottie shakes away those nerves and sets her sights on the very grave Imogen started. The one ordered to be dug by The Coterie—by *Mackenzie*.

The same one Lottie has since finished. Body-ready.

Lottie clutches the magick book. Mackenzie's magick book. *The* magick book.

Having only been able to fully research a few of the pages within the monstrous tome, she steals the chance to glance at new insights even now. Here. Under the moon that watches them.

It's this book that showed her how to avoid suspecting eyes by becoming another shadow in the night. It's this book—this terrible, dangerous, fascinating book—that makes it possible to bury Mackenzie's body properly: six feet deep and in secret. It's the same book, Lottie has come to realize, that taught Craven how to slip a sedative past unsuspecting lips inside the dark underbelly of a bone bothy.

"I did a little research," she tells to the carcass. "From my grandmother's grimoire. And your book helped, too."

Blistered palms drop a shovel as Lottie kneels beside a macabre Mackenzie.

"'Dirt of bones,'" she recites. "That's a curse of death, did you know? The very soil where a body rotted. Bone dirt, full moon, intent laced with rage. That's what it took. And that's what you got. Pumped through your veins." She glares at the statue-still face. "I bet that was uncomfortable."

Dirtied fingers start shoving, pushing the limp limbs toward the fresh grave.

"Maybe even as uncomfortable as being tortured, again and again, by someone you thought was a friend."

Sweat beads despite the chill of the night. Moisture clings to the air as another storm threatens.

"Maybe as infuriating as having your mind invaded—your sanity stolen—just to be someone else's pawn."

Almost there. The night is quiet. And dark. Lottie ignores the nearby graves and weathered headstones, spooked by Imogen's memory of unsealed souls—false as it may be.

"You, though," she seethes, as the sickly white limbs plop into the hole with a thud, "I was happy to kill. And now,"—sweeping hands push the dirt back in—"you're going to rot."

"First, the maggots will come."

Scattered earth rains down.

"Then the worms."

Another pile.

"They'll invade your body, then your brain."

Fingers vanish.

"I'm sure you'll appreciate the irony."

Almost done.

344

"Then you're going to ooze and rot and be nothing but bone and dirt…"

Lottie stands now—breathless, relieved, and still so angry. It scares her, this anger. Has been scaring her, and still does. Because she hated Mackenzie. Still does.

And that feels dangerous.

Magick isn't a maker. She can see the words as if the beginner's textbook were open in her hands. *It only magnifies what's already inside.*

So she gave it rage. Gave it guilt. Gave it grief.

Her insides are festering. Maybe she's all rotten, now.

"Ill will meets ill will," she reminds to whatever souls are listening. "Yours was ill will, Mackenzie. Mine is balance. And protection."

I'm not like you, she insists. *But I'm like this because of you.*

She spits on the grave, sealing it secret.

"I'll come back for you, someday. When I need another Buried Secret."

Looking to the spellbook, Lottie stands straighter, trusting its guidance. Trusting Mackenzie to stay a secret—locked beneath dirt and spellwork. Forgotten by the rest of the world.

Just another thing in the ground.

www.ingramcontent.com/pod-product-compliance
Lightning Source LLC
Chambersburg PA
CBHW030239120726
47903CB00005B/1542